Bread Over
Troubled
Water

Bread Over Troubled Water

Winnie Archer

Kensington Publishing Corp.
www.kensingtonbooks.com

KENSINGTON BOOKS are published by

Kensington Publishing Corp.
119 West 40th Street
New York, NY 10018

All Kensington titles, imprints, and distributed lines are available at special quantity discounts for bulk purchases for sales promotion, premiums, fund-raising, educational, or institutional use.

Special book excerpts or customized printings can also be created to fit specific needs. For details, write or phone the office of the Kensington Sales Manager: Attn.: Sales Department. Kensington Publishing Corp., 119 West 40th Street, New York, NY 10018. Phone: 1-800-221-2647.

The K and Teapot logo is a trademark of Kensington Publishing Corp.

First Printing: December 2022
ISBN: 978-1-4967-3356-6

ISBN: 978-1-4967-3359-7 (ebook)

10 9 8 7 6 5 4 3 2 1

Printed in the United States of America

Friendships and meaningful connections come from unlikely places . . . and when you least expect them. This book is dedicated to you, Mary Crooks, Tracy Hartman, and Annette Cutler, because sometimes social media works its magic and brings strangers together, turning them into friends.

Chapter 1

Working in the hospitality industry, in whatever form that comes, means the customer is always right. Yeast of Eden, Santa Sofia's artisan bread shop, was no exception. So it was particularly unnerving to walk in to the scent of yeasty sourdough straight from the oven, only to be accosted by the raised voice of Olaya Solis, the bread shop's proprietor, baker extraordinaire, and generally a very zen woman.

Olaya had her back to the door, the house phone clutched to her ear with one hand, and the other waving around furiously, communicating something all on its own.

I raised my brows at Zula Senai—who stood close to six feet tall in her flats, had legs that went on for miles, and worked half-time at Yeast of Eden—and mouthed, "What's going on?"

Zula shrugged and threw out an *I have no idea*

look as she finished up with the customer at the front of the long line of bread lovers. When a bread shop is your home away from home, the customers become a kind of family. Olaya ran her shop like a well-oiled machine. Felix Macron and his morning crew, along with Olaya, started the day's bake. Janae Jackson, Felix's girlfriend, who was a firecracker in a pint-sized woman's body, Taylor Wilson, a long-legged and Kim Kardashian–curvy twenty-one-year-old blonde who looked and acted like she'd rather be catching a wave than kneading mounds of dough, and Mae Spelling, a short, kind of squat woman with dark hair and apple cheeks, did a bang-up job. I helped with the bake, too, but lately I'd been working more with Zula, a graduate of Olaya's Bread for Life class, helping run the front of the store.

It takes a village.

Zula stepped back and stuck her head through the swinging door. Calling for help, I presumed. I pressed my palm to my chest. "*I* can help," I said, but Zula was back, shaking her head, and already assisting the next customer with an order of two baguettes and six plain croissants.

Olaya's voice rose above the happy sound of customer chatter. "It cannot be—"

She broke off just as the old-fashioned cash register drawer slid closed with a ding. At the same moment, Esmé Adriá glided out from the kitchen through the swinging doors. I waved at her, my face breaking into a smile. Maggie, the girl who'd worked at Yeast of Eden all through high school and her first year of community college, had gone to live in San Francisco with her boyfriend, which had left Olaya needing a new employee. She'd turned to the women who'd been in the first group of her Bread for Life program. She'd designed the project as a way to reach out to low-income and immigrant women in the area to help them develop hirable skills. Supermarkets, other bakeries, and manufacturers were only a few of the places where they'd be employable when they finished the program. That alone could help boost their self-confidence. The friendships they formed with one another were an added bonus. The whole thing was like group therapy centered around an activity, but instead of crocheting or bunko, they baked breads from their different cultures and backgrounds.

Esmé had been in the same Bread for Life cohort as Zula. Where Zula was a boisterous and strikingly beautiful woman from the East African country of Eritrea—and could run circles around any of us—Esmé came to the United States from Zacatecas, Mexico, had escaped a bad domestic situation, and now was back on her feet. While I missed Maggie's youthful antics, Esmé brought a calm serenity to the bread shop, which balanced out Zula's brightness. She was an excellent fit.

Esmé tied the strings of her white apron, sneaking a look at Olaya and raising her brows at something Olaya had muttered in Spanish. I leaned over the bakery display case, beckoning to Esmé and raising my brows. "What's she saying?"

Before Esmé could respond, Olaya slammed the phone down and spun around. She pointed at

Esmé. "*Ayudar a los clientes con Zula.* Help the customers." Then she directed her fiery eyes at me. "*Mija, por favor,* I need your help."

With my own mother gone, Olaya, along with Penelope Branford, my eighty-something neighbor, had been slowly filling in the hole in my heart. "Anything," I said. I had my camera-bag strap slung over my shoulder. I perpetually snapped photos. The breads, the kitchen staff, the customers, the park, the ocean, the sand, the flowers. You name it, I photographed it. Now I swung my camera bag onto my back and followed her into the kitchen, leaving Zula and Esmé to the growing line of customers.

Olaya marched through the sleek, stainless-steel-heavy kitchen without even a sideways glance at the morning crew. She didn't need to worry about what was happening. The place ran with precision and expertise. Felix, Olaya's protégé in the truest sense of the word, worked the grain mill, an enormous pine and millstone contraption, turning heirloom wheat into hundreds of pounds of flour each and every day. Rye. Spelt. Cornmeal. Buckwheat. Olaya wanted an array of freshly ground grains, and the Osttiroler mill did the heavy lifting.

As the person in charge of the bread shop's website, I'd done a lengthy write-up on just how important the Osttiroler was to Olaya Solis and the bread she baked. "The quality of the flour is the heart and soul of any loaf of bread," she'd once said, a statement I'd put online. "A bread shop that grinds its own wheat—compared to flour in the supermarkets? It is like comparing apples and

oranges. They are two different things altogether."
Working here, even part-time, I'd learned a new
set of vocabulary words, too. Terroir. Noun. How
soil and climate and sunlight affect the flavor and
character of wine grapes. It holds true for wheat,
I'd learned. No two wheat fields are the same.

Felix was in his mid-twenties, pretty much lived
in his three-quarter-sleeved chef shirt, and had a
Pillsbury Doughboy belly. He was a jolly sort, true,
but he was an old soul, and he was a magician. He
was Rumpelstiltskin, turning stalks of wheat into
finely ground powder rather than gold, which he
then used to bake the most divine bread this side
of . . . well . . . anywhere.

His girlfriend, Janae, was almost five feet, had
skin the color of a sable, brown eyes rimmed with
gold, and braided hair piled close to six inches
tall on her head. She wore one of the bread
shop's aprons and bopped her head in time with
whatever song played on her earbuds as she
rolled out buttery sheets of dough, folding each
leaf into thirds. The croissant dough required
massive amounts of butter, which was rolled into
the dough, which in turn was folded, chilled, rolled,
then repeated. Each time the dough was rolled
and folded, a new melt-in-your-mouth, flaky layer
was formed.

I heard Olaya's voice in my head. "Cage-free
eggs. Organic produce. Freshly ground flour. They
are in the same category of artisan ingredients."

It was true. She and Felix packaged several types
of flour to sell in the front of the bread shop. It always sold out by midday.

Mae Spelling and Taylor Wilson rounded out

the morning crew. Mae had a bounce in her step and seemed to love early mornings in the kitchen. She was on the short and plump side—the complete opposite of Taylor, who was model tall. Mae thrived in the bread shop's kitchen, even though it meant waking up at five AM. It was clear, on the other hand, that Taylor wished she was back in bed. She had dark circles, lackluster skin, and was visibly jittery—probably from too much coffee. She didn't wear early-morning work shifts well.

The two young women bickered. "You're supposed to be working on croissants," Mae said when Taylor tried to elbow her way into Mae's workspace. Taylor retorted, "I don't listen to my parents anymore. I sure as hell don't need to listen to you."

Janae and the rest of the morning crew kept their distance. No one wanted to cross Taylor when she was bearish. Only Felix dared. He gave a sharp whistle to get their attention and said, "She's right, Taylor. I need you on croissants this morning."

Taylor's tired eyes pinched tightly, and she opened her mouth to object—but she changed her mind, clamping her lips together.

Olaya slowed her steps and surveyed Mae and Taylor, and for a second, I thought she might stop to intercede. She didn't, though. She nodded to Felix, then carried on, almost purposely blind to the inner workings of the kitchen. The fabric of her palazzo pants snapped against her legs as she marched into her office, a space big enough to hold only a small desk and chair, a mounted bookcase, and a mini filing cabinet. She held the door open for me. I slid past her and sat in the single, ladder-backed chair facing her desk. "What's going on?" I asked, more concerned now that I saw the dark circles around her eyes set into her drawn and pallid face. In the time I'd known Olaya, she'd never raised her voice to anyone. It wasn't in her nature, except that I'd just witnessed it, and in front of customers no less.

She drew in a slow, shaky breath. She exhaled and said, "Oh, Ivy. Life, it is not always good."

I'd also never heard Olaya speak so forlornly. It shook me. "What do you mean? Are you okay?"

"Me? Yes, yes. It is my brother, Guillermo, and my *cuñada*—my sister-in-law, Alessandra."

I couldn't help but react. I knew Olaya's two sisters, Consuelo and Martina, but none of them had ever mentioned having a brother and a sister-in-law.

Her lips quivered unexpectedly, and her eyes glazed. "They . . . they were in an accident a few days ago," she said. "Both . . . both are dead now."

I'd also never known Olaya to be a particularly religious person, but the moment the words left her lips, she crossed herself, holding together her thumb and forefinger as she pressed them against her forehead, her chest, then from her left shoulder to her right shoulder. She muttered something in Spanish before adding, "God rest their souls."

Shock and sadness surged through me. An accident. Her brother and sister-in-law, gone in the blink of an eye. I cleared my throat, swallowing my emotions. "I'm so sorry, Olaya. Can I do anything to help?"

"Guillermo and Alessandra, they have . . . *had* . . . one child. She is my goddaughter, Pilar," she said, pronouncing the *i* like a long *e*, rolling the *r* at the end. "She is fourteen."

"Oh no," I breathed. I knew what it was to lose a parent. And she'd lost two. My heart instantly broke for the girl.

Olaya rubbed the center of her forehead with the tips of her fingers. She let out a deep sigh. "We are her family now. She is coming here. To stay."

"Do you need to go get her?" I stood up and slung my camera strap over my shoulder. "Where do they live? I can drive you."

Olaya shook her head. "No, Ivy, *pero* I thank you. Consuelo and Freddy, they will bring her from San Diego. Soon. Very soon."

I sat back down, dropping my bag to the floor. "Okay. So what can I do?"

She heaved a heavy sigh. "I am not a mother, Ivy. None of us are. Only Guillo and Alessandra had a child."

Oh God. She was worried about how she'd be able to parent her niece. "You're a natural, Olaya. She must already love you—"

I broke off when Olaya pressed her lips together. Her nostrils flared as she drew in what looked like a bolstering inhalation. After an equally strong exhalation, she said, "Alessandra and I, we did not get along well. Because of this, I have not seen Pilar for ten years. More, maybe. I have not seen my brother. Guillermo has been a stranger to me."

They'd been estranged? This was, perhaps, a bigger shock than learning about Guillermo, Alessandra, and Pilar in the first place. Olaya was sanguine and even-tempered. I'd never seen her lose her cool . . . until this morning on the phone. How could they not have gotten along? "None of that matters now, does it? They're gone," I said softly.

"Pilar, she does not know me, or Consuelo, or Martina. We do not know her."

"She will get to know all of you. And she'll fall in love with you, just like I did." Olaya forced a small smile. It was clear she didn't believe what I said, but I doubled down. "Olaya. Your niece needs you and Consuelo and Martina. *You* are her family now."

She sighed, resigned. "Yes. This is not as it should be, but you are right. We cannot undo the past."

"You said you needed my help?"

"Yes, yes. Pilar, she will start school here in the fall. Until then, she will not know anyone. Maggie, she is no longer here. Consuelo and Martina and I, we all work. Too much work, but we must."

I stretched my arm across the desk, reaching for her hand. "It'll work itself out," I said. They'd all adjust eventually. "I'll help. I've been through what Pilar is going through."

"If I need to leave suddenly to help her—"

She broke off, the words clearly strange for her to utter. Olaya rarely took time off. She planned her days well, organizing her time carefully to ensure that all the baking she needed to do for her restaurant orders, catering jobs, special events, and the regular daily bake were completed. Errands during business hours didn't factor in, but Felix was always in the kitchen overseeing the morning bake, and if Olaya's niece needed her, that had to take priority over the bread shop.

"I can be here at a moment's notice," I said.

Chapter 2

If Olaya was the mother of the bread shop, her sisters were the beloved aunts. They came by frequently to grab a cup of coffee before they headed to their respective jobs, or for a croissant or sweet roll between real estate deals Consuelo was making or during lunch for Martina. This morning, at just a few minutes before eight, Martina came in, stopping at the door to scan the tables. Only half were occupied, so there was plenty of room for her to stay for a morning treat. That had been her regular habit until a few weeks ago. "I am too busy these days," she'd said when Olaya commented that she hadn't been around as much lately. On the mornings she did come, she arrived earlier and earlier.

Of the three Solis sisters, she was the quiet one—and the youngest. Where Olaya and Consuelo were fairer and green-eyed, Martina was olive-complected and had big, dark eyes. Olaya had let her short hair go steel gray, Consuelo dyed hers dark brown, but Martina's long wavy locks were almost black. Olaya's bohemian and statuesque vibe contrasted with Consuelo's casual jeans and T-shirt look. On the other end of the spectrum was the refined Martina. I was a few years away from forty, but I knew I could learn a few style tricks from the much older Martina. She was in her late fifties, but she looked a decade younger. Despite their differences, the three women depended on each other the way flour depended on yeast.

"*Buenos días*, Ivy. *Buenos días*, Zula," Martina said. Behind her, the bell dinged. Martina turned to look at another early-morning customer entering before turning back. She drummed her fingers on the counter.

"*Kemay haderki* to you," Zula said, wishing Martina good morning in Tigrigna, the language she spoke in Eritrea.

"*Kemay haderki*, Zula," Martina repeated in a practiced tongue. They'd been offering each other this greeting for months now, sometimes alternating with Spanish, Martina's native language. She pointed to the upside-down stack of "to go" cups. "Just coffee today."

Zula handed her a cup. A perk of being the owner's sister meant everything was gratis. She moved aside to chat with someone while the next customer stepped up to the counter.

If the leaders of the Yeast of Eden village were all the people working for Olaya, the villagers themselves were the customers. We had a slew of regulars for whom Yeast of Eden was part of their daily routine. The A group came, bought, and left. Group B hung around for a little while and socialized with people who had become friends after so many encounters in the shop. And the C group settled in at tables and conducted their daily business.

When I worked the front of the shop with Zula, we took turns, one of us manning the old-fashioned register Olaya still used, while the other handled the customers' bread from the cases. This morning, I had on my nitrile gloves as I pulled and bagged sourdough rolls, croissants, baguettes, or whatever else was ordered. I'd come back to Santa Sofia to mourn the loss of my mother. Now I was engaged, worked part-time at Yeast of Eden, and was building my burgeoning photography business. And I'd grown an extended family from the ground up.

I smiled at each customer as they came up to the counter. One by one, we worked through the long line. The first several customers were soundly Group A. They bought and left. I caught the eye of Julia Prudell, who stood six deep in line. Group B. She'd made acquaintances over the months she'd been coming here, so she usually stayed to talk with one of the other regulars. Julia was one of those women who didn't appear to age. I couldn't say for sure whether she was thirty, forty, fifty . . . or somewhere in between. Her dark hair shone, she had flawless skin—and in a beach town where people worshipped the sun, wrinkles and age spots be damned, that was saying something. I lived and died by my SPF 50 face cream.

Nina Blankenship ran the mini-mall antiques store across the street and down a few storefronts. She was on the boisterous side of Group B, staying, chatting, laughing, and generally lifting the spirits of anyone who was around. She was like Mrs. Claus—a little round and a lot jolly. People like Nina changed it up every time they came in. I could rarely predict what Nina would order on any given day.

Kristin Spelling came in once a week. Like so many of the other Group A folks, there was no hemming or hawing. She knew what she wanted. She constantly scanned the dining area, her gaze often landing on one attractive man or another. A few weeks ago, she'd seemed especially committed to her search. I'd asked her if she was looking for someone in particular. "Just admiring the scenery," she'd said as she waggled her brows in the direction of a particularly handsome customer named Josh Prentiss. She'd thrown out a hearty laugh as she refocused on me and bent in conspiratorially. "Actually, my daughter works in the kitchen, but I don't want her to know I am here. She's doesn't like me eating bread. Too many carbs," she'd said, and then patted her ample hips.

The only two young women who worked in the kitchen were Mae and Taylor. Even if their matching surnames didn't give it away, the short stature and matching doughy bodies shared by mother and daughter did.

She'd lowered her voice to a whisper. "Don't mention to her that I was here, okay, dear?"

I'd turned an invisible key at my lips.

After that first meeting, she began putting her

thumb and forefinger to her lips whenever she saw me, pinching them together and turning them as if she was locking the dead bolt on a door. She wanted her visits to the bread shop to be our little secret. I figured it was only a matter of time before Mae figured it out. In the meantime, it wasn't my business.

Now, next in line, she stepped up to the counter, shooting a quick glance at the swinging door separating the front of the bread shop from the kitchen. It was perfectly still, no sign of Mae. I bagged Kristin's order and held it out to her. But her face suddenly paled, and she took a step back, leaving my arm suspended in midair, the bag of goodies dangling from my fingers. Her eyes had bugged and were glued to the swinging door. I turned to see it opening. Taylor, tall and blond, dark circles still under her eyes, poked her head out. She surveyed the dining room, her gaze darting from table to table to table. She then scanned the line of customers.

"Taylor," I said with a hiss, "what are you doing?"

She focused on me and gave a faint scowl. "What, am I not allowed to take a break?"

Of course she was, but the kitchen had racks of baked goods waiting to fill the display cases when they ran low, from which any of us could snag a treat; there was a walk-in refrigerator stocked with sparkling water, and there was a Nespresso coffee machine for the kitchen staff and employees to use. Plus there was a conference room, which people used as a break room, and there were a small bistro table and two chairs just outside the kitchen door, nestled in one of the flower gardens. There was no reason for Taylor to come to the front of the shop. It seemed to me that she was looking for someone. Before I could step over to her and check her attitude, she withdrew, her head disappearing back into the kitchen. The door swung shut, and in front of me, Kristin let out the breath she'd been holding.

For now, Mae was none the wiser about her mother's visits to Yeast of Eden.

The morning at Yeast of Eden had been swamped, and the afternoon was just as busy. I managed to fill my insulated water bottle with cold water, grab a morning cookie, and sit out front at one of the cute little green outdoor bistro tables.

I'd snapped a few pictures of the busy summer street traffic and now had my notebook open, my list-making skills in full effect. I started with a list of things to do:

1. Photograph the park for the engagement party.
2. Map out table layout for party.
3. Menu (bread wall!).
4. Decide where to live.

That last one was a biggie. I'd been married and divorced, had moved from California to Texas and back, and had saved my money for years. I'd been able to buy my dream house—a red, Tudor-style crafted of old brick with a half-timber exterior. A steep gable and a high-pitched roofline, the red, wavy-edged siding at the gable peaks, and the cobbled walkway leading to the arched front door made it look straight out of a fairytale. Looking at the house filled me with happiness. Living in it was a dream.

But—and it was a big but—Miguel's house was pretty darn spectacular. His was a beach bungalow with a view of the Pacific Ocean. It was situated in the Upper Laguna District, between Riviera and Malibu Streets. There was no shortage of bungalows in Santa Sofia, but Bungalow Oasis held the vast majority. It was a quaint, hilly area full of charm and beach views.

Miguel had bought the place as a fixer-upper. And he'd fixed it up. The house, which seemed to be built into the hill behind it, had stucco walls. Terra-cotta-colored steps, an abundance of flowers in overflowing pots, and draping greenery made the outside about as welcoming as a house could be. Plus there was a front deck with an expansive view of the Pacific.

He'd tackled the interior, too. The house had an open living room filled with light. It opened onto the front deck, making the space double in size. The galley kitchen had a six-burner professional range. Miguel had made the kitchen efficient and welcoming at the same time. A sunroom led to a tiered backyard with just as many flowers and plants as the front.

Miguel and I spent about half our weeknights together, alternating between his bungalow and my old Tudor. We were getting married, but it was a toss-up as to which house we'd live in. Maybe we'd just keep both.

I detected a shift in the air and looked up. Walking down the street in a line that took up the width of the sidewalk were five women. Their eyes were focused and intense. The woman in the center pulled a half a step in front of the others, turning their line into a V, as if they were a flock of birds and she was in the lead. If she made the slightest adjustment, they would all follow. I could almost see the scene shift into slow motion as if they were the stars of an action film—all cool and hip, silver hair blowing gently as they threw their heads back confidently. I tried not to gawk, but I confess, I was a little bit awed. Who *were* these women?

Sometimes Hollywood showed up in Santa Sofia. Streets shut down. People were pulled in to be extras. Films were shot. I thought maybe I'd gotten caught up in a film shoot. I looked around, half expecting to see sound and video crews moving in.

The women didn't register my existence. They walked right on past me. I expected them to keep going, but the one in the lead made a sudden turn, and they descended on the bread shop as a group. All for one, and one for all.

I watched them through the window, from the outside looking in. Once inside, they broke apart and fanned out, walking through the space as if they owned it. They moved around the tables, then came back together. The one in the lead gave the slightest movement of her head. One of them queued up to buy a loaf of bread. The others waited while Esmé rang her up, and then they left as a group, the air settling as they retreated the way they'd come.

My break wasn't over yet, but I left my water and notebook on the table to go inside. "Who was that?" I asked Esmé.

She'd come around the counter and was wiping down the tables, something we did multiple times a day. She looked up. "Who?"

"Those women," I said, throwing my arm wide as if they were still here and I was gesturing to them. "Those five women who swept in, then swept right back out."

Esmé clearly wasn't nearly as taken with them as I'd been. She shrugged. "I don't know. Customers. One rustic wheat loaf."

I wanted more. "Have you seen them before?"

"Ivy, I just started working here," Esmé said. "I do not know people yet. Maybe Zula—"

"I have never seen them before, ever," Zula said. She'd been crouching down, but stood now. "They were like movie stars or something, though, weren't they?"

Or something, I thought. Their presence at the bread shop felt off. Puzzling. I couldn't put my finger on it, so I let it go.

Chapter 3

Sometimes the days ran together. If I didn't have a photo shoot, each day was pretty much like the last. I awoke. Walked Agatha. Arrived at Yeast of Eden. The crew baked in the kitchen. I helped until it was time to fill the display cases with every kind of bread imaginable. The ever-present heady scent of yeast hung in the air. And once the doors were unlocked, the line of customers almost never stopped.

Martina and Zula had had their morning greeting, and now Martina filled her coffee cup at the self-serve counter.

Kristin Spelling sat at a table enjoying an item from her carb-loaded bag of goodies. Everything was just as it should be.

The bell on the front door tinkled, and I glanced at the clock on the wall behind the counter. Some of our customers were like clockwork, coming in at exactly the same time every single day. Josh Prentiss, who had, in the past several months, had become like the mayor of the bread shop and who was a representative of Group C, was one of those people. He showed up every day to conduct his morning business at a back table. It was eight o'clock on the dot. The bell on the door dinged, and there he was, sweeping in like a ray of sunshine. Right on time. From the looks of it, he'd already begun his workday, his satchel slung diagonally across his body, his cell phone glued to his ear.

Martina topped off her coffee, and as she headed to the door, Josh lowered the phone against his shoulder as he held the door open for her. Ever the gentleman. She paused for a long moment as he smiled and said something to her. She had her back to me, so I couldn't see her response, but after a moment, his smile wilted, and the connection he'd tried to establish was broken. He watched Martina for a moment as she walked down the street, then went back to his phone call, queuing up at the end of the line of customers.

Poor guy. Martina had been seeing someone for quite a while, and when it ended, she went into a funk. She'd come out of it, and I didn't know if she was still technically on the rebound, but from the way she shot Josh down, it looked like she wasn't ready for his particular kind of charm.

Like Olaya did, I'd started identifying people not only by their names, but by what they ordered. Josh was a man of routine. Sourdough on Tuesday. Plain croissant on Wednesday. Morning cookie on

Thursday. And blueberry cornmeal cake on Friday. He always took a cup of black coffee to accompany his order.

I'd offered him butter and jam the first time I'd served him, but he'd refused both. "I don't want anything to interfere with the bread."

Olaya had dipped her head with respect when she'd heard that. He was a man after her own heart—if she and her heart weren't already besotted by my father.

As Josh waited on line, he sipped from a disposable water bottle. He ended one call, only to take another. With this one, his smile instantly vanished. He shoved the bottle under his arm as he muttered something and sucked in a breath before answering. His voice was low and terse. No bright sunlight shining from him today. As the line moved and he stepped closer, I caught bits and pieces of his conversation. "Absolutely. Not a problem. I can get it." He listened for a moment, then gave a stone-faced nod. He usually had a smile carved into his face, so the solemn look was off-putting. "Let's meet at eleven—" He stopped. Pursed his lips. "Right. At the ga—" He paused again and listened. "Right. Fine. I understand, Br—"

He broke off as he stepped up to the counter, his turn in line. "Morning, Josh," I said with a smile.

With his dirty-blond hair, square jaw, warm brown eyes, and usual high-wattage smile, he could have made it in Hollywood. He was probably somewhere in his forties, but like so many leading men, he was kind of ageless. The man's typical state was happy and upbeat, but at this moment, the smile he offered me in return was strained. His eyes were darker than usual, and he blinked against the morning light. "Give me a minute," he said curtly into his cell phone, pulling it away from his ear. With his attention fully on me, the tension melted from his face. He finished off his water, the plastic crackling as he handed it to me to toss in the recycle bin. "Ivy, looking lovely, as always."

From the mouth of a lot of people, the greeting might have come across as hollow. But from Josh—even when he was distracted with a phone call—it felt genuine. Of course, with my ginger curls piled on top of my head in a messy topknot and the lack of makeup on my freckly face, I really wasn't looking as lovely as I might. I thanked him anyway.

It was Tuesday, so I placed a sourdough roll on a small white plate and slid it across the counter to him, along with a cup for him to fill at the self-service carafes at the far end of the shop.

"And a cup for water, please," he said.

"It's getting warmer, isn't it?" I commented, handing him a clear disposable cup.

"Summer," he said with a chuckle. He handed me a five-dollar bill, enough for the roll, the coffee, and a bit leftover to add to the day's tip jar. He smiled at Julia Prudell, who was next in line, then dug into his pocket, pulling out a ten-dollar bill, which he laid on the counter. "On me today," he said to Julia. This was a more overt attempt to garner Julia's attention. Josh had been flirting with her for the last week and a half. "Keep the change, Ivy."

Julia rolled her eyes. She was independent and strong, and it was clear she didn't want the unsolicited attention of a man. Not even one as handsome and charming as Josh Prentiss. Where other women went weak in the knees at his wooing, Julia was immune. She stared at him, standing eye to eye. For a moment, I thought she might smile and say thank you. Instead, she blinked. In an instant, she snapped out of her momentary shock. She held up her other hand, a twenty-dollar bill clutched in her fist. "Thanks, but no thanks. I got it." She picked up the tenner and handed it back to him. "I can pay for my own."

Josh's smile faltered—he wasn't used to rejection, I thought—and after his brief conversation with Martina, which had looked like a brush-off, he was two for two. That *had* to be unusual for him.

"My bad," he said. He took his coffee cup and headed toward the self-serve carafes, leaving the adorable Julia—and she *was* adorable in her white canvas sneakers and pale yellow sundress—to order. She held a cell phone, had a book tucked under her arm and a small white purse slung over her shoulder. Her bottle-blond hair was pulled into a ponytail, which swung behind her as she moved. Her dark roots showed, but in a way that gave the tiniest edge to her girl-next-door look.

"Julia Prudell," I mock-scolded, "you didn't even let him down easy. He's heartbroken."

Julia shrugged, completely unconcerned. "Not my problem. I get tired of men thinking they can do what they want, when they want it." Her voice carried, but Josh didn't look up. While she perused the display case of breads, he filled his coffee cup with our strongest brew, then went to his usual bistro table—one in the back corner. He put his satchel on one of the chairs and his plate and mug on the table. He gave a last, fleeting glance at Julia, his brow furrowed, his ego bruised. Finally, he took a deep breath and held the phone to his ear, returning to his phone call.

A little girl came up to the front of the line. Her hair was pulled back in a ponytail, and she wore a yellow sundress, just like Julia. "We're twins!" the girl exclaimed.

"Tara! Come back here. It's not our turn!" I followed the voice to the back of the line. The little blond-haired girl was the spitting image of the woman calling her.

"It's fine," Julia said to the girl's mother, and then, Josh and his unwanted attention forgotten, she crouched down in front of the girl. "We *are* twins," she said. "Oh! What's that?"

The little girl startled, looking over her shoulder. "What? What?!"

Julia reached to the girl's ear and pulled a quarter out of it.

"Magic!" The girl, Tara, clapped in delight.

"Oh! Look! There's another one!" Julia reached her other hand to Tara's ear, revealing another quarter. This time Tara squealed. "Can I keep them?"

Julia stood and smiled. "You bet. Now, you better get back to your mom."

My eyes trailed the mother and daughter. Miguel and I had discussed having kids. It was a definite possibility, and seeing the sweet interaction between Julia and the little girl made my biological clock tick.

"She's a cutie," I said.

"Isn't she? Not in the cards for me, but I love 'em."

"Why not? I bet you'd be a great mom."

She smiled wanly. "Maybe. I've been on my own for too long, though. When you don't have a family, it's hard to know how to make one of your own," she said, opening up to me as if I were a bartender or hairdresser. I had that effect on people. The empathy factor.

"Sounds like you've spent a lot of time thinking about it," I said, admiring how self-aware she seemed.

She brushed a wayward strand of hair away from her face. "I wanted kids." She looked around at the other children in the shop. "It's just not my destiny."

"You never know," I said, then changed the subject to something less emotionally wrought. "Where'd you learn to do tricks like that?"

Her smile turned momentarily chilly, as if she didn't like the question I'd asked. "My dad was an amateur magician. Makes for a great party trick. For kids, anyway. His *big* trick was running off with his assistant. But he taught me everything he knew before that." She fluttered her hand, waving away the memories. "Enough about that. How's the engagement party coming?"

I'd invited a few of the regulars, as well as the bread shop's entire employee roster. And, of course, my octogenarian neighbor, Mrs. Branford, the Blackbird Ladies, my brother, Billy, and his wife, Emmaline, who also happened to be my best friend and Santa Sofia's sheriff, my dad and Olaya, Consuelo and Martina, and a slew of other new friends. "I'm going to check out the park this afternoon. The weather is supposed to be beautiful on Saturday. Olaya's got some bread secret up her sleeve. All in all, I think we're almost ready."

"Can't wait," she said.

Someone behind her in line cleared their throat. I threw up an apologetic hand. It was so easy to get lost in conversation with customers who had become friends. Julia's gaze skittered over the bread-filled display case as she tapped her index finger against her lips. "I think I'll have a sourdough—" She stopped and looked around at what the other eat-in customers had on their plates, shook her head and tapped her fingernail against the glass. She was unperturbed by the restless people in line behind her. "No, make that a morning cookie."

I reached for one.

"No, wait! Maybe I'll have the blueberry roll."

Someone groaned. My hand froze just before clutching a cookie between my fingers. "Go with the sourdough," Josh called from his table, flashing his signature smile. He wasn't ready to concede defeat with Julie Prudell.

Julia gave him a withering stare and said, "I'll take the morning cookie." This time her tone was definitive. I suddenly knew she'd give hell to anyone who catcalled her as she strolled down the street. Julia didn't put up with any shenanigans. I gave her the cookie on a small plate.

She moved off, and the next person in line stepped forward muttering, "Finally," under his breath. From the corner of my eye, I saw Julia stop at Josh's table for a minute. She put her cup and plate down. Maybe she was going to apologize for being so abrupt with him. He smiled, but then she said something and gave a stern wag of her finger. She'd brushed off his attempts to engage with her for weeks. Now it seemed she'd finally had enough. Her voice rose loud enough for everyone to hear her. "You have to treat women with respect. Your smooth operator act is only going to get you so far."

His smile slipped away, chagrinned. "Have a good day," she said as she picked up her things and sauntered off to the coffee bar. She filled her cup, then found a table near the windows.

The line had already been long, and with each passing minute, it grew longer. I cut out the chitchat, and, together, Zula and I served up croissant after croissant after croissant, by far our most popular morning item. Esmé came in from the kitchen, tying her apron and donning her gloves. She greeted us with a quiet *hola*, then went to check the coffee and cream. The three of us worked the counter with speed and efficiency.

Next in line, Nina Blankenship scooted up to the counter. She had told me not six months ago—and quite matter-of-factly—that Olaya's bread was going straight to her hips. She hadn't cared then, and she didn't seem to care now. She was plump and happy and had an ever-present smile. She stepped up and placed her hands on the counter, her elbows locking.

Zula's voice was naturally loud and contagiously

up-lifting. "Good morning, Nina!" she said, her voice inflected with her distinct accent. *"Kemay haderki."*

"Good morning to you, too!" Nina gave Zula a run for her money in the exuberant category. "I'll take two chocolate croissants, two ham and cheese croissants, and three morning cookies."

Zula's smile grew. "A hearty order today, my friend."

Nina grinned happily. "I believe in living life to the fullest."

The morning cookies were a new item Olaya had recently added to the bread shop's offerings, and a pivot from her usual stance of not baking yeast-free sweets. She'd built her bread shop on the principals of traditional long-rise doughs, wild yeast, and fresh grains. Everything she created had a bit of magic baked in, though I couldn't figure out how or why that was the case. It was like an unspoken gift that only she possessed. Over the years, word had traveled, and now people came from far and away just to sample her offerings. Her bread was said to mend broken hearts and to heal sadness. For stress, she recommended her lavender tea bread. Upset stomach? She packaged up a lemon mint loaf. For someone with eye troubles, she'd bake a special batch of her black currant scones. Whatever ailed a person, Olaya Solis had bread that could help. It was as if she spoke incantations over each bit of dough before it went into the oven. I know that wasn't *actually* the case, but her special magic seemed to swirl through the kitchen, infusing everything baked there.

One morning, on a whim, Olaya had baked a

dozen morning cookies for my father to put in his freezer. The second dozen sat in a corner of the first display case in the bread shop. They were gone in less than forty minutes. Since then, they had become a permanent offering. They were naturally gluten free, made with extra-thick oats for chewiness, and oat flour Felix ground once a week. Her favorite mix-ins were cranberries and walnuts, but she also made them with raisins, dried cherries, dried blueberries, chocolate chips, or pecans. Each batch was different, and that first bite was always a joyful surprise.

Zula packaged Nina's selections in a small white pastry box, sealing it closed with a Yeast of Eden sticker. "Until tomorrow!" she said as Nina moved away and the next customer sidled up to the counter.

A movement behind me drew my attention. I turned to see Taylor Wilson from Felix's morning crew. Just as she had last week, she stood in the doorway between the kitchen and shop. This time, though, after her gaze darted around, she zeroed in on Josh Prentiss, transfixed. I snapped my fingers, breaking the trance. First of all, the guy was too old for her, and second, she looked like a raccoon caught in the headlights, what with the dark smudges under her sleep-deprived eyes. It was a weird distraction for the customers. "What's going on, Taylor?" I said. "Do you need something?"

"Not from you," she said, then she sashayed past me, around the counter, and right up to Josh. He smiled as she approached. She bent to whisper something to him, then ran her fingertips over his sleeve.

I stared, slack-jawed, in part at her insolence, but also because . . . oh no. Surely not. Josh and Taylor? A shudder ripped through me. He was old enough to be her father—or pretty close. Taylor turned and came back behind the counter. She paused at the swinging door to the kitchen and looked back at him. Josh must have felt the intensity of her stare because he looked up and met her gaze head-on. He smiled, but it seemed off. Strained, as if alarm bells were going on off in his head. Their gaze stayed locked like that for a solid ten seconds before I hissed at her, as if that single sound would be enough to sever whatever was going on with her and Josh.

She threw up one hand with a dismissive, "Yep, yep." Then she disappeared back into the kitchen, and I forced my attention back to the customers.

Zula, Esmé, and I were in the zone, moving around each other like dancers doing the waltz. We slid nitrile gloves on and off, bagging up baguettes and rolls, plating scones and croissants, slicing loaves of sandwich bread, and walking new customers through our offerings.

Out of the blue, Nina's exuberant voice rose over the din of the chatter. I glanced over to see the lid to the bakery box she held askew in the crook of her arm and her nibbling on one of the morning cookies she'd bought.

Josh had finished his phone calls. Now his leather notebook cover was open, and he was jotting something down on the pad. From the corner of my eye, I saw Nina behind him, staring at his open computer. After another few seconds, her voice rose above the low chatter of the customers again, directed at Josh. "Here you are again. We *have* to stop meeting this way."

Weird, since she'd been behind him for a solid minute or two without saying anything. He looked up at her, startled, but smiled when she winked.

Her gaze dropped to his computer screen, then her eyes widened to circles. "Is that . . . Wow, Josh, those numbers are amazing!"

He gave a self-deprecating nod. "Yeah, we did well."

"I'll say!" she practically bellowed. "Finally, a new coach, right? And the marquee? Finally, a way to show who our teams are playing!"

He cringed and quickly scanned the room, as if he was embarrassed at the volume of Nina's voice. Josh relished attention, but I had always gotten the impression that he liked to be in control of that attention. I hadn't noticed it earlier, but he looked tired, his eyes drawn, the half-moons beneath them smudged dark with sleeplessness. After two rejections and his heated phone call, I got the feeling he wanted to be left alone. He heeded Nina again, though, as he closed his laptop and flashed a slightly dimmed version of his thousand-watt smile. He said something, but at a volume that was much lower than hers had been. Too low to hear. She tilted her head and gave him a coy grin, then put her index finger to her mouth in a "mum's the word" symbol.

Even when he was tired, Josh's smile was beguiling. Truly, it was a gift. He could make a person feel as if they were the only one in the room. He said something else to her, causing Nina to throw her head dramatically to the side, as if she was catching an invisible kiss right on her cheek. "The boosters are *so* lucky to have you. That new marquee'll be paid for before you know it!"

Someone clearing their throat brought me back to the line of customers. Finally, the woman with the little girl, Tara, was next. "A skull! Look!" Tara pointed to one of Olaya's *día de los muertos* cookies nestled between the croissants.

"You spotted it, so it's yours," I said. I used a fresh waxed sheet to retrieve the painted sugar cookie and handed it over. As Tara munched, the little girl's mother stared at Josh. He might as well have been Robert Redford, the way women fawned over him. I cleared my throat, and she snapped back to Zula and me, her cheeks tinted pink with embarrassment. She twisted her wedding band as she ordered a baguette. Despite the ring, I got the feeling she would relish a little attention from Josh. She paid, then left with her little girl and a lingering backwards glance.

Kristin Spelling was next, anxiously tapping her fingers on the counter and glancing around. "Mae's in the back," I said.

She blew out a relieved breath. "Perfect. I'll take a blueberry roll."

Zula reached for it, but froze as the swinging door separating the kitchen from the shop swung open. Suddenly, Mae, short and soft and the spitting image of her mother, was there screeching. "Mom! What are you doing?"

Chapter 4

Kristin stumbled backward as Mae barreled around the counter and into the dining area. It was like a comic farce. Kristin dodged tables as Mae pursued her. "Mae!" I soft-shouted, sending a placating smile to a mid-thirties couple dressed in biking gear who came up to the counter next. From their padded spandex bike shorts, helmets braced against their sides, and stiff bike shoes clicking against the floor, they looked like they fell on the serious end of the biking spectrum.

The commotion died down. Kristin had nowhere to go. Mae backed her up against a chair where Josh was sitting, shoving it against his table. The table rocked, jostling his computer, sloshing his coffee. He grabbed for the laptop a split second before the heavy white mug tipped precariously, more coffee landing on the table. He was not having a good morning. Josh gaped at them. "What are you—"

Mae's hand flew to her mouth. "Oh my gosh, I am so sorry." She spun to Kristin. "Mom! Look at the mess!"

Kristin's eyes went wide. "I'm sorry, too! We'll clean it up."

Mae grabbed a handful of napkins from the coffee bar to soak up the spill. She handed another pile to her mother, then took the cup and topped it off for Josh.

With the crisis averted, Josh sat down with his coffee cradled in his hands. His face had paled in the commotion, and he watched warily as Mae dragged Kristin out of the way as if he was afraid they might barrel back toward him and crash into his work space again.

The bicycle couple at the counter recaptured my attention. A sheer glow kissed their sun-drenched skin. They each ordered a croissant—one ham and cheese, the other chocolate. They paid and click-clacked back outside. Another couple—this one in their twenties—stepped up. They bickered back and forth over what to order for their picnic lunch, but it was playful and kind of endearing. They landed on two baguettes. I bagged their bread in paper sleeves and handed it over. The young woman gave a mischievous grin. "We'll be back to try everything else—"

She broke off at the sound of chair legs scraping against the floor. I looked over in time to see Josh jump up at the same moment the plate with his half-eaten sourdough roll landed on the floor, breaking into thick shards against the tile. Another puddle of coffee had sloshed from his cup.

Kristin was on the floor. Mae already had her arm reached out in order to help her mother stand up. Julia had been heading for the door when the commotion happened. She had been caught in the crossfire, and now she stood there, frozen. Everyone in the bread shop fell silent for a long second. Josh raked his hand through his hair.

"Oh God, I am *so* sorry," Kristin said. "I didn't mean to . . . it was an accident . . ."

Josh waved away her apology. "It's fine." He patted his flat stomach and managed a wink. "I needed to cut back on the carbs anyway."

Kristin giggle-guffawed. "Oh you . . ."

Mae yanked her mother to standing as Julia bent to pick up the shards of the broken plate, grimacing as a corner of the sharp ceramic cut into her finger.

"Are you okay?" Josh asked. His brow furrowed as he took her hand, turned it over, and examined the bleeding finger.

"I'm fine. It's just a scratch," she said, more brightly than I think she felt. Then she propelled herself into motion and disappeared into the bathroom. I left her to tend to her cut.

Josh stared blankly, looking bemused. I left Zula behind the counter and hurried over to him with a tray, two rags, a broom, and a dustpan. He crouched down and started to put the broken ceramic pieces and the remnants of his pastry into a pile on a napkin. He looked up at me. He didn't seem any worse for wear, but the color was gone from his face. "Sorry about the plate."

I waved away his apology. "Oh, no problem. Accidents happen. Are you okay?"

He managed a smile. "Oh God, yeah. Fine. Julia, though . . ." He looked at Mae and Kristin, who had gone off toward the front door to the bread shop and were bickering. His gaze shifted to the swinging doors leading to the kitchen, then to the direction of the restrooms. Yeast of Eden had been hit with chaos, and Josh had been in the center of it. Definitely not his morning.

"What happened?" I asked.

Josh flashed a self-deprecating smile. "I don't know, actually." He looked at Mae and Kristin again, his forehead crinkling even more as he pressed his palm to the back of his head. "Something hit me, I think. Maybe? I don't know."

I searched the airspace in the room. No flying bugs that I could see, thankfully. I righted the fallen chair and swept the remaining ceramic chunks and the nearly invisible slivers into the dustpan. Josh held his hand out for one of the rags. He proceeded to wipe up the bit of spilled coffee, while I emptied the broken pieces into the trash can by the bussing station.

When I came back to the table, he was crouched down, searching under the table. "Everything okay?" I asked.

"Yeah, yeah. Just looking for my book—"

I grabbed the dirtied towel from him. "Let me get you a fresh cup and a new pastry," I said.

"Mmm. No, thanks." He rubbed his temples and squinted his eyes. "I . . . uh, yeah, I'm just gonna go. I'll see you tomorrow."

I finished the cleanup, taking the dirty towels

and broom to the back. By the time I returned to the counter, Freddy Martinez, a stocky man with a flat nose and a thinning hairline, had opened the door, holding it while Olaya's sister, Consuelo, and a teenage girl passed through. Freddy stayed outside. Smart man to steer clear of whatever emotional toil he anticipated with Consuelo, Olaya, and their niece.

Everything else was forgotten as I watched Pilar Solis. I'd expected a girl haunted by the sudden and unexpected death of her parents. The reality was so much worse. She stared at the floor, looking up only when Consuelo gently touched her arm and whispered something to her.

Pilar looked up at her aunt and tried to smile. It really was a valiant effort, but instead of her lips curving up on either side, they stretched out, reaching for her ears and puffing up the apples of her cheeks, but not with any mirth. Her nostrils flared slightly as she relaxed her face muscles and looked down again.

She was about my height at five feet six inches. Her chestnut hair fell like a sleek waterfall down her back. Her olive skin was clear and glowing, but sadness seemed to permeate through her.

Olaya kept her hair short, but Consuelo had the same almond-shaped eyes, the same nose, curved down very slightly at the end, the same lips, and the same hollowed cheekbones. She was the most boisterous of the three sisters, while Martina, the youngest, was the quietest. Olaya fell somewhere between them.

At this moment, though, Consuelo's demeanor

mirrored her older sister's. She bypassed the line and came up to the counter where I stood and spoke softly. "Could you get Olaya for me?" She glanced over her shoulder, giving Pilar an encouraging smile.

I hurried to the kitchen. Olaya wasn't one to sit by and let her kitchen staff do all the work. She worked right alongside them—whether that meant mixing, shaping, or baking. She found the entire process meditative and cathartic. This morning, it looked as if she was working through her grief from the loss of her brother, as well as her concern for Pilar, by digging her hands into a bowl of dough. She looked at me and immediately read my face. "They are here?"

I briefly glanced over my shoulder, nodding.

"*Bueno.*" She cleaned the dough from her fingers, then crossed the kitchen to wash her hands. I rejoined Zula and Esmé behind the counter. Once again, the line went all the way from the counter to the door. Consuelo and Pilar stood off to the side near the self-serve coffee bar. A minute later, Olaya was with them. The three women huddled together in a tense conversation. Their voices were low and eclipsed by the animated chatter of happy customers, Zula's joyfulness, and another customer's ongoing phone call.

After a few minutes, Consuelo hugged Pilar. She gave Zula, Esmé, and me a quick smile before heading out to the sidewalk. Through the large windows, I saw Freddy appear from the shadows and fall into step with her, walking until they disappeared from sight.

Olaya came up to the counter. "Ivy. Zula. Esmé. This is my *ahijada*, Pilar."

I raised my brows in a question at the unfamiliar word.

"She is her goddaughter," Esmé whispered.

Olaya extended her arm toward us. "This is Ivy. This is Zula. And this is Esmé."

The three of us offered smiles, but Pilar's expression remained blank, as if the effort of trying to smile a minute ago had completely zapped her ability to offer another. "I must settle Pilar at my house," Olaya said. "I will be back soon."

Zula shot a surprised glance at me, but Olaya had prepped me for this. "No problem. We'll hold down the fort." Yeast of Eden was in good hands.

"Yes," Zula chimed in. "We will be fine here."

Santa Sofia was a well-planned community, and not just because my dad was in city planning. Beach towns were notorious for their lack of parking near the ocean, but we had small lots along the coastline, as well as lots behind the businesses on each major street. Olaya's car was parked in the lot behind the bread shop. She flashed us a grim look as she led Pilar to the kitchen, where they'd go through the rear door.

I continued to handle customers, while Zula cleared and wiped down vacated tables.

Finally there was a lull, and even the regulars were clearing out. Julia had come back from the bathroom, looking none the worse for wear. Her empty plate clattered against the other dirty dishes at the bussing station. She studied her phone intently. A baby in a stroller cried. The bell on the door dinged. "Five olive loaves," a woman ordered.

"We have four left," I said, after sticking my head into the kitchen to double-check with Felix that none were tucked out of sight somewhere.

"That'll do," she said. I donned a new pair of gloves and bagged the loaves up. The next time I looked up, Josh was packing up his satchel, tucking in his computer and notepad. He wiped the table down with a napkin, then he slung his satchel strap on his shoulder. A moment later, several other customers vacated their tables.

Someone else stepped up to the counter—a middle-aged man, thick-necked and stocky, his belly protruding slightly over his belted pants. I'd noticed him earlier, standing by the door, waiting for the line to shorten. Finally, he'd decided to take his turn. "What can I get for you?" I asked him.

He leaned against the counter, his back to the dining area. He turned his head long enough to take in the bread shop with an all-seeing sweep of his eyes. He paused for a moment when he saw Josh. "I'll take one of those," he said, coming back to me and pointing to the morning cookies.

The woman with the olive loaves left. I held the cookie with a thin sheet of parchment paper to the man at the counter. "Would you like a bag?" I asked.

No response.

The bell on the door dinged as Josh opened it. I started when the man with the cookie thrust a five-dollar bill at me, the ring on his pinkie finger glinting slightly in the sunlight. He hurried to the door, catching it, and stepping back to hold it for little Tara, her mother, then Julia to pass through. "Your change!" I called to him.

"Keep it," he said without even a backward glance, and then he was out the door, heading north in the same direction Josh had gone.

Chapter 5

Once the morning shift was over, I revisited my To Do list. I hadn't crossed anything off of it, but today I was determined to do just that—starting with photographing the park for my and Miguel's engagement party. I'd gone home to pick up Agatha, and now my little fawn pug and I hiked uphill toward Skyline Park. I'd parked down by the pier so Agatha could get in a little extra trotting time. Her tail was curled into a spiral, and her bug eyes practically glowed with pleasure. There was nothing better than a beautifully temperate summer day in Santa Sofia.

We maneuvered around tourists. I knew they were tourists by the Santa Sofia swag they wore, the way they dillydallied, cupping their hands at their foreheads to gaze through shop windows, and by how they exclaimed at the wafting breeze kicked up by the Pacific. The locals weren't exactly jaded by the breeze and the faint crashing of the waves, but they weren't in constant awe, either. Truthfully, we just kind of took it for granted because the bliss of living in coastal California was our everyday life. We could appreciate it without experiencing the rapture of a tourist.

I say this, but I admit that I walked on the beach regularly, always mesmerized by the vastness of the ocean and the frothing whitecaps slicing through the water. I had a favorite spot near the pier where Baptista's Cantina & Grill, an upscale Mexican seafood restaurant on the pier, was located.

This spot on the beach, and these huge rocks dotting the landscape, had been my mother's favorite place to think and just . . . be. It had become mine, too. Agatha and I started there, then took side streets to avoid some of the meandering people.

The farther from the beach we got, the fewer people we encountered. On such a clear day, everyone wanted to be on the sand or in the water. The businesses along Pacific Coast Highway and near the public beaches were bustling. But Agatha and I, we were heading east and away from all that congestion.

By the time we reached Skyline Park, we were both panting. Those hills are harder to climb than they look. They can be killer. We stopped at the entrance to the park, where there was a human and dog drinking fountain. I turned on the low spigot for Agatha. As she lapped, I bent to the fountain to quench my own thirst.

I turned my back to the park and took in the

panoramic view of the Pacific before me. From the vantage point of the park, it was spectacular. Once I'd gotten my fill, I turned on my heel, gave Agatha's leash a gentle tug, and we headed into the park. Before long, I was clicking away, taking shots of the park from different angles. It was as much an exercise in capturing the light as it was in envisioning the space filled with friends and family.

The white gold of the engagement ring on my left hand glinted in the sunlight. My father had proposed to my mother with this ring. Thirty-nine years later, Miguel had proposed to me with it. He'd hidden it in an ornament that he'd surreptitiously hung on my Christmas tree, surprising me with it on Christmas Eve. Sometimes I had to pinch myself. I'd gone to college in Austin, Texas, started a business, married Luke Holden—then divorced the cheater—and had moved back home to Santa Sofia after my mother's tragic death. Rekindling a relationship with Miguel had been the furthest thing from my mind, yet that's exactly what had happened, and now happiness fluttered inside me like joyful butterflies flapping their colorful wings.

Because now Miguel and I were getting married! In a million years, I never could have predicted a future with Miguel as one of the outcomes of moving back home. It goes to show you, life is full of unexpected surprises.

Before the wedding, though, came the engagement party. And Skyline Park was the perfect location for the shindig. I spun around. Whoever had done the landscape design for the park deserved an award. Pink and white crepe myrtles lined the walkway, creating a veritable wall of flowers encircling the gazebo. Columbine, daisies, and native orange and yellow poppies gave low-lying color. Meticulously shaped boxwoods lent a sense of permanence to the flowing beds, and beautiful white flowers hung like bells against a decorative lattice wall.

The gazebo itself was the location of the town's Christmas tree. It didn't come close to rivaling the one displayed in Rockefeller Center each holiday, but it was beautiful, nonetheless.

I turned to face west again, the expanse of the Pacific before me. This was the clincher. On a scale of one to ten, the ocean backdrop made the location a ten and a half.

The party was timed to capture the setting sun in the distance. At twilight, the twinkling lights in the trees would create a magical feeling. The spot was beyond perfect.

It was also just a few blocks from the bread shop. Convenient, given the fact that Olaya was planning a bread wall—a concept that I was sure she had invented and that would become Pinterest and Instagram famous by the time she was done with it. It had happened with her Van Dough Focaccia, flatbread she decorated with veggies to look like Van Gogh paintings. I had every reason to suspect it would happen with the bread display she'd conceived.

She also had something extra special planned for the event. It was top secret, and no matter how many times I'd tried to sniff out a clue, she had her lips sealed tight. I was stumped—and I was pretty good at sniffing out clues, if I did say so myself.

Agatha trotted along beside me, stopping when I paused for a photo op, moving again when I did. She was my shadow. "It's perfect, right?" I asked her, bending to scratch her head.

She looked up at me with her marble-sized eyes. Her perpetually downturned mouth and saggy jowls gave the impression that she wasn't interested and that she was terminally depressed. Her curlicue tail told a different story. It was the barometer by which I gauged her happiness. Pugs didn't wag their tails. They hung straight down if they were scared or unhappy. At the moment, Agatha's tail was curled into a tight spiral, an indication that she was a very happy camper.

I took that to mean she approved of the location. "Good call. I agree, one hundred percent," I said to her. I started walking again. She pulled out ahead. School was out, so anyone who *could* be at the beach *was* at the beach. That meant the park was blissfully empty. I let out some slack, giving Agatha a wide berth. She took advantage of it, stretching the retractable leash attached to her purple harness to its full fourteen feet. While she sniffed the bushes and plowed through the flower beds, I continued to snap pictures from different spots. The bread wall—which Olaya had explained to me, but which I couldn't quite visualize—would face east, the ocean behind it. We'd set up pub-height tables, eliminating the need for chairs and encouraging mobility and conversation. It was harder to park yourself at one table if you were standing. At least I hoped so.

"Ivy!"

I turned to see all six feet of my fiancé approaching from the parking lot on the east side of the park. If I had to describe him, he'd fall somewhere between Enrique Iglesias and a youthful Mark Harmon, only far more handsome than either, separate or melded together. His olive skin contrasted with my fairer coloring, his hair about a million shades darker than my mop of tousled light paprika curls.

I lifted my camera again and pressed the button. Capturing Miguel—or anyone—unposed was my favorite kind of photo to take. He swung his arms, his gait steady and determined—a perfect reflection of him.

"One day you're going to get tired of taking my picture," he said as he came up to me.

He cracked a smile as he said it, and it widened as I replied with a saucy, "Never."

He planted a kiss on my cheek, then bent lower and said, "Hey there, Ags," as he rubbed his fingers over Agatha's back. Standing again, he draped one arm around my shoulders and gazed at the Pacific. "Nice."

We never got tired of living on the coast. "It is. Absolutely perfect."

"I have less than an hour," he said, pulling me into motion. As the owner of Baptista's Cantina & Grill and its sometime chef, mid-afternoon was just about the only time Miguel could sneak away.

Despite his limited time, we ambled along the park's walking path, Agatha alternatively leading the way or lagging behind as she sniffed and marked her territory. At the cross path to the gazebo, the leash grew taut again. Agatha had her nose buried in a cluster of poppies. I tugged the leash, pressing the lever to retract some of it, but she resisted. Her stout body was stronger than it looked. She held her ground, pulling me forward instead of the other way around.

"What do you see, Ags?" Miguel asked. Agatha ignored him. She scooted deeper into the flower bed, her head disappearing behind a shrub. The curlicue of her tail had unfurled, her tail now pointing straight down.

I drew in the leash so I'd have more control once I got close enough and could get her to come with me. A few seconds later, Miguel and I stood just outside the bed. Agatha was having nothing to do with listening to me. "Agatha! Come!" The command was solid, but I'd never consistently trained her, so she didn't actually listen.

I stepped gingerly into the bed of poppies so I could grab her, trying hard not to trample them anymore than Agatha already had. I retracted the leash so it grew shorter still, and I yanked again. She was solid and strong, and she stood her ground against my effort. She sniffed at something. "Come on, Agatha," I started to say, but the words froze on my lips.

"Oh no. Oh my God." I spun around, my free hand flapping in the air at Miguel. "Call Em. Call

York." I felt the color drain from my face. "Hurry. Call 911!"

Miguel didn't ask for a reason. He dug his phone from his pocket and placed the call, only then galumphing through the poppies, not caring one iota if he stomped them into the ground. When he reached me, he pulled up short and drew in a breath. Because he saw what I saw—and what Agatha had apparently smelled.

The toes of a pair of shoes poked out above the yellow and orange petals, reminiscent of the Wicked Witch of the East's ruby slippers pointed skyward. These shoes were attached to a pair of legs, which led to a torso, and ended with a head.

The face at the top of the body was that of Josh Prentiss.

Captain Craig York folded his beefy arms over his chest. He stood with his feet wide and looked quite a bit like the trunk of an old oak tree firmly rooted in the ground. His feathery blond hair fluttered in the light breeze. He looked more like a '70s TV star than a modern-day deputy sheriff. "You have an uncanny ability to find dead bodies, Ms. Culpepper," he said acerbically, which seemed to be his standard way of speaking to me.

I guess I couldn't really blame him for his general abrasiveness. After all, it was true that I'd stumbled across more than my fair share of corpses since I'd come back to my hometown. If I could share the wealth, I certainly would. "Agatha actually found this one," I said.

York looked around. "Agatha who, and where is she?"

I scooped up my pug, who I'd finally managed to extricate from the poppy field. I lifted her into the air. "Captain York, meet Agatha." I turned my gaze to the pug. "Agatha, this is Captain York."

York let out an exasperated sigh that effectively communicated just how much he didn't appreciate my . . . well, my anything. York and I weren't friends. We weren't exactly enemies, either, but I hadn't been able to look past the fact that in the not so distant past, he'd set his sights on Miguel for a murder he obviously hadn't committed, and York couldn't . . . or *wouldn't* . . . get past the fact that I'd helped exonerate Miguel of said crime, pointing him in the direction of the real killer.

It also didn't help that I was besties with his boss. At best, he and I tolerated each other. I pointed to the flower bed, where a uniformed officer had cordoned off the area. "The body's over there."

"So I see," he said dryly, as if it wasn't completely obvious where the corpse was.

He left Agatha and me behind and plowed straight through the already pulverized flowers. Emmaline had arrived about ten minutes prior, and since Miguel had to get back to the restaurant, she had already pulled him in front of a nearby crepe myrtle, interviewing him first. A short while later, Miguel gave me a kiss on my cheek. "See you later," he said, followed by an entreating, "and maybe consider *not* getting involved in this?"

I gave a wry chuckle, because not only did I

have the uncanny ability to stumble across dead bodies, in the words of Captain York, but because I'd also had a hand in bringing a few people to justice. And by a few, I mean seven. Or eight, depending if you count the crime or the people involved in said crime.

"Falling on deaf ears, am I?" Miguel asked, reading my expression.

I wrapped an arm around his neck, hugging him and Agatha at the same time. "No, you're not. I don't plan to get involved." And that was true. Other than the fact that Josh Prentiss was a Yeast of Eden regular (Group A), I had no connection to the man. Which meant I had no stake in solving his murder.

Other than the fact that a killer was at large in Santa Sofia, of course.

As soon as Miguel left my side, Emmaline strode up. She hummed a few bars of "Here I Go Again," an old Whitesnake song we'd warbled along to once upon a time. She stopped humming, looking me square in the eyes. "And here *we* go again. What is it with you and dead bodies?" she asked, her words mirroring Captain York's sentiment.

"It's not like I go around planting them so I can discover them later."

She cocked an eyebrow. "So I can eliminate the possibility that you're actually a serial killer and everyone we've arrested for murder since you came back to Santa Sofia is really innocent?"

I dipped my chin in a solid yes of a nod. "It would be very bad for your reputation as sheriff if your sister-in-law was a deranged sociopath. Rest assured, I'm one hundred percent *not* a serial killer."

A little humor broke the tension, but Em got serious again as she turned to look at the evolving crime scene. "Tell me what happened."

So I did, retelling the same story Miguel had just shared with Captain York. "Miguel and I booked the gazebo for the engagement party, which you know. We met here to scope it out and finish up the planning. The party is Saturday. Which you also know. We walked around with Agatha on her leash. When she went into the flower bed and wouldn't come out, I went in after her. That's when I saw the body. Miguel called 911, and we stood guard until your people got here."

"Not many folks in the park today, so that's good."

A small consolation that mattered not one bit to the deceased. Still, I nodded.

"Thanks, Ivy. We've got it from here. I'll need an official statement—" The word "again" was implied. She raised her arm and called to one of her deputies. "Deputy Johnson, take Ms. Culpepper's statement." She looked back at me. "After that, you're free to go."

In the blink of an eye, Emmaline had gone from the familiar and relaxed interaction with a friend and sister-in-law to the steady, professional, and mirthless Sheriff Davis. I'd seen it happen more times than I could count. "Okay," I said as she headed off to join the team around the body. Fifteen minutes later, I finished telling my story again to Deputy Johnson, a forty-something woman with straight dark hair pulled into a tight ponytail and equally dark eyes that bore into anyone caught in their line of sight. She asked for my full name, address, and cell number. "In case we need to reach you later."

I thought it strange that she wouldn't know my connection to Emmaline, who already had my information. Maybe she was new. Then again, she probably needed it for the official paperwork. I gave her the info. "And Agatha," I added, watching her write down my pug's name.

She grimaced. "I've never seen the appeal of pugs. Flat-face snorers. No offense."

Agatha snorted, clearly affronted, but I said, "Oh gosh, none taken." I'd heard it all before. People either thought pugs were adorable . . . or abhorrent. There wasn't much in between. It was true, the breed tended to snore. How could they not, what with their distressed airways? And then there were the skin folds and bulging eyes, two things many people found unappealing.

I was firmly in the *pugs are adorable* camp. It wasn't *their* fault they'd been selectively bred to have these problems. It also wasn't their fault they'd been overbred. They still needed love and care, and I was happy to give Agatha every ounce of love I had in me, whatever anyone else felt.

The deputy left me, striding off for further instructions from one of her superiors. I sat on a bench on the opposite side of the walkway, the grassy expanse separating me from the crime scene. From here, I watched the beginning of the investigation unfold. More of Emmaline's people came. They kept the growing crowd of lookie-loos away from the bed of crushed poppies and the dead body.

I stayed and watched for another thirty minutes. By that point, I couldn't see through the throng of people surrounding the cordoned-odd area. I stood and tugged on Agatha's harness. She grumbled, but rose to her feet. With her tail curled again, we left the park.

Chapter 6

That evening, I sat on the patio at my childhood house, sipping on iced tea. I could have gone for something a little stiffer, but I stuck with the tea for the time being. Billy sat across from me. My dad bustled around, moving in and out of the house, bringing chips and salsa, refilling drinks, and generally keeping busy. "Dad! Take a load off, come on," Billy said before turning to me. "Miguel at the restaurant?"

"Yep. Late nights most nights," I said. "I guess Em'll be pretty busy till . . ."

"Yeah," he said. "Till this case is solved, she'll be burning the midnight oil, as they say."

I didn't actually know anyone who said that—and I had no idea where that idiom came from—but I understood. I'd been hoping Emmaline would take some time off for a family dinner, but the death of a community member meant her meals would happen at her desk or in her car or wherever she could squeeze them in.

"Any leads?" I asked Billy, knowing that four hours was hardly enough time to file an official report, forget about Emmaline taking the time to fill in her husband.

Billy just shrugged. "Not as far as I know. The guy was pretty well liked."

I piggybacked on that, relaying how generally popular he was at the bread shop, today excluded, how he practically held court there, and how I'd miss the constant chatter of him on his cell phone.

"Sounds like a decent guy," Billy commented.

"Generally, I think," I said. The thought of him snapping at the guy with the cell phone passed through my mind. I didn't know what that was about, but in terms of Josh's overall demeanor, it was a blip.

My dad finally listened to Billy and sat in one of the patio chairs. Owen Culpepper had gone from dark hair to salt and pepper after my mother died. He'd lost weight and struggled to get by, but slowly, the fog had lifted. He still had moments of melancholy, but the blossoming friendship between him and Olaya Solis had helped bring him back into the present. "His girlfriend was devastated," he said.

I spun my head to face him. Josh had been a very handsome man, so I don't know why it surprised me that he had a girlfriend. It did, though. In the time he'd been coming to Yeast of Eden, I'd learned that he was separated from his wife. I'd seen him flirt and charm and generally make women swoon. I never suspected he'd already recommitted to a single woman. "His what?"

My dad took a sip from the bottle of beer he held, switching up his crossed legs. "I was in line at the market to get those"—he pointed to the chips and salsa on the table—"and overheard a conversation. The woman in line ahead of me was talking to someone on her cell phone. I think she'd just gotten the news. She was barely keeping it together. I really felt for her."

I could see the empathy of their shared experience written on his face. I leaned forward and squeezed his hand. He smiled, squeezing back.

"What did she say?" I asked.

"Mostly she was crying. Kind of frantic. She just kept saying, *What am I going to do without him?*"

Something about the crying woman didn't sit right. Just that morning, I'd seen Josh Prentiss pointedly talk to Martina Solis. He'd flirted with several women at the bread shop. I'd seen his hands often enough over the past weeks. No wedding ring. Still . . . "Maybe it was his wife," I suggested.

"Could be," my dad said skeptically, "but I did notice that she didn't have a ring on."

"Maybe she just doesn't wear it," Billy said.

"Don't think so, son. She had on diamond earrings and a ring on her right hand." He gave a self-assured nod. "No. I'd venture to say that they weren't married."

"Don't suppose you caught her name," I asked, not holding out any hope that he actually had, but apparently I got my detecting chops from my dad, because he smiled and said, "In fact, I did. That's the other reason I think girlfriend and not wife. Her name is Jeanne. Pole or Pewl. Something like that."

I beamed at my dad. What a guy. He'd made a mental note to remember the name.

"I felt bad for her," my dad said. "She was lamenting her retirement. Without him, how was she going to be able to live like she did? How would she ever retire? Of course, I don't know what her career is, and then there were the diamonds, but still. A woman should have her own money."

I had to agree. Being able to support yourself was important. As a woman, it was essential. "Ten more years to work?" I asked suddenly. I didn't know Josh's age, but he wasn't anywhere near sixty. That much I knew.

My dad seemed to have read my mind. "I'd venture it was a bit of a May–December romance," my dad remarked. Now Billy and I both looked at him, waiting for him to elaborate. "Mmm, I'd place her close to her seventies."

My jaw dropped. That put her closer to Penelope Branford's eighty-something years than to Josh's late thirty- or forty-something. If this woman, Jeanne, was close to seventy, that meant Josh was, at *minimum*, twenty years younger than his paramour.

I couldn't say why, but that didn't sit well with me.

Chapter 7

I hadn't slept well last night. I'd tossed and turned, and when sleep finally *did* come, nightmares supplanted my normally peaceful dreams. Miguel and I walked through a dark park straight out of a dream-core video. Instead of a clear blue sky, my nightmare turned it ominously dark. The air undulated in visible, ever-moving inky streaks. As Agatha poked her nose into the Salvador Dalí poppies, I saw my mouth open to call her back, but my voice was slow and inaudible and came out sounding like, "Mwah mwah mwah."

Josh's body itself was surreal, hovering above the flowers, eyes wide. His mouth opened, and a tear rolled down his cheek. I reached down to feel his pulse, and he disintegrated before my eyes.

The faint sound of birds chirping seeped into my consciousness. They grew louder and louder still. My eyelids fluttered open, and I registered the singing of the birds from outside my window. The bright morning light filtering in from between the slats of my plantation shutters finished the job of waking me up.

It came back to me with harsh clarity. Agatha sniffing around Josh's body. His face looking dead, dead, dead. Murder. My hand found Agatha. Her steady breathing calmed me, settling my thrumming heartbeat. I picked up my phone from the bedside table. 5:30 AM. I scrubbed my hand over my face, pressing my fingers against the corners of my eyes, hoping I could push the images of the nightmare back into the recesses of my mind. I'd lived through discovering Josh Prentiss's body in real life. I didn't want to relive it in dreams that were straight out of a Tim Burton movie.

I arrived at the bread shop a full hour before I normally did. Felix was working the grinder. Janae mixed ingredients in three separate mixers. She stood five feet tall. Where Felix was a little portly from one—or ten—too many croissants, Janae was a pixie. They fit together, though, like flour and yeast.

They both looked up as I entered through the back door from the parking lot. "Ivy!" Felix looked at the wall clock. "You're early."

"Couldn't sleep," I mumbled.

"Olaya, too," Janae said. She motioned toward the office. "She's been in there for a while, though. Maybe she's finally getting some rest."

Olaya not sleeping was as unusual as her leaving with Pilar the day before, but her holing up in her office instead of being in the kitchen, her arms elbow-deep in dough, was downright concerning.

"Back in a minute," I said, walking past the morning crew members and their various tasks. I'd jump in where I was needed when I came back out, and once the shop opened, I'd transition to working behind the counter. I was a Jill-of-all-trades when it came to my part-time work at Yeast of Eden.

I rapped my knuckles lightly against Olaya's office door. Her response was quick. "*Adelante.*" My Spanish was rudimentary, at best, learned nearly twenty years ago at Santa Sofia High School. Miguel, though, was fluent, as was Olaya. Between the two of them, I'd been picking up words and phrases, understanding more than I could actually say. *Adelante.* Come in. So I did.

Olaya sat at her desk, one hand moving a black computer mouse around a rectangular mousepad. She wasn't quite a late adopter of technology, but neither was she first in line for new things. No trackpad for her, even though I'd suggested it. "I have no need," she'd stated, firm and sure.

"You are here too early," she said, looking at me. "And you have dark circles."

"Murder has that effect. What's *your* excuse?" I asked.

I'd expected her to say her anxiety had to do with Pilar. Instead she answered with, "The same."

At this, I cocked my head. Olaya didn't know Josh Prentiss any better than I did. She liked his philosophy that butter and jam masked the depth of flavor in a piece of sourdough, but other than that, I couldn't remember a time when I'd seen the two of them talk. "Are you okay?" I asked.

Her brows knitted together in thought, as if she

had to consider how to answer the question. Before she could answer, though, a loud clatter sounded from the kitchen behind me. It was like a gun fired in the dead of night. I jumped, spinning around. Olaya was out of her chair like a bullet, running past me and through the door. I went after her, nearly plowing into her when she stopped short. Four stainless-steel baking trays were upturned on the floor, smashed pieces of dough splayed out around them.

They used to be dinner rolls, neatly shaped, with a slash down the center. Now they were mangled and unusable.

"*Qué pasó . . . ?*" Olaya pressed her palm to her forehead and muttered, "*En nombre de Dios, qué pasó?*" She repeated her question in English, her voice on the edge of control. This mess would set them back a good hour. "What happened?"

Felix stepped up, his thin lips pressed together. His hands fisted around a white kitchen towel. "A mistake," he growled. "I'll take care of it. It won't happen again."

Olaya leveled her gaze at him, but she was more Rita Moreno than Linda Hamilton. Even when she was angry, there wasn't much bite to her words. She opened her mouth to speak, but changed her mind, instead drawing in a calming breath and beckoning to him. "Come."

He followed her into her office. The door closed behind them. I ignored the low murmur of their voices, instead crouching to help Taylor and Mae, who were at the center of the mess. Taylor stacked the trays and set them aside to wash. I used a dough scraper to get as much of the sticky, misshapen dough off the floor as possible. Mae did the same. "So what *did* happen?" I asked.

Mae, a short, slightly plump twenty-eight-year-old with remnants of acne scars on her forehead, bit her lower lip. "I just . . . I didn't see her, and—"

"Bam!" Taylor clapped her hands together. "You need to look where you're going."

"It was an accident," Mae squawked.

Taylor, who was about the same age as Mae, albeit a solid foot taller, had darker under-eye circles than mine. She blew an insolent raspberry. "Whatever. They're just stupid rolls."

Mae gaped. "Hey! I worked hard on those rolls. You need to look where you're going."

Taylor's nostrils flared. "Whatever. One less for you to knock your mother down over," she said.

I gawked. It was clear Taylor had come into the dining area and had seen Mae chase her mother around the bread shop's tables the day before. It was also clear that everyone knew Kristin Spelling liked to sneak our bread behind her daughter's back, so that was a low blow, but Mae came right back. "Oh yeah? Better than having daddy issues."

Taylor saw red. Her nostrils flared and she lunged at Mae. "You little—"

"Stop!" I jumped up and inserted myself between them.

Mae flung her arms around, trying to reach Taylor. I managed to hold her back, but she snarled. "I'm going to—"

Taylor smirked. "What? You're going to what? I'm a model, and I do yoga, like, every day. My core is rock solid, and my balance is perfect. You're just a little freak."

I was still holding Mae back, but Taylor's words made me spin around. "Hey! That is *not* cool."

Taylor looked at me with all the disdain she could muster. "Who even *are* you? You're too old to be hanging around this place all the time."

I stared. This girl was Jekyll and Hyde. I'd never seen this nasty side of her. The other three people in the kitchen—Janae, Ryan, and Rochelle—had stopped their dough prep and were staring at Taylor and Mae. I'd faced down my ex-husband, his mistress, and a fair number of murderers. I was so *not* in the mood for *this* snarky girl. I looked her square in the eyes. "I think you should stop before you say something you regret."

But she was too far gone to stop. She threw down the mound of mangled dough she'd gathered up from the floor, then wiped her hands on her apron. "For real, though. This is the worst. Job. Ever. Four-flipping-thirty in the morning? Seriously?" She huffed. "I don't even *need* this job."

"Then why are you here?" Mae muttered. "Do us all a favor and just go."

Taylor spun on her. "Because my stupid *parents* won't give me any *money* till I work for six. Straight. Months." Seething steam almost spewed from her nostrils. "So. Lame. It's *my* money. God, I can't *wait* till I'm outta here."

There was a change in the air behind me, then Felix spoke, controlled anger clear in his voice. "Consider this your lucky day, then." We all spun to see him and Olaya framed in her office doorway. Felix continued. "Get your things. I'll see you out."

A collective gasp sounded, and for a few seconds, it was so quiet you could have literally heard dough rising.

Taylor had frozen at Felix's words. Now she suddenly jolted back to life. Rage bubbled at the surface. "What the hell are you talking about? You can't *do* that."

"Of course he can," Olaya said. "He hired you. He can most certainly fire you."

In three strides, Felix was by Taylor's side, escorting her to the small employee area, where her personal belongings were. He took her apron from her as she shoved a book into her purse, grabbed her cell phone, and practically stomped toward the back door Felix held open. "I'll mail your final check."

"Karma's a bitch," she snarled, first at him, but then her eyes skittered here and there, and she spat. "You'll get what you deserve."

I had no idea if she'd been talking to Felix, Olaya, Mae, or all of us as a collective. Regardless, a chill slithered up my spine. The girl seemed to be more than a little unhinged. I felt sorry for whoever hired her next so she could serve her parentally imposed six-month sentence.

The ruckus in the kitchen had blinded all of us to the time, slowing it down as the drama unfolded. With the slam of the door, reality jolted back into place. The second hand on the large analog wall clock ticked, ticked, ticked in a steady rhythm. There was bread to bake, including rolls to remake. As Mae and I finished cleaning up the mess on the floor, I pressed her for details on her squabble with Taylor. "She flipped out," Mae said.

"Just completely flipped out. She ran into me on purpose, I know she did."

"But why?" Surely Taylor was smart enough to figure out that an outburst like that would jeopardize her job.

Mae shrugged. "I have no idea."

A few minutes later, I had my apron on and flour in the mixer. My thoughts spun round and round in time with the dough hook attachment. Now Josh wasn't the only person taking up space in my brain. Taylor was there, too. Despite her vitriolic outburst, I had to think that something had triggered it. She had never been particularly pleasant, but neither was she usually that mean-spirited. I had to let it go, though, since she was no longer an employee of Yeast of Eden.

Once the dough was mixed, I turned it onto my floured, stainless-steel counter and dug my hands into it, kneading and pulling and turning until the gluten was good and stretched. As I formed the dough into rolls, placing them on a baking sheet, I couldn't stop my mind from drifting to Josh and what had happened to him. I didn't know how he died. There had been no obvious indications on the parts of his body I'd seen. No bashed-in head. No blood. No marks on his neck. I had no answer to that. I slid the baking sheets onto one of the racks to rise and immediately got to work on the next batch.

Meanwhile, Olaya worked on her skull cookies, a labor of love for her. She'd started the tradition of the *día de los muertos* cookies one October years ago. Since then they'd become the one sweet

Olaya offered on a regular basis. Well, those and
now the morning cookies. She made a batch every
other day or so, taking the time to pipe icing onto
each and every one. She then hid them amid the
breads in the display cases for the children who
came into the shop to find. I watched her from the
corner of my eye. She bent over the tray of cookies, tuning out the low chatter between the bakers.
I knew that Pilar having lost her parents, her own
responsibility to now care for her niece, along with
Consuelo and Martina, and Josh's death had all in-
vaded Olaya's thoughts. Now the incident with
Taylor and Mae had likely planted itself there as
well. Icing the cookies was meditative for her, but
even the repetitive process didn't ease the strain
evident on her face. No, it was clear that Olaya
Solis was not herself.

By nine o'clock, the kitchen was back on sched-
ule. I tossed my flour-covered apron in the laundry
basket Olaya kept in the back corner, donned a
fresh one, and headed to the front of house to
help Zula, who'd waltzed through the kitchen and
to the front a few minutes earlier. I stopped short
at the swinging doors. Zula stood frozen near one
of the tables, staring out the front windows. I followed her gaze and drew in a sharp breath. Outside the bakery windows, the sidewalk was crammed
with people. I'd heard that a few people had
shown up at the park the night before in an im-
promptu vigil, lighting candles, and propping up
photographs of Josh, who seemed to be one of
Santa Sofia's native sons.

But this gathering was something entirely different. It seemed every one of Josh Prentiss's friends

knew that he spent his mornings at Yeast of Eden conducting business. It also seemed as if a secret missive had been sent out alerting every one of those friends to show up this morning with hand-made signs that said *Justice for Josh* and *Josh Was Murdered.* But the worst one—and the one that explained the crowd's presence here—was *Yeast of Eden: Bread That Will Kill You!*

Chapter 8

I barreled past Zula and yanked the door open. The bells jangled ferociously from the force. I was met with a wall of people. One of them, a young man whose thick neck supported his square-jawed head and who looked like he was still in high school, spun around. I watched as he zeroed in on the Yeast of Eden logo on my apron. His eyes narrowed, and his expression turned hostile. "You work here?"

I reacted to his animosity by rooting my feet to the ground and slamming one of my hands onto my hip. "Yeah. I do." I let my gaze dart around and flung my other arm wide. "What the hell is all this?"

He looked at me as if I was off my rocker. "My best friend's dad is dead, that's what this is."

"Yeah. I found the body," I said. I channeled

Taylor Wilson with my heavy pauses. "In. The. Park."

This bit of news momentarily stunned him, but he recovered and growled. "So? Maybe *you're* the one who poisoned him."

I took a step backward at the accusation. "What are you talking about?"

"Poisoned bread. It's what killed him—"

I gaped at him. "Whaaat?"

The kid rolled his eyes. "Oh come on—"

I held my palm out to him. "Nooo," I said, drawing out the word. "*You* come on. There's no poisoned bread here."

He reached for my wrist to yank my hand away from his face. I jerked it back before he could touch me. I turned, ready to leave this kid behind. "The local paper is all over it," he snarled.

This stopped me in my tracks. The *Santa Sofia Daily*, our local newspaper, was saying Josh Prentiss was poisoned by bread from Yeast of Eden? "You cannot be serious."

"Look it up," he said, then he motioned overhead. "Murderer! Murderer!" He pointed at me. "Murderer. This one right here. She's a murderer!"

I backed away, waving my hands at him. "Whoa. Dude. You don't know what you're talking about."

For every step backward I took, he stepped toward me. "It makes sense to me."

By now, a few people had filled in around the guy. "Murderer!" they chanted.

"It makes *no* sense. I hardly knew the man. And he *wasn't* poisoned by bread from Yeast of Eden."

The piercing wail of a siren cut through the noise.

A police cruiser appeared, slowly forcing the crowd to disperse. It split apart, giving me a straight-line view across the street, where a local news crew had set up. A TV reporter had her back to the crowd, while her cameraman pointed his giant camera at her. I watched as the reporter shifted, stepping out of the way so the cameraman could get a wide shot of the bread shop and the crowd with their signs.

I darted to the left to get out of the line of sight, at the same time looking for the thick-necked high schooler I'd been talking to. I searched the crowd for him, but he was gone. When I turned again, I ran smack into the back of Nina from the antiques mini-mall. She spun around, her eyes as wide as quarters and her mouth agape. Her shoulders hunched in relief when recognition hit. "Oh my God, Ivy! This is crazy!"

That was putting it mildly. Mayhem? Chaos? Pandemonium? A surreal nightmare? Any of these words felt a little stronger and more apropos. Despite the presence of law enforcement and the way the crowd had broken apart a few seconds ago, it now seemed to expand before my eyes, as if the pavement had taken a big breath in and exhaled a dozen more people swinging their signs around to make sure they could be seen from every angle. The chants grew louder. "People think Olaya's bread actually killed that poor man," I muttered. It was unbelievable to even contemplate.

Nina pointed past me and toward the plate-glass windows of the bread shop. "I just saw him yesterday," she said. "Right there. How can he be dead?"

It felt like days had passed, not just twenty hours or so. Just yesterday, Josh had been on the phone with someone, then he'd chatted with Nina. He'd been *alive.*

And now he wasn't.

My temples throbbed in time with the chanting. *Olaya's bread kills. Olaya's bread kills. Olaya's bread kills.*

"No it doesn't!" Nina caterwauled, issuing her own response to the protestors. Amid the rising volume of the demonstrators, the keening sound was lost.

"The boosters," she cried, spinning to face me. "They're going to be so lost without him. That man single-handedly changed the football program at the high school. He was a master fundraiser. My son is going to miss him. They all are."

I raised my brows in surprise. I didn't even know Nina had children, let alone a high schooler. "Do you have a son on the team?"

She flung her head around in an untethered nod. "Sure, sure. Seth is a junior. When he heard the news . . . oh, Ivy, he's devastated. Dev-a-stat-ed. The whole *team* is. Josh went to practices. Well, not all the time. He was a busy man. But when he was there, he cheered on every kid, not just his own . . ." She trailed off and slapped her hand over her quivering lips. "Oh, his poor son. Brendan."

I thought about Miguel asking me to not get involved in Josh Prentiss's murder. At the time, I had only a thin connection to the man as a customer of the bread shop. But now, on a dime, things had changed. These people, with their posters and chants, actually thought Josh's sourdough roll had been, what, a vehicle for poison? Suddenly, I felt as if I *had* to be involved. Rumors in a small town traveled faster than Sha'Carri Richardson slaying at the Olympics. I had to stop it from getting out of control before all the life was choked out of Yeast of Eden and Olaya was destroyed.

"I'm sure his mom will do everything she can," I said, hoping it was true. A strong, supportive network to help the boy cope was the thing that would get him through.

"Oh God, Tracy's got to be devastated, too. They were reconciling—"

"Oh. That's . . . wait. They are? I mean, they were?"

"That's what I heard."

"Why were they separated in the first place?"

Nina shrugged. "I don't have any idea about that. Like I said, Josh was a great guy."

Not to everyone, I thought. There was a pretty solid belief that if one person in a marriage was killed, the chances were good that the spouse had a hand in it. My thoughts shot to the probability that Josh's wife—Tracy—was involved. Maybe they'd been reconciling, but maybe she'd gotten wind of her husband's girlfriend, Jeanne.

An unnatural silence fell over the crowd. I turned to see Olaya standing in front of the bread shop's door. "I have to go," I said to Nina.

She looked over my shoulder, giving Olaya a sad smile. To me, she said, "I don't believe it, Ivy, and neither will anyone else."

I hoped she was right, but as I made my way back to the storefront, I saw the reporter who'd been across the street. She was now plowing down the sidewalk with her arm extended, her microphone clutched in her hand ready to shove right into Olaya's face. I approached just as the reporter said, "Ms. Solis, people are saying your bread contained the poison that killed Josh Prentiss. What do you have to say about that?"

All the color drained from Olaya's face. Her normally olive skin was pallid and chalky. "It is a mistake," she said gravely. "A man is dead, and you are here to blame me? I am telling you now, it had nothing to do with me or my shop." She spoke to the reporter, but her eyes bore into mine as she said, "Go. Go find the truth about what happened to that man."

Chapter 9

Things went from bad to worse in a matter of a few hours. If we'd thought the vultures were circling before, now they were in full attack mode. The local news station had come around asking questions, and the *Santa Sofia Daily* had tried to get statements from Olaya, Zula, Esmé, and Felix, all to no avail. The news station had aired their report on scene, capturing the protest. By noon, the crowds had finally thinned out, but Marcus Brolin, a reporter from the local tabloid, *The Scout*, was hanging around, talking incessantly to any and every person who came and went from Yeast of Eden. When he tried to talk to the bread shop's employees, he'd started out professionally, asking politely for a statement, on the record. With each refusal, he became more and more agitated. By the time *I* marched across the street to confront him, any pretense of politeness was gone.

"Is Olaya Solis concerned about the accusations against her that she poisoned Josh Prentiss?" he demanded.

It had gone from bad to worse. Now Olaya was being directly accused. "There are no accusations," I said.

"The community won't let this rest until justice has been served."

I stared at him. From his deep tan, it looked like he spent a good amount of time either on the beach or in a tanning salon. And from the stubble on his face and his red-rimmed eyes, he'd gotten very little sleep the night before. The death of Edward Yentin popped into my mind. He'd been a reporter for *The Scout*, too, and it had ended badly for him. If this guy, Marcus Brolin, wasn't careful, he might end up with the same fate. I felt my nostrils flare. "Justice will be served when people start looking for the real killer. Olaya had nothing to do with it."

I tried to walk past him, but he sidestepped, blocking my path. "Is it a coincidence, then, that you discovered the body of the man your employer is accused of killing?"

"She's not accused of killing him!" I blurted. "The man was a customer, that's it. She has no other connection to him."

"That's not entirely true now, is it?"

I balked. "Of course it's—" I stopped abruptly when his lips curved up in a triumphant smile. "What?" I demanded, thinking this guy was way too cocky for his own good.

"There is another connection between the late

Josh Prentiss and Olaya Solis." His smile turned smarmy. "I'm surprised she hasn't told you."

I knew he was baiting me, but I couldn't help myself. "Tell me what?"

And then he dropped the grenade he'd been holding. "Josh Prentiss had a relationship with Ms. Solis."

My brain sputtered. That certainly couldn't be true. First of all, Olaya was dating my father. And second, she was far too old for Josh Prentiss. But then my father's story about Josh's older girlfriend, Jeanne, came to mind. I pushed away the very idea. After all, Olaya had scarcely ever spared a single glance for Josh Prentiss.

A niggle of worry wormed into my mind. That, in itself, was unlike her. She usually greeted her customers warmly, but other than her approval of him saying he wanted to savor her bread without jam or butter, he was a person she had rarely spoken to. Surely that wasn't a cover because they actually *did* know each other. Overcompensation?

"I don't know what you're talking about," I said to Marcus Brolin, managing indignant.

"Then I'll say it again. It appears your boss was closer to Josh Prentiss than she let on." He paused, knowing full well the dramatic effect it caused. I waited with bated breath for him to continue. "Jilted by him is what I heard."

"That is simply not true," I said. He was fishing. He had to be. Still, his words played on repeat in my mind. *Jilted by him.* Aside from the fact that it would break my father's heart, if by some cruel twist of fate what Marcus Brolin said *was* true, that gave Olaya motive, which meant the idea that she'd been the one to poison Josh Prentiss wouldn't be so far-fetched. *I* knew she could never commit murder, but that didn't mean the rest of Santa Sofia would believe it.

Without warning, what Olaya had said to me earlier came back. *Go. Go find the truth about what happened to that man.*

The impact of those words sank in. "She knew," I muttered.

Like a quick-moving lizard, Marcus Brolin's head snapped toward me. "What's that?"

"Nothing," I said, all the while thinking, *No, no, no. Olaya knew. She* knew *she'd be a suspect when her connection to Josh Prentiss came out.*

"You need to separate yourself from her. Don't let her drag you down," Marcus warned.

He'd be the type of person to leave a loved one in a burning building, saving only himself. I wasn't that person. I'd risk life and limb to help the people I cared about. I stuck my elbows out to the sides and ducked my head, pushing past him. "No comment."

On a normal day, the bread shop would have been hopping. Even though the protestors were gone, the lack of normalcy continued, and the dearth of customers remained. Other than the woman Zula was helping, the place was still empty.

I kept my head down and fast-walked past the counter and into the kitchen. The low morale was palpable. Felix stood at the grain mill. He turned when he heard me enter, giving a small wave. His usual smile and good cheer were notably absent.

Janae had removed every bowl and kitchen tool from the stainless-steel shelves. They were laid out in front of her on the shiny silver counters. She stood on a stepladder, her arm outstretched as she wiped down the shelves with a white rag. "Deep cleaning," she said when she saw me. Right. Because there weren't enough customers to keep the normal bake load going.

Mae was a the only other late-morning crew member present. Felix had apparently let everyone else go for the day.

My head buzzed. Rumors about Olaya and the possibility that her bread had caused Josh Prentiss's death were affecting business to a degree I'd never have imagined. Yeast of Eden simply *was*. It was an institution in Santa Sofia. It had been here forever, and it had gone without saying that it would continue to be here forever.

Only now its enduring existence was in question.

I raised my brows at Felix in another unspoken question. Where was Olaya? He gestured with his head. She was holed up in her office. I rapped my knuckles lightly against the closed door. A few seconds later, it slowly opened. I'd expected to see Olaya. Instead, it was my father looking back at me. I felt my eyes bug. "Dad?"

"Ivy," he said, and he opened the door wider, closing it again after I entered.

Olaya leaned forward in her chair, one elbow on her desk, her fist propped under her jaw. She looked up at me. Her normally sanguine eyes looked tired. I glanced from her to my dad, then back. Something was going on, but I still couldn't bring myself to believe what Marcus Brolin said was true. My dad pointed to the chair facing Olaya's desk. "Sit down, Ivy."

I squeezed into the narrow space and sat facing Olaya. My dad leaned against the door. If it was true that Olaya had been seeing a much younger man behind his back, he was awfully calm about it. "What's happening here?" I asked.

"Things are a little complicated," my dad said.

He couldn't have said anything truer and, at the same time, less helpful. "I'll say. That hack Marcus Brolin? From *The Scout*? He's outside and he's saying—" I swallowed. Regrouped and directed my gaze at Olaya. It hurt to even say the words, but I forced them out. "He's saying you were involved with him. With Josh."

Olaya pressed her lips together as her spine stiffened. She sat up straighter. "It is a lie, Ivy." She looked at my father and gave a slow blink.

"Tell her," he said, his tone supportive and encouraging.

Olaya blinked again before returning her gaze to me. "About that he is wrong, Ivy. *I* did not have anything to do with him."

A wave of relief flowed through me. If she said she didn't have anything to do with Josh, I believed her. It wasn't Olaya. She hadn't broken my father's newly mended heart. "Oh, that's good news." I exhaled a loaded breath. "Such a relief!"

But my dad and Olaya didn't look relieved, and suddenly I knew it wasn't as simple as Olaya saying she wasn't involved with Josh. A rush of anxiety climbed from my chest to my throat. There was more to the story.

Olaya gave me the same slow blink she'd given my father a few seconds ago, as if she needed the extra second or two to garner up all her strength. "He was not seeing me, Ivy. He was seeing Martina," she said.

"Oh." I stared, then said, "Oh," again, this time cupping my hand over my forehead as I processed this bit of information. Just a few months ago, Martina had been seeing Vicente Villanueva, a businessman investor in town. She'd been smitten, maybe even in love, but Vicente had lost a bundle in a bad deal and had moved to the East Coast to head up a new hotel operation. He'd wanted Martina to go with him, but she hadn't mustered up the gumption to leave her coastal California home.

I caught my father's eye and heard his voice in my head telling me to remember the woman he'd overheard in the grocery store.

"Right."

Olaya looked at me, puzzled. "What?"

I left her question unanswered as I processed through my thoughts. Josh Prentiss had been a rebound for Martina, only Marcus Brolin had ID'd the wrong Solis sister. But *that* wasn't my top concern. No, what bothered me the most was that—at least from where I sat—it looked like Josh Prentiss had been stringing at least two women along— Martina and Jeanne, the woman at the grocery store. Not to mention reconciling with his wife, if Nina was to be believed.

"There's more," my dad said. He dipped his chin—silent encouragement for Olaya.

Olaya closed her eyes for a beat. When she opened them, her nostrils flared. "Something happened between them last week, and Martina ended it."

I looked from Olaya to my dad, eyebrows raised. "What happened?"

Olaya shook her head. "She won't say."

She broke it off. After losing Vicente, I thought, filling in the blank.

"She will not tell me more than that."

Olaya's earlier directive haunted me again. *Go. Go find the truth about what happened to that man.*

Go find the truth about that man who'd hurt her sister.

In order to do that, I had to get answers to two questions: Had Martina found out about Josh's wife? Or about Jeanne?

Chapter 10

Emmaline had confirmed that Josh Prentiss had been poisoned, but I didn't believe for a minute that Yeast of Eden's bread had anything to do with his death any more than I believed Martina was involved. Sometimes the truth, though, didn't matter. The fact that Martina had full access to Yeast of Eden didn't bode well for her. Once Marcus Brolin figured out he had named the wrong Solis sister, it wouldn't take long for the court of public opinion to weigh in . . . more than it already had, that is.

If people continued to spread the story that bread from Yeast of Eden had been the vehicle to deliver whatever poison had killed Josh, Martina might rise to the top of the suspect list. She had a key to the bread shop. She knew how to make bread. Not as well as Olaya, and without the infusion of magic, but still, she could measure and mix and knead and bake.

Another thought hit me like a punch to the gut. Olaya might actually be seen as an accomplice. My father, Olaya, and I stared at each other, each at a loss as to what to do. Finally, with no other solution materializing, I said, "We need to call Emmaline."

Olaya shook her head. "No, no, no." Her fingers pulled at her short, iron-gray strands of hair and hissed. *"She did not do this."*

"Of course she didn't," my dad said. He moved to her side and sank down to his haunches. "We can trust Emmaline. She's like a daughter to me. Hell, she *is* my daughter."

True, because she was married to his son.

"We can trust her," he said again.

It wasn't Emmaline I was worried about. It was Captain Craig York. He was a "develop a theory, then figure out how to prove it" kind of man. If he got a sliver under his skin that told him Martina—and, by association, Olaya—had something to do with Josh Prentiss's murder, he'd worry that sliver till he dug it out, blood and infection be damned.

But I had utter and complete faith in Emmaline. If *she* trusted York—which she seemed to—then I had no choice but to put my confidence in him, too.

Olaya called Martina. The conversation was in Spanish, short, and sweet. Forty minutes later, Olaya, my dad, Martina, and I were crammed into Emmaline's office. My best friend sat at her desk, a model of professionalism despite the fact that we'd known each other since we were kids building sand castles on the beach. Once again, she adeptly separated her position as sheriff from her role as my friend and sister-in-law. Her long braids were woven into her dark curly hair. She had them pulled back and wound together with a hairband. Before her career in law enforcement, she'd alternated between keeping her hair natural—giving it a break—and alternating between teal and lavender and blue braids. Now subdued red was as adventurous as she got. It suited her, adding a little bit of spark to her otherwise ordinary sheriff's uniform.

Captain York stood by her side, as tall and thin as ever. Every time I saw him with his long sideburns and flyaway blond hair, I thought again how he seemed to live in the wrong decade. I wanted to tell him that the 1970s were calling, but I couldn't quite bring myself to do it.

"Thank you for coming forward," Emmaline said to Martina.

Martina gave the slightest nod. Her usual refinement had been replaced by tired eyes and a sallow undertone to her olive complexion. At the moment, she mirrored the exhaustion of her eldest sister. But, like Olaya, she was stoic and controlled. No tears fell, although it looked to me like they might have already done so in the privacy of her own home. She and Olaya held hands. She clasped tighter, her knuckles turning white, as she told the story. "I met him at a real estate mixer. I'd never seen him before, and he was very ... attentive. This was about four months ago. I remember because my boyfriend—" She stopped. Regrouped.

"My *ex*-boyfriend had moved away a few weeks before that. He was interesting and successful. That's when it started. We met at the park a few times to walk and talk. Then we started having lunch together once in a while. He met me during my break at a little mom and pop's place nearby. Off the beaten track, he always said. After a while, we stopped meeting in public at all. He wanted to keep things quiet. Josh was very private. He told me right away that he had two kids and an ex-wife. He didn't want to be public with our . . . *relationship*."

She put an emphasis on the word, as if she wasn't sure what they'd had actually had *been* a relationship.

From the slight movement of Emmaline's head, I knew she picked up on it, too. She didn't press the issue, though. "Where did you usually meet, after you stopped meeting in public?" Emmaline asked.

Martina usually wore lipstick and eyeliner, and under normal circumstances, she would have looked more put together than everyone in this room combined. Right now, though, she pulled a face with unmascaraed eyes and nude lips. "At my town house."

"And how often did you meet?"

"In the beginning, just once a week. Then we started seeing each other more often. Two or three times a week."

"Until . . ." Emmaline pressed, because from Martina's tone the *until* was implied.

"Until a week ago."

"What happened a week ago?" Emmaline asked.

Martina's eyelids did an odd fluttery thing as she looked up to the ceiling. "He left his cell phone on the table when he went to the bathroom. A mistake, I am sure. He was not careless like that. As soon as I looked at it, I knew why he was always so careful. A few texts came through while he was gone." She paused and inhaled, her nostrils expanding with the effort she was putting into controlling her emotions. "They were from two other women. Someone named Jeanne, and his wife, Tracy."

A silence fell in the office for a solid ten seconds, as if in respect for Martina in the face of Josh's betrayal.

Captain York spoke for the first time. "So you thought you were exclusive in your . . . *relationship?*"

"Yes. *I* thought we were, but apparently we were not."

"What happened next?" Emmaline asked.

From where I sat, I could see Martina's fingers tightening their grip on Olaya's hand. "When he came back, I showed him the phone with the texts. I asked him about his wife first. He said they were divorcing. I do not know if that is true or not, but that wasn't the thing that made me doubt him. I asked him about the other one. About the woman, Jeanne. He said she was a friend. She had borrowed some money and was going to repay him."

"But . . ." York said, because there definitely seemed to be a *but* coming.

"*But* . . . I don't know. It did not seem right.

Truthful. The text from the woman said he could come over to see her and get the check then."

"Is that when you stopped seeing him?" Emmaline asked.

"Yes, but I did not know it then. Not until after—" A small sound escaped from Martina's throat as she broke off. Olaya clucked. "*Está bien, hermana.* It is okay. You will be okay."

"Until after what?" Em coaxed.

Martina's shoulders had started to slouch. "I followed him—"

"*We* followed him," Olaya interjected.

My dad and I had been standing quietly, like wallpaper in the room, but Olaya's admission took me by surprise, and I let out a small gasp. Whenever I wanted to dig deeper into something, it was Penelope Branford who played Watson to my Holmes, not Olaya. But, apparently, she'd given a turn as the good doctor when Martina had decided to be Sherlock for an evening. I turned to my dad and cocked one eyebrow. He gave me a single nod in response. It had really happened, and he knew about it.

"*We* followed him," Martina amended. "Straight to this woman's huge house. She met him at the door with a hug and a kiss, and then they went inside."

"We waited there for more than an hour," Olaya said. "He did not come out. Finally we left."

Martina scoffed. "They were *not* just friends."

"Could you find this house again?" Emmaline asked, but Martina shrugged helplessly. "It was dark."

Em turned to Olaya. "Could you?"

"No," Olaya said. "I wish I could, but no. The hills, that is all I know."

"What did Mr. Prentiss do for a living?" York asked, redirecting the interview.

"Banking and venture capital," Martina said.

Something about that answer sent up a red flag in my mind, but I couldn't pin down what had triggered it. I hadn't known what Josh Prentiss's job was, aside from being one of the football boosters, but from the amount of time he'd spent on the phone, spreadsheets pulled up on his computer, banking seemed to fit the bill.

As Emmaline and York shared a knowing glance, I felt like I was two or three steps behind them both. Emmaline cleared her throat. "Did he ever ask you for money, Ms. Solis?"

She hesitated, giving me time to ponder the question. Why would Josh ask Martina for money? It bounced around in my head. The moment Martina answered Emmaline with a slow nod and a quiet, "Yes," *bam!*, I got there. In the blink of an eye, I came up with a theory. What if Jeanne hadn't borrowed money from Josh? What if it had been the other way around?

I looked at Emmaline. We'd known each other almost our entire lives. We couldn't quite read each other's minds, and we couldn't communicate telepathically, but we were darn close on both counts. My head waggled, and my eyes popped open wide. "*He was a scammer?*" I mouthed.

Whether or not Emmaline actually read my lips was debatable. But she knew what I was asking, nonetheless, and she gave one succinct nod.

"And did you give him any money?" York asked.

Again, Martina said, "Yes. Seven thousand dollars. For an investment opportunity. A new tech company. That was before . . ."

"Before . . ." York prompted.

"Before the texts. Before I realized something was not right."

York nodded. "And did you earn any returns on that money?"

"Not yet," she said quietly.

My head suddenly felt full of cotton as I remembered what my dad had said about Jeanne, the woman at the grocery store—presumably the same woman whose name Martina had seen on Josh's phone. She'd been woeful about her retirement. Without Josh, how was she going to maintain her current lifestyle? How would she ever retire?

Josh Prentiss had been her retirement. I thought that had meant that maybe they were going to get married, odd though it was, and his retirement would then become hers as well. I could see now that made no sense. He was too young to retire. He was already married. And he was seeing more people than just Jeanne.

But what if she had given him money with which to invest? What if *that* was her retirement? And now that Josh was gone, so was her money.

Emmaline tapped her index finger against her lips. It was one of her "thinking" tells. "When did he start coming to the bread shop?" she asked, directing the question to the room.

I spoke up first. "It was about three . . . maybe four months ago."

Then Martina spoke. "I didn't want to see him

anymore. I told him that, but he started coming in the mornings, working there for a few hours."

"After you saw the texts on his phone?" York clarified.

"Yes," Martina said. "I had broken it off, but he knew my sister owned the bread shop, and he knew I stopped there most mornings. He kept trying to talk to me. *To explain*, he said."

Now we knew why Josh had become a fixture at Yeast of Eden.

Martina gave a heavy sigh. "He was there every morning. I did not want to talk to him. I stopped coming in as frequently."

Another puzzle piece fit into place. Josh's presence explained Martina's decreased visits to Yeast of Eden, and also her earlier arrival times.

"Why do you think he wanted to keep seeing you after you realized he was seeing someone else and wasn't actually getting divorced?" Emmaline asked.

Martina glanced at Olaya, who squeezed her hand. "I told him I wanted my money back or I was going to tell his wife about the affair. He . . . he . . . was trying to convince me not to do that."

My heart sank. If Martina and Josh had argued over it, things could have gone badly. It was thin, but it was a potential motive. From the hard line of Captain York's lips, I got the feeling he'd come to the same conclusion. "Ms. Solis," he said, "where were you yesterday between the hours of ten AM and twelve PM?"

All I could think was, thank *God* Martina had an office job. She'd come in for coffee that morning and had rushed right back out in a hurry to get to work.

And then I remembered something else. Martina and Josh had crossed paths at the bread shop door. She was leaving, while he was entering. He'd been talking on his cell phone but stopped and pressed it to his shoulder while he and Martina spoke briefly.

I waited for Martina to answer York's question, but instead of piping up with an airtight alibi, she wilted under his steely gaze. "I saw him that morning at Yeast of Eden. I already had told him I wanted my money back. Over and over, I told him. I asked him again yesterday morning, and he said he would get it for me."

"Did you plan to meet?"

"Yes," she said. "We were supposed to meet at the park at eleven thirty. I took an early lunch and got there at eleven twenty-five."

"And? Did you get your money back?" York asked, but at the moment, I got the feeling he was like a lawyer who never asked a question he didn't already know the answer to.

"No—"

He interrupted her with a curt, "Mmm hmm. And to be clear, your meeting was at the same park where his body was found a few hours later. Skyline Park."

It suddenly felt as if I was part of a strongman carnival game and someone had used a hammer and pounded the lever hard enough to catapult my heart to my throat, but now it went into free fall, straight to the pit of my stomach. Despite the circumstantial evidence, York couldn't possibly think Martina had really killed the man. I looked at Em, trying to catch her eye, but she was focused only on Martina. Surely *she* didn't believe it.

Martina and Olaya's grasp tightened. Martina swallowed. She did her best to lift her chin and meet York's gaze. "I waited until twelve o'clock, but Josh—" Her voice broke, her emotions finally breaking through the stoicism. "He never showed up."

"Right," York said. The implication of that single word was crystal clear. Josh Prentiss had not shown up because by that point, he was already dead.

Chapter 11

Ever the gentleman, my father escorted Olaya and Martina back to the bread shop. I stuck around to talk to Emmaline. After York left her office, I closed the door and sat across the desk from her. "You can't possibly think Martina killed that man," I said, blurring the lines between Emmaline the sheriff and Emmaline my friend.

"Ivy, this is a murder investigation. We have to look at all the potential suspects. And let me tell you, there are a few. Do I think Martina did it? No. Do I have to investigate every lead to the best of my ability. Damn straight."

"She didn't do it. She isn't capable of murder," I said, underscoring the impossibility of it.

But Em wasn't so easily persuaded. "Everyone is capable of murder if the right buttons are pushed at just the right time. It might be accidental. But under duress . . . under the right circumstances, you, me, or even Martina Solis could be driven to murder."

My head swam at the idea that anything would push me to that breaking point. "Maybe," I conceded after a minute. "But I don't believe she did it."

"Like I said, we're investigating all the leads we currently have."

I knew she had to do her job, and I knew she'd do it well. "You have the time of death?" I asked, thinking about the narrow window of time York had asked Martina about.

"We do."

The picketers and their insistence that Olaya's bread had killed Josh came to mind. "You're sure it was poison?" I asked, hoping she'd tell me that, in fact, no, his head had been bashed in.

"One hundred percent. Stomach contents of coffee. Bread. Strawberries. Sugar. Eggs. Level of digestion—"

I waved, not needing to hear anything more. "So the idea is that he didn't eat anything after the bread shop."

"Before—the eggs and strawberries. During—bread and coffee. But probably nothing after."

"What kind of poison?" I asked, as if I knew arsenic from cyanide.

"Atropine and scopolamine. ME thinks they came from a flower."

"A flower," I repeated blankly. I'd read of poisonous flowers, of course, but I didn't know of any. "So definitely not from the bread."

"We can't rule that out. He injected it somehow. The specific flower is Angel's Trumpet," Em said. "It's often used as a hallucinogen. From the nightshade family. Can definitely be fatal. Apparently every part of the flower—from roots to leaves to petals—is toxic. And not exactly difficult to find since it grows well in Santa Sofia's climate. And here's the kicker. There is some growing in Skyline Park."

I'd been at the park admiring the flowers before Agatha had found Josh Prentiss's body. I called up an image of the only trumpet-shaped flower I could recall. "Do you mean the bell-shaped ones?" I asked, visualizing the hearty stalks up against one of lattice barriers.

"One and the same."

A chill wound through me. Murder was murder, but the idea that someone had taken a part of an Angel's Trumpet and somehow figured out how to get Josh Prentiss to ingest it made it very, very premeditated. I voiced that thought to Em.

"Oh Ivy," she said with a small smile. "I've said it before, but I'll say it again. You missed your calling. You have a knack for getting to the heart of the matter."

I basked in the glow of the compliment as much as I could, given the morbid circumstances, pretty sure my dad was happy I'd missed that particular calling. Putting myself in the way of a murderer didn't bode well for personal safety, and parents always wanted their children to be safe. Billy handled Emmaline's high-power job with grace, I thought. He was all about wanting her to be true to herself in every possible way. Miguel was the same. He didn't love when I got involved in the dastardly doings that sometimes happened in Santa Sofia, but he supported me, nonetheless.

"Do you think Josh was scamming a lot of women?" I asked, still trying to get my head around the fact that the man wasn't, in fact, one of the good ones, like I thought he'd been.

"It seems likely. I have a computer forensics guy scouring his laptop."

"Martina didn't do this," I said, circling back to my earlier proclamation.

"I hope not, Ivy, but like I said, she's someone we have to look at. She was with him that morning—"

"Briefly! They crossed paths at the bread shop as he was coming in and she was leaving."

"And she admits to meeting him at the park—"

"But he didn't show up."

"So she says."

"What happened to innocent before proven guilty?" I asked, holding back my frustration. "You're acting like York."

Emmaline leveled an even gaze at me, not fazed by my outburst. "It's personal for you. I get that. And believe me, no one is being found guilty here—"

"What about the press? That buffoon Marcus Brolin's pointing the blame right at Olaya. Pretty soon he's going to redirect it to Martina."

"We can't stop him from printing whatever BS he comes up with, Ivy. You know that. Freedom of the press. All we can do"—she waggled her finger from her to me—"is find out what really happened. That will exonerate the innocent and bring justice to the guilty."

Easier said than done.

*   *   *

Later, at home, I replayed the morning of Josh's death, wondering if I'd missed anything. He'd arrived right at eight o'clock, as usual. He'd held the door open for Martina and spoken to her for just a moment. Long enough to make a plan to meet at the park.

But, I remembered, when he arrived at the front counter, he'd been on his phone and was *also* making a plan to meet someone else—at eleven o'clock. Where? I racked my brain, trying to remember. The letter B or G kept resurfacing. At the beach? No. I racked my brain. At a gate somewhere? If so, what gate, and where? There wasn't one at the park. At the Grotto? The touristy restaurant was nowhere near the park. If he'd planned to meet this person at eleven at the Grotto and Martina at eleven-thirty at the park, he'd been cutting it awfully close. That could explain why he didn't show, except that he *would* have gotten there by noon, so that couldn't be the reason he didn't show.

Of course, I knew the reason he didn't show was because he was already dead.

Let's meet at the g . . . g . . . goooo . . . ge . . . . ga . . . It came to me like a thunk against my forehead. The gazebo! Or course. Skyline Park had a gazebo. If I was right and he'd planned to meet up with someone before the eleven thirty appointment with Martina, that would clearly point the finger at someone else. So maybe this mysterious person, whoever he or she was, had met him at the park and had somehow gotten him to ingest poison.

Regardless of the how, it could have happened. Whoever did the deed could have hung around to make sure Josh would meet his demise after taking in the Angel's Trumpet. After that, his body could have easily been dragged to the flower bed.

With the possibility of a Suspect X firmly rooted in my mind, I moved on to the poison itself. I'd never heard of Angel's Trumpet. I typed the name of the flower into my laptop's search bar and immediately landed on a link, which took me to the symptoms of ingesting the poisonous flower.

- Muscle weakness
- Dry mouth
- Rapid pulse
- Dilated pupils
- Fever
- Hallucinations
- Convulsions
- Confusion
- Excessive thirst
- Difficulty breathing
- Memory loss
- Paralysis
- Coma

The list was long and horrible. Why in the world would anyone have such a deadly flower in their yard? More than that, why would the city plant it all over the park? Both were unanswerable questions, but the fact that Angel's Trumpet was planted around the city meant anyone had access to it. The suspect field was very wide open.

As I drifted to sleep, though, another horrible realization struck. I'd only been in Martina Solis's backyard a few times, but the image hit me bright and clear. She had Angel's Trumpet planted along the fence line.

Chapter 12

By the next morning, the pall that had fallen over the bread shop had taken root. Over the entire town, truth be told. Apparently, Josh Prentiss was popular in some crowds, and his death seemed to have caused a heavy shroud to settle over all of Santa Sofia. Even though he was only a regular at the bread shop for a few months, his Group A presence at Yeast of Eden, along with his constant chattering into his cell phone, were both conspicuously absent. They'd been replaced by random speculation and gossip dropped by one or two of our few remaining customers. *My son plays football with his son. He was so involved in everything. He was so good at his job. He was going to hook me up with a sure thing. I saw him at the market just last week. His poor family.*

The local police had shooed the protestors away, but by that time their presence had already

taken its toll on Yeast of Eden. The local newspaper carried the story of the protestors on the
front page, right alongside the murder of Josh
Prentiss. Comments on the paper's online forum
spewed vitriol, condemning the bread shop and
convicting Olaya as if there'd been a trial and she
and the bread shop were O. J. Simpson. They were
being tried in the court of public opinion, and
they were losing. The press coverage also brought
out the lookie-loos, who cupped their hands over
their foreheads to stare through the window. They
looked, but not many ventured in. Not even Nina
showed up for her morning treats. The line was
usually long and steady, but today we had only a
spattering of customers.

The whole thing resulted in an unusual—and
disconcerting—lull.

Felix and his crew manned the kitchen, adjusting the day's bake quantities. Zula and Esmé had
the morning off. I busied myself in the front of the
bread shop. First, I restocked the sweetener pack-
ets, napkins, and mugs at the coffee bar, then came
back around behind the counter to straighten the
disposable cups and sleeves. Finally, I grabbed two
spray bottles of cleaner—one for the glass, the
other for the bistro tables and chairs—and set to
work. I started with the glass doors and the storefront windows, hoping the bells would tinkle, sig-
naling a customer. I finished all the windows, and
there was nary a customer in sight.

I moved on to the furniture, taking the time to
wrap the cloth around each spindle on the back of
each chair, trying hard not to think about which
ones Josh Prentiss had sat in since he'd frequented

the bread shop. By the time I made it to the last table and chair, a small group of people had gathered on the sidewalk just outside the shop. I wiped each table leg, watching them from the corner of my eye as they talked, looked at the door, then talked some more. It was as if they were debating whether or not to come in on the off chance the bread *was* poisonous.

I tried to ignore them, focusing on the cleaning. One thing I'd noticed during the time I'd worked part-time for Olaya was that people left things. Umbrellas. Books. Jackets. Hairbands. Cell phones. Keys. Wallets. The list went on and on. Olaya had told me she'd once found a well-worn toothbrush, a child's retainer, and even a pair of dentures. People set things down, didn't check their space before leaving, and departed with fewer items than they'd had when they'd come in. Case in point, this morning I'd collected two black hairbands, which would promptly go into the trash bin, a lancet from a blood-sugar kit, an abandoned novel half hidden under the coffee bar, and a broken umbrella. I glanced at the sky outside. Not a rain cloud to be seen.

Finally, one of the men outside spun on his heel and plowed through the front door, sending the bells into a riotous clanging. I saw him coming, but I still jumped. "Hello there!" I said as I gathered up the spray bottles, the rag, and the detritus I'd collected. I hurried back behind the counter, depositing the spray bottles where they belonged. I shoved the book, umbrella, and hairbands, along with the cloth, on the shelf under the cash register, squirted hand sanitizer to clean my hands, and focused on the people, all of whom had now come inside.

The man was tall. His legs were long and thin, and he had his pants belted under his round and protruding belly. "Big selection," he commented, scanning the nearly full display cases.

He wasn't wrong. Felix had baked almost everything he normally did. The difference was that there were not racks and racks holding more of everything in the kitchen. "More to choose from," I said brightly.

Something about the way he raised his brows and glanced at the man and two women who'd come in with him struck me, but I couldn't say why. He let his eyes skitter over the breads before he settled on me again. "Makes sense. Guess business is down. After what happened."

I bristled. Was this guy even here to buy bread? I forced my small smile to stay put.

He gave a little laugh. "I guess we'll stay away from the sourdough rolls." He threw a smug look at his companions. They gave churlish chuckles.

"You'll be missing out, then," I said, not willing to play their game.

Just then Mae came out from the kitchen, running the back of her hand across her forehead. She couldn't have stood much over five feet. She would have had to stand on tiptoes to really see over the display cases housing all of the yumminess she'd helped create. "Ivy, Olaya's on the phone, and Felix is . . . I don't know, somewhere. I have to run home. My mom, she's diabetic, and she's not feeling very well today."

"Yes, of course," I said, turning my back on the faux-customers for a moment. "Is she okay?"

"Oh yeah, she's fine, I'm sure. She just needs to rest until her blood sugar comes down."

A lightbulb came on above my head. Mae's frustration with her mother's carb habit suddenly made so much more sense. "You go. I'll let Felix know."

As she disappeared back to the kitchen to leave out the back door, the bells in the front tinkled again. I turned around to see the retreating figures of the mocking man and his companions.

Once again, the bread shop was empty.

Chapter 13

Funerals, as a rule, are somber affairs. Even the tiny bit of levity in the scene in *Love Actually* when Liam Neèson plays the Bay City Rollers in tribute to his wife—even *that* doesn't erase the fact that his sweet Joanna is gone.

This one had been put together lightning quick. In just a few days, to be exact. Miguel was stuck at the restaurant, and although he could leave for such an important thing, he didn't really know Josh Prentiss. Mrs. Branford agreed to be my plus one, so Miguel was off the hook.

"I'll bring the tissues," she said when I called to ask if she could join me. It wasn't as if I couldn't go to the funeral alone, but having Mrs. Branford by my side bolstered my resolve to dig into a dead man's life.

I started to say that I didn't know Josh well enough to break into tears, but I thought better of it. The fact was, I *had* known him—even if it was only in the context of coffee and sourdough rolls.

Josh's funeral was the stuff of movies. It was held at one of the largest churches in town. If I had to guess, I'd say it seated close to five hundred. Given the short notice, I thought the showing would be on the paltry side. I was wrong. Every pew was filled. Despite the very low rumble of voices, an odd kind of silence filled the room. Sniffs and light sobs were like a music score playing in the background. I saw strangers alongside familiar faces. Some bread shop regulars, as well as some of the employees. Zula and her colt-legged daughter, Ella, who'd been a tween but was now fully a teen, sat on the end of one of the back pews. I smiled at them both as Mrs. Branford and I made our way up the center aisle. I caught a glimpse of our former employee, Taylor Wilson, and in the same pew, although on the opposite end, sat Mae and her mother, Kristin. I caught a glare between Taylor and Mae. Enemies at the bread shop, and still enemies here. Taylor was stone-faced, and Mae and her mother both clutched tissue to their noses. They were opposites in every way.

The number of people in attendance was, frankly, shocking. Santa Sofia was a small coastal town. Josh, clearly, was well-known. I couldn't imagine how he'd managed to juggle a wife and his kids, an affair with the elusive Jeanne, and even Martina. Then again, Martina had said they usually met at her place after the initial meet-cute period.

A rogue thought shot through my head: *At Martina's place, where there was Angel's Trumpet.*

I searched for any open seats, hoping we could

find a spot. Beside me, Mrs. Branford relied heavily on her cane. She'd been just fine walking from her house to my car at the curb, then from the car to the vestibule. Once we'd come inside, though, her gait became considerably slower. I knew from experience that Mrs. Branford put her cane to good use whenever she felt the need. Usually that need was not actually physical.

"Penelope!"

We both stopped and turned toward the general area the whisper-yell had come from. An older woman had stood up in the middle of her row. She had one arm raised up halfway. She waved at us, beckoning. "Come. Sit here."

Mrs. Branford reached back and grabbed my wrist with one hand, tucked her cane safely under her arm and out of the way, and pulled me with her. We bumped the knees of the sea of grieving guests dressed in black as we inched our way toward the empty seats. Over and over, I repeated, *Oh, sorry. So sorry. Whoops, sorry.* Finally, we made it to the middle of the row and took our seats—me, then Mrs. Branford, then her friend.

"Ivy, this is Lorinda Mulvaney. Lorinda, Ivy Culpepper," Mrs. Branford said in the same low voice I imagined she'd used during testing when she'd taught at Santa Sofia High School.

Lorinda looked a decade or so younger than Mrs. Branford, but her skin was dewy and beautifully taut. Under different circumstances, I might have commented on it and asked her secret. As it was, I smiled and said hello.

Lorinda leaned in front of Mrs. Branford, her voice falling somewhere between silence and a whisper. "I know exactly who you are. You are keeping Penelope young."

"She doesn't need me for that," I whispered back.

The faint notes of a song began over the church's speaker system, replacing the funeral silence. Only the sniffling could be heard as the classical piece played. I focused my attention on the massive photograph of Josh resting on the ledge of a dark wooden easel. In the photo, Josh was dressed in a suit and tie, although in the time he'd been coming to the bread shop, I'd never seen him dressed so professionally. Usually, he'd worn a tracksuit, changing it up sometimes with jeans or khaki shorts. I had no idea where he went or what he did after he left the bread shop each day. Maybe he changed into his professional attire and carried on with the second half of his day, but from what I'd seen, Josh wasn't the buttoned-up type. To my mind, the picture didn't really represent who he'd been in life.

I let it go. The decision of what funeral photo to use hadn't been mine to make, and whoever had made it, I presumed, made it for a reason. A man in a black suit with a white shirt stepped to the front of the altar. He held out both of his hands, palms to the ceiling, and raised them. Immediately, the rustling of movement filled the church as the congregation stood.

Like in a wedding, we all turned as a woman in a black, knee-length dress entered from the vestibule. Josh's wife, I suspected. On either side of her were, I supposed, her children. One was a thick-necked teenage boy who looked to be just under six feet. He wore a dark suit and white shirt. The resemblance between him and Josh was uncanny. The boy was his father's mini-me. On the other side of the woman was a younger girl I placed in middle school. Her black dress hung on her thin frame, hiding her shape entirely. It looked as though it was wearing her, rather than the other way around. The three of them were linked by their arms. As they moved slowly toward the altar, more sobs escaped from the mourners.

Josh's three family members sat in the front row. After a few more moments, the pastor began. He spoke about what a wonderful father Josh had been, first and foremost. "He devoted untold hours to Santa Sofia High School, serving in all positions on the board of the football boosters, from president to secretary and everything in between. His son, the players, and the coaches will miss him. His absence leaves a huge void in the organization."

He paused for people to absorb the sentiment. Someone coughed. More sniffles. Another sob. The pastor went on. "Josh put his family above all else. He and Tracy were separated for a short time, but they never stopped loving each other. In fact, they were in the process of reconciling." He hung his head for a moment.

I felt my brows pull together as I pondered the idea that Josh had been reconciling with his wife.

Mrs. Branford elbowed me. "What's wrong?" she mouthed.

I raised one shoulder in a puzzled shrug. Something about the reconciliation didn't seem right. What about Jeanne, the woman my dad had overheard at the market? And Martina, with whom he'd had a relationship? Had Josh been stringing his wife along, promising to get back to her, all the while happily seeing these other two women? Or was it the women he'd strung along, keeping from them the fact that he was back together with his wife.

The pastor looked back out at the mourners and continued. "Josh took care of his children, Brendan and Beth." This time when he paused, he looked at the huddled family, making eye contact with each of them in turn. "He adored them. He adored being a father. That, he told me, was his life's work. There was nothing else."

The pastor talked for another ten minutes, sharing anecdotes about Josh passing the football with his son from the time the boy was just three years old, about cheering on his daughter during swim practice, about dressing up with them every Halloween, about taking everything he did seriously, staying up till all hours of the night to give one hundred percent to each and every commitment.

The quiet was broken by someone blowing their nose. Someone else coughed. Rustling came from one area, then from another. The entire congregation seemed to be in some sort of grief-stricken synchronized motion.

The pastor continued. "There are so many people who want to share stories about their friendship with Josh. We'll begin with Tracy Prentiss, mother to Josh's beloved children, and his loving wife."

Brendan stood, holding his hand out to his mother. She stood, steady on her feet, but still relying on her son to guide her. Her face showed the strain her husband's death was taking on her. She was drawn, with ruddy cheeks and hollow eyes. A shadow of herself, but underneath it all, I could see *her*. Brendan led her to the altar stairs, walking up to the podium with her before returning to his seat. That sweet gesture brought a new wave of tears to the already weepy mourners.

Another cough. More rustling. Another loud sniffle. A woman scooted out from the pew opposite ours, her head down, a wad of tissue in one hand. She walked toward the vestibule.

Tracy Prentiss started. Stopped. Started again. "When I met Josh, it was love at first sight for me. Not necessarily for him. I mean, look at me . . ." She gave a self-deprecating laugh as she pointed to the huge photograph. "And look at him."

Someone tittered. A few people laughed with Tracy. In the front row, Brendan shook his head, and Beth bent hers down. I could imagine them both closing their eyes against their mother's self-directed criticism in the face of their father's death.

Tracy continued to talk, first telling the story of how Josh had won her heart, and then about how he'd sat vigil when Brendan was born and became jaundiced. More coughs. More rustling. Two people climbed over knees and feet, extricating themselves from their pews, sobs racking their bodies as they stumbled up the aisle and disappeared into the vestibule. Tracy kept talking, somehow managing to keep her voice steady, also managing to keep any tears at bay. She talked about Josh's long work hours. About him insisting he be at every football practice, and every game. About him missing their anniversary two years in a row.

The room was silent again. Tracy stared over the heads of all the people who'd come to pay their respects. Her eyes glazed, and I saw a visible shift in her. Her expression grew still. Stony. "He wasn't the perfect man you all think he was," she said softly. Then louder, "He was not perfect. He was far from—" She broke off as Brendan bolted up to her. "Mom. Stop," he said, his pleading voice echoing through the speakers. He wrapped his arm around her waist and pulled her away from the microphone and the podium.

Tracy's head swiveled, and her glazed eyes cleared. She snapped out of whatever trance she'd sunk into. Her knees buckled, but Brendan held onto her and led her back to their seats, where Beth sat, tears streaming down her face.

Tracy Prentiss hadn't been able to say it a second time, but her message had come through to me loud and clear. Josh Prentiss had more skeletons in his closet.

Chapter 14

Two more people spoke—friends of Josh. I scanned the front row, wondering if his parents or a sibling might bury their emotions enough to speak, but no one else stood. I let my perusal of the front row extend to the rest of the left side of the church. More familiar faces. People from the bread shop. People I recognized from around town. Young football players from the Santa Sofia High School team.

My gaze followed yet another person leaving their pew. I tracked the woman as she retreated, pushing through the door in the back of the church and disappearing. "I'll be right back," I whispered to Mrs. Branford.

I started to stand, but her hand came down on my knee like a claw, forcing me back down. "Where are you going?"

"To the bathroom," I said, my voice still hushed.

She arched a grayed eyebrow at me. "Hmmph." The sound said it all. She didn't fully believe me, but she loosened her fingers and patted my leg. "I'll let you know if there's any more drama while you're gone."

"Thanks." I whispered apologies and thank-yous as I scooted past the rest of the people in the pew, going out the way I'd come. Once I stood on the red carpet of the aisle, I hurried toward the back of the church. Another tall and thin woman was in front of me—there were plenty of them here. I squinted my eyes to peer at her. Could it be . . . was it Taylor? Her skirt was short. It fell past her finger-tips, but barely. As she flew through the door to the vestibule, I suddenly spun around to search the sea of mourners. I searched where Taylor had been sitting, but I couldn't find her. Or Mae, for that matter. I was too far back to identify anyone in the sea of heads. A few seconds later, I was through the door and—

I pulled up short. A bevy of black-clad women stood huddled together. If I hadn't known better—and if they weren't in a church—I would have said they looked like a coven gathering on the winter solstice. The harsh whispers flying between them came to an abrupt halt, as if they were a choir and the conductor had drawn a hand out to the side, pinching fingers together.

Silence.

I stared at them.

They stared at me.

"Another one," one of them spat.

Then from someone else: "He did it to you, too?"

The question came from the tallest of the women. Her tailored mourning dress hit just above the knees, and her low pumps were traditional and made her look tame and put together. Her mussed, shoulder-length hair told a different story. She crunched a black hat in her hand, clearly recently wrenched from her head. I didn't know for sure what she was talking about, but given Jeanne, Martina—and what Tracy Prentiss had said at the podium about her husband not being such a great guy—I had my suspicions. I went with it and threw my hands up dramatically. "Can you believe it?"

My theatrics didn't register as excessive because they occurred in the midst of their own histrionics. One of the women burst into gasping tears. Another spun on her low heel and stormed out the church door and into the sunlight. A third shot daggers at me. "You're not his type," she said with a sneer.

Another look at the gaggle of women confirmed what she said. They were all very well-dressed and tearful, but, most importantly, they were all middle-aged or older. My mid-thirty status didn't fit the bill. Tracy Prentiss's words rose like a beacon in my head. *He wasn't the perfect man you all think he was.* The truth clicked into place. "He was dating *all* of you," I asked, then added a disbelieving, "too?"

The woman with the disheveled hair stepped toward me. "Every single one of us," she said.

The door from the nave opened, and in strode Mrs. Branford. She swung her cane as she walked, but she didn't use it for support. She saw me and started to say something, but stopped as she took in the lay of the land. I saw the moment it clicked for her, and the very next second, she fell into character. "Do not tell me. My sweet Josh, he . . . he . . ." Her voice faltered. She gave a small shake of her head and closed her eyes for a dramatic beat. She pressed her palm to her chest. "Good grief, tell me it isn't so."

I had to bite back the smile that threatened. Mrs. Branford was anything but subtle.

The wailing woman took one look at Mrs. Branford and sank further into misery. She gasped for air and ran the back of her hand under her nose. "You, too?" Then she repeated, this time with unabashed disbelief. "You? Too?"

Mrs. Branford offered a forlorn smile and tsk'd. "One of the many, I see. Tell me, how did you meet him?"

She directed the question to a woman standing in the back of the group. When she realized Mrs. Branford was talking to her, her eyes popped wide, and she took a step backward. "Me?"

Mrs. Branford moved toward her, deciding to up her frailty quotient by using her cane. "Yes, dear," she said to the woman, who was probably just ten years younger than Mrs. Branford's eighty-some-odd years. She looked at each of the women— excluding me—in turn, landing back on the wide-eyed woman. "Do you think he used the same ruse on all of us?"

The timid woman blinked. Her lower lip quivered. She stammered. "I m-met him through M-Meet Your M-Mate dot com."

"I did, too," one of the other women said.

The wailing woman let out a hearty howl. "Me, too."

"Same," said the tall woman.

"Oh my," said Mrs. Branford. "Tsk, tsk, tsk." She let her lower lip quiver as she said, "What gullible old women we are."

They let that register before they all spun and shot me a collectively expectant look. I felt glacially slow compared to Mrs. Branford, but I managed to move my head in a nod-shake combo. "Right," I said, hoping that was enough of an affirmation. "Meet Your Mate dot com. Same here."

The outside door opened, and the woman who'd stormed out a few minutes ago stormed back in. She stopped, took one look at Mrs. Branford and me, and barked, "What in the name of heaven is going on here?"

The tall woman responded. "Two more of Josh's . . . victims."

The gray-haired woman stared.

And I stared, because it suddenly hit me. These women—I'd seen them before. They'd been the group who'd been like a flock of birds moving down the sidewalk when I'd been on my break at the bread shop. They'd gone into Yeast of Eden, looked around, and left again.

Had they been looking for Josh?

"Two more . . ." the woman said. She spun around again, and for a second, I thought she was going to charge back outside. Instead, she made a full 360-degree turn and faced us again. "Meet Your Mate dot com?"

Mrs. Branford and I both nodded. I was fully invested in the ruse now. "What are your names?" I asked, wondering if one of the women was Jeanne.

They rattled off their names. The tall one was

Sharon. The weepy one was Peggy. Linda had stormed out, then back in. The timid woman was Betsy. And the last one, who'd melted into the woodwork, was Darlene.

"I am Penelope," Mrs. Branford said. She gestured to me, feigning ignorance. "And you are—"

"Ivy," I offered.

The women's eyes were all on me again. "You're too young," Sharon said, repeating the general sentiment Linda had expressed.

I shrugged, playing it like there was no accounting for Josh's taste.

"Do you have money?" Linda demanded, then looked at the others. "She must have money."

"Ah, you are all wealthy women," Mrs. Branford said, coming to the same realization I had.

"And widowed," Sharon said.

"Wealthy and widowed." Linda scoffed. "How could we be so stupid? He played us all."

Martina and her seven thousand dollars surfaced in my mind. Josh, it seemed, had a pattern.

Darlene's gaze skittered toward the nave. "Do you . . . do you think there are more?"

The question made me catch my breath. Peggy's sobs stopped with a hiccup. "M-more?"

Mrs. Branford blew out an audible breath. "Oh, I imagine so."

"Undoubtably," Sharon said dryly. "I suppose it would be rather inappropriate to burst in to the church and ask if other women were duped by the deceased, but if we did, I suspect we'd find a good many shocked women who would join our company."

"I-I have to g-go," Betsy said. She wiped a new flurry of tears from her eyes, and three seconds later, she scurried out the door.

I thought timid Peggy might follow suit, but it was the one who'd been nearly invisible, Darlene, who walked out behind her.

"And then there were five," Sharon said dryly.

"Four," I said when the door opened again, and Linda melted into the sunlight.

Mrs. Branford, Sharon, Peggy, and I stared at one another, speechless, until, once again, the door from the nave opened. This time, though, instead of another unwitting victim of Josh Prentiss's, Captain York stepped into the vestibule.

Chapter 15

Captain York stared at me. I stared at Captain York. If I didn't act quickly, he'd blow my cover, and I didn't want that to happen. If they found out I wasn't one of Josh Prentiss's victims, I'd never get anything more out of them, and that was my one and only goal at the moment.

The problem was, Captain York was not part of my fan club. In fact, the opposite was true. Still, I had to try. I reacted, but if felt as if I was moving in slow motion. The sounds around me heightened. Sharon spoke, her voice sounding like one of the adults in a *Peanuts* special. The crumpled tissues Peggy had been holding fell to the floor at her feet. As York opened his mouth to speak, Mrs. Branford stamped her cane once . . . twice . . . three times. The sound reverberated like an echo inside my skull. And, still, I moved toward him at a glacial pace.

I tried to communicate with my eyes, telling him to act like he didn't know me. Not something easily done nonverbally. His head slowly swiveled from me to Mrs. Branford. He came back to me, then let his eyes focus on Sharon and Peggy in their mourning clothes.

"What's going on out here?" he asked, keeping his attention on the actual grieving women. "Are you ladies okay?"

Oh, thank God. I still had time to divert him. "Officer, these women—"

"Uh, you, too, Ivy," Sharon said, waving her finger in a circle.

I felt heat flame my cheeks. "We all . . . *knew* . . . Josh Prentiss."

"I would assume so. You're at his funeral, after all."

Smart man. "Right. What I mean is that—"

Sharon elbowed in next to me. "What she is trying to say is that *all* of us were suckered by Josh."

We'd already had his attention, but now his head snapped up as if a puppet master had yanked a set of strings attached to the crown. "What's that now?"

"Let me lay this out for you, officer," Sharon said, her voice quite prickly. "We all met Josh Prentiss on Meet Your Mate dot com. We all dated him, unaware that he was also seeing"—she spread her arm wide as if she was a game show host presenting a litany of prizes—"other women."

York narrowed his eyes as he processed what Sharon had said. He looked at me for a long second. After a moment, he went back to Sharon, tilted his head to one side, and said, "You don't say."

Sharon jammed one indignant hand on her hip. "I do say. And there were others."

"What others?"

"You just missed them."

"There were Darlene, Betsy, and Linda," Mrs. Branford said. "Of course, we didn't get each other's last names. We were all rather shocked, as you can imagine."

He grimaced. "Oh yeah, I can imagine that just fine." He pulled a small notepad from his jacket pocket and flipped it open, sliding out a miniature pencil. He cocked one sarcastic brow at Mrs. Branford—if a brow can be sarcastic. "And you are?"

"Penelope Branford," she supplied.

He'd met Mrs. Branford at my house once when he'd stopped by to tell me to mind my own business. It was clear he recognized her. That sarcastic brow again. He shook his pencil, and the corner of his mouth tipped up. "Right. Mrs. Branford. I believe we've—"

"I'm Sharon Steward," Sharon interrupted, impatient to get on with things. Thankfully. "And this is Peggy—"

She dipped her chin at Peggy. "Oh. Martin. Peggy Martin."

"I'm Ivy Culpepper," I offered before he could show familiarity.

"Riiight," he said. He made a point of writing down my name, saying it slowly as he wrote each letter. "I . . . vy Cul . . . pepp . . . er."

Sharon turned a suspicious face to look at me. "Have I met you before somewhere?"

There were several places she might have seen me. The bread shop was the most obvious one. The town's art car show, which I'd photographed, or the holiday bazaar, or the Spring Fling. Who knew? I didn't mention the time she'd strode down the sidewalk and into Yeast of Eden while I'd been sitting outside. "I don't think so," I said.

"Hmmph." She frowned, reluctantly turning back to York. "I gave the man money."

A choking sound escaped from Peggy's throat. "I did, too."

"I imagine we all did," Mrs. Branford said. She looked at York. "You might want to write this down, young man."

I cringed, hoping York wouldn't whip out a pair of handcuffs and haul Mrs. Branford away for insolence. Instead, he gave a mirthless chuckle and nodded. "Got it."

"I believe the deceased has probably left a long string of swindled women in his wake," she said. For a brief second, I wondered if she was aware of the pun she'd used, and then I pulled a face. Of course she did. She was a former English teacher. She knew the many definitions of wake and had probably used the word intentionally.

"Right. Peggy, Darlene, Linda, Betsy, Sharon, Ivy, and you." He nodded at Mrs. Branford as he ended the list.

"We are only the ones taken aback by his wife's proclamation that he was far from perfect. I have to agree with that, by the by," Mrs. Branford said. "If I were a gambling woman, which I am, as it happens; I do like a good game of poker—I'd bet all the money I have left that there are plenty more women Josh did this to."

York turned to Peggy. "You said you gave him money, ma'am?"

I had to admit that I was impressed by York's kid-glove treatment of Peggy, and of the situation. I hadn't really expected him to go along with my ruse. Despite York's gentle voice, Peggy's skin lost its color. She said something, but so softly I couldn't hear.

"What was that?" York asked, turning his head so one ear was directed toward her.

Peggy sucked in a shaky breath. "I gave him fifty thousand dollars," she whispered, this time just loud enough to carry to our shocked ears.

"I thought I was nuts at eleven, but fifty thousand dollars?" Sharon gawped. "Are you out of your mind?"

I'd thought the tears and hysterics had gone when Betsy left the church, but Peggy's face crumpled, and she broke into quiet sobs. "So stupid," she muttered. "So, so stupid."

I couldn't comfort her because I was supposed be just as stupid. But fifty thousand? That was stupefying.

From the way everyone else stared at Peggy, I wasn't alone in my disbelief. York jotted something down in his notebook. I sensed he was taking the moment to school his expression, wiping away his own display of shock. "Excuse me, ladies," he said, then he pulled Peggy off to the side to question her. When he was done, he escorted her out, then pulled Sharon aside. Mrs. Branford and I shot each other raised-eyebrow looks as we waited for our turn.

It came too soon. York led Sharon to the door. She gave us a backward glance, her attention resting on me for a long second before York closed the door on her.

He turned around slowly. As he came closer, he spoke, his voice just as measured as his gaze on us. "If I've read the situation correctly, neither of you met Josh Prentiss on Meet Your Mate dot com, neither of you gave him money, and neither of you were his victim in any way. Am I right?"

"Right on all counts," I said, and Mrs. Branford tapped the tip of her nose with an arthritic finger.

"So you're playing undercover, like Charlie's Angels?"

"Yes," Mrs. Branford said at the same time I replied, "That reference is a little dated."

He scowled. "Veronica Mars. Nancy Drew. Agatha Christie. Take your pick. You're going to get in over your head. Once again."

There it was. The chastisement I'd been waiting for—if you could call it that. It was a tame scolding. I treaded carefully, wondering if I'd misread the passiveness of his comment. "They assumed, and we just didn't correct them."

"You know what they say about people who assume," he smirked.

"I do," I said. He waited, as if he wanted me to actually tell him what people said. I obliged. "You make an ass out of you and me."

"Exactly. You're lucky I didn't call you out."

"Why didn't you, Captain York?" Mrs. Branford

asked, tilting her head in a way that conveyed her true interest in his answer.

"Ma'am, that is a very good question." He cupped one hand around his chin. "The best I can say is that it was entertaining watching you both"—he swung his gaze to me—"especially you, Ms. Culpepper."

"Why me?" I asked, not sure if I should be affronted by the confession.

"I think you were quite worried I was going to pull the rug out from under you."

My hackles fluttered to life but settled down again just as quickly. Maybe York was lightening up. "This is a good discovery," I said. "What Josh Prentiss's wife said was right on. He wasn't what he seemed. These women can prove that. Maybe one of them is the killer."

"Ah. I see. This is proactive on your part. Almost a bait and switch. If one of them is guilty, that means Ms. Solis is not."

He was smart, I had to give him that. I figured it wouldn't be too hard to follow the bread crumbs we'd just provided. I was already moving on. "What if Tracy Prentiss found out about all of her husband's women? *She* might have snapped."

"Poison *is* premeditated," York said. "It's possible."

It was. Josh's betrayal could have forced his wife past the tipping point. If anyone could administer poison, a spouse was the most likely person. I said as much to York. "Point taken," he said.

I pointed to the exit door. "And then there's all those women."

"There were two more, you said."

"Three. Darlene, Linda, and Betsy. Linda was livid. Betsy was like a deer caught in the headlights of a speeding car. And I think Darlene was in shock."

He jotted the names down in his notebook. "We'll look into it."

"There's at least one more," I said.

Mrs. Branford and Captain York both looked at me, waiting.

I relayed the story my father had told Billy and me. "He said her name was Jeanne. Last name begins with a P."

"Hmm," he said unenthusiastically, but he wrote down the information.

A minute later, the two sets of doors between the church and the vestibule opened. The low murmur of the mourners grew louder as the somber people left the nave. "Ladies," Captain York said with a dip of his chin.

"Captain," Mrs. Branford returned.

We all turned and watched the people stream past us and out the front doors to congregate in front of the church. I searched for Taylor and Mae and Kristin Spelling, but couldn't spot them in the crowd. I tried to catch Zula's attention as she came into view, but she led her daughter through the throng without a backward glance.

The people moved as one grieving mass. Who else among them had also been a victim of Josh's online dating game?

From the intent expression on Captain York's face, I suspected he was wondering the same thing.

Chapter 16

"It's like we came to an unspoken truce," I said to Mrs. Branford. We sat on my back patio, sipping iced tea and nibbling on raspberry scones I'd made that morning. Agatha lay on her side in a sliver of sunlight slicing across the grass.

"Nobody is all good or all bad," Mrs. Branford said. "We've seen Captain York's irritable side. Perhaps now that he's been in Santa Sofia for a little while, he's feeling less threatened and more settled."

"And less like a cranky bear."

"Precisely."

"Let's hope it lasts."

"Well, he did *not* tell us to keep our noses out of the investigation," Mrs. Branford noted.

That was true. He said we were going to get in over our heads, but that didn't translate to *butt out*.

"I'm so curious, aren't you?" I said, opening my laptop.

As I typed, she said, "About Meet Your Mate dot com? But of course."

"Amazing," I said with a smile, then swung two fingers back and forth between us a few times. We were on the same wavelength.

A few scant seconds later, I was on the website. I hesitated, though. I was in love with and engaged to Miguel. Even under the pretense of amateur sleuthing, I didn't want to create a profile. That felt a little skeezy.

"Here. Let me," Mrs. Branford said, clearly sensing my hesitation. She stretched her arm across the table, reaching for the laptop.

I pushed it toward her, then slid my chair over until I was right beside her. "We have to set up an account. The first week is free. We could make up a fake name," I suggested, wondering why Josh hadn't done that. If he had, he might not have been found out. At least not right away. Probably eventually, but none of those women would have known their paramour was dead and shown up at the funeral if he'd gone by different names.

"Pshaw," Mrs. Branford waved away the idea. "I'm free, single, and in my twilight years. Who knows, maybe my perfect mate is out there. Other than Jimmy, of course." Jimmy was her long-deceased husband. Mrs. Branford had recently reconnected with an old teaching colleague, but other than that, she didn't *date*. Creating an online dating profile, though . . . oddly . . . didn't feel too far outside the realm of possibility with her.

"Okay," I said.

She leaned forward, peering at the screen, then moved back, her chin pressed to her chest, her eyes narrowing even more. Finally, she slid the computer back to me. "I don't have my glasses."

"I got it," I said, and began typing. "What do you want to put for your interests?"

"Poker," she said. "Texas hold 'em, five card draw, and Caribbean stud, specifically."

I'd heard of the first two, but not the third. "What else?" I asked.

"How many spots are there?"

"There's no set amount," I said. "Just whatever you want to put. It doesn't really matter since we just want to be able to look at Josh's profile."

She pshaw'd again. "Of course it matters. As I said, perhaps my perfect mate is waiting for me out there."

I'd thought she was halfway kidding, but she was taking this seriously. We spent the next twenty-five minutes filling out her other interests (bridge, Words with Friends, Wordle, gardening), her ideal date (an early dinner out, followed by a game of poker), and what she wants in a man (intellect, curiosity, and get-up-and-go to match her own). After that, we set out to find a few photos to include in her profile. Luckily, I'd taken quite a few of her over the last few months. I hunted through my files until I found one of her at the poker game in the basement of a local bar, another of her swinging her cane while she walked, a little Charlie Chaplinesque, and a third with her nose to nose with Agatha. We added her education, former occupation, and all the other information they asked for, including her contact email.

We hit SUBMIT, then sipped our tea and ate our baked treats while the site processed her information and created her profile. "Now, how can we search for our gigolo?" she asked after she finished off the last of her scone.

"He used his name, so it should be easy." I didn't think MeetYourMate.com would have taken down his profile yet, but that could happen at any time. I typed in Josh Prentiss. Five profiles of men with that name popped up. When I narrowed it down by region, only *our* Josh Prentiss was left. He had used several photos—one of him on the sidelines of a football game, arm pounding the air in triumph, one smiling right into the camera, and a third with his shirt off at the beach. He'd created an appealing profile. I read some of his information aloud. "Forty-five and looking for love with a mature woman."

"Mature being code for older, I assume," Mrs. Branford said.

I lightly backhanded her arm. "You know what people say about using the word *assume*."

"Pshaw," she said for the third time. "In this case, I *assume* I am correct, so no one is an ass."

I grinned. "Right you are, Mrs. Branford."

"Penelope," she said.

She had been trying, in vain, to get me to call her by her first name. I just couldn't do it. "Mrs. Branford."

"Penny."

I smiled. "Mrs. Branford."

"One of these days, Ivy. One of these days."

"Don't count on it," I said, then went back to the profile. "He put down that he prefers women sixty years of age or older."

"He looks young and virile in the photos he posted. To a mature woman needing an esteem boost, I suppose that would be appealing. Cougar love."

My mouth pulled into a frown. I wouldn't have thought so many women would be in need of external validation from a stranger, so much so that they stopped seeing things clearly and could be exploited. I hoped my self-confidence didn't ever need that kind of bolstering.

"What did he include in his profile?" Mrs. Branford asked.

"He listed his interests as slow strolls through the park, gardening, puzzles, and doting on the special woman in his life."

Mrs. Branford rolled her eyes. "What a master manipulator. Those poor women."

Really, I thought. "Really," I said. It seemed believable that women with the emotional fragility of Betsy, Darlene, and Peggy could be easy targets, but he'd also fooled someone as seemingly tough as Linda, who'd stormed out of the church. And someone as pulled together as Sharon, who'd looked disgusted with herself, had been hoodwinked. All of Josh's victims had to be questioning their judgment, questioning how they'd been beguiled to the point of blindness. I know I was, and I'd only been charmed by him peripherally.

We spent a few more minutes poking around the site, but it didn't give us any other information about Josh. On a whim, I typed in the name Jeanne Pewl, then Jeanne Pole, but nothing came up. I dropped the surname, but there were too many even in our small region to begin to guess which one—if any—was the Jeanne my father had overheard at the market.

Without her in the mix, the suspect pool of disgruntled women was large enough. None of the women had seemed to understand that they'd been deceived by Josh, but who knew. Maybe one of them had been pretending, or another one of Josh's victims had figured it out and snapped.

I wasn't feeling very optimistic that we'd ever figure out what had really happened to Josh.

Chapter 17

The next morning, I was back at Yeast of Eden. Business was still slow, but a tiny bit better than it had been before the funeral. People had short memories. They also had other things to spend their time worrying about.

It also helped that the *Santa Sofia Daily* had written an article about the women Josh Prentiss had bamboozled. That went a long way toward discrediting the idea that the bread shop had anything to do with his death.

We'd adjusted our bakes, so by mid-afternoon, we were close to sold out. The bells tinkled as the door opened. A woman appeared. The sunlight backlit her, obscuring her face for a moment, but as she stepped inside, I immediately recognized her. Tracy Prentiss, Josh's widow.

She scanned the shop. When her eyes landed on me, they stayed put. "Hi," she said.

"Hi." I didn't think she was here to buy bread, but it seemed easiest to act like I did. "What can I get for you? Stock's a little low at this time of day, but—"

"I don't want any bread," she said.

"Oh." I blinked. So much for feigning happenstance.

"You're Ivy Culpepper?"

"Yes," I said, wary. What could Josh Prentiss's widow want with me?

"You were at my husb—" She stopped. Started again. "At Jo—" She closed her eyes for a long second, then finally said, "You were at the funeral."

"I was. Jo—er, he came in here almost every day to work."

She scoffed. "To work. That's a riot."

I tried to school my expression so I wouldn't show my surprise at her bluntness. This woman was hurt and angry. The notion that she was a murderer flitted through my mind. She'd been betrayed by her husband, not just with an affair, but with a series of affairs. Very intentional affairs. And from what I'd gathered from Sharon and the other women at the funeral, there had been fraud, too. So Tracy's husband had been both a cheat and a thief. And a cougar hunter, as Mrs. Branford and I had discovered.

"I'm sorry, Mrs. Prentiss, can I help you—"

"Don't call me that." she said.

"Oh. Um, of course."

"I can't . . . I told my kids I can't keep the name. I'm going back to McCall. I know conventional wisdom says you should keep the same name your kids have, but Brendan and Beth are old enough to understand. Their father betrayed me. He betrayed them, too."

"Of course," I said again.

"Go," Zula said, pushing me out from behind the counter. "Go sit."

It was the end of the workday for the front of the bakery. Olaya and her small afternoon team were finishing up the afternoon bakes. Olaya had several contracts with restaurants in town, including Baptista's Cantina & Grill and the brand-new Sofia's Chophouse. Business was better, but Zula could easily handle the customers who might trickle in.

I led Tracy Prentiss, née McCall, to one of the tables. At the last second, I realized it was where Josh had always sat. I did an abrupt turn and maneuvered to an open spot by the window. She didn't seem to notice the about-face and just followed me. We sat facing each other, and I waited for her to tell me what she wanted to talk to me about.

"I recognized you, but I couldn't figure out from where. And then in the middle of the night, it came to me. I saw your name and photo in the newspaper when that murder at Eliza Fox's house happened over the holidays. I found one of the articles online about it and tracked you to here."

A little amateur sleuthing on Tracy's part. Apparently I wasn't the only one who'd missed her calling.

"Mmm hmm," I said, hoping to encourage her to continue. I couldn't fathom *why* she had sought me out.

She propped her forearms on the table, leaned

in, and peered at me. "Did you . . . were you one of Josh's—?"

Her meaning was instantly clear, even though she didn't finish the question. I drew back sharply, waving my hands in front of me. "No. I wasn't. I hardly knew him. He worked from here most mornings, that's all."

"Why here?" she asked, letting her gaze drift from one end of the bread shop to the other.

"The bread is excellent," I said. Obviously. The bread was more than enough of a reason for someone to set up shop here.

Of course, there could have been more to it. He'd met Martina here. Maybe she hadn't been the only "in real life" pickup. Maybe Yeast of Eden was the perfect hunting ground for a man seeking vulnerable women. Women like Kristin Spelling, I thought randomly. Women who didn't have someone at home. Women who needed someone to bolster them up. Women who had time on their hands and no one to spend it with.

"He never liked to be holed up in an office or cubicle. Even when we first met, he liked to work from home, from the dining room table. I think he felt like he might get trapped, like his father left his family trapped."

"His dad left them?"

She nodded. "He was a showman. In theater or something. He left his family. Such a cliché. Fell in love with the woman he worked with. It tore the family apart. Then Josh's mom died. Josh went away to college and didn't come back till we bought our house here. Inheritance and his early earnings. I never thought we should come back here, but it was like he needed to make new memories. Then again he was always gone, as if he was trying to *escape* his memories."

"A bit of a conundrum," I said. "Maybe he wanted one thing, all the while wanting something else at the same time."

"Maybe," she said. "All that time, I thought he was traveling. But no, he was off screwing other women and stealing their money. He was playing a risky game."

Everyone had their baggage. Sounded like Josh had had a deadbeat dad. Maybe that had set him off on a self-destructive path.

"Was he always in . . . investments?" I asked.

"He was a financial planner," she said. "He started as an accountant, but after he got his MBA, he moved into investments. He landed with Beacon. Lucky for him, because they didn't make him stay in the office. As long as he brought in the clients. And he did. Josh grew up here—in Santa Sofia, but we met in LA. He was determined to get back here. To paradise, he always said."

I thought about all the money those women had lost to Josh. There were probably others. Where was all that money now? Tied up in the Prentiss's house in the hills? Bernie Madoff came to mind. I remembered the story, although the amount of money reportedly lost was so far beyond the scope of anything I could even comprehend. Sixty-five billion, from what I recalled. That made Josh Prentiss small potatoes, but Peggy's fifty thousand and Sharon's eleven weren't peanuts to them. Jeanne

P.'s retirement was most likely gone. Would Emma-line and York be able to follow the money trail and get it all back for them? Would Tracy Prentiss keep her house in the hills? I studied her now, wondering just how much she knew about her husband's business dealings.

"Can I help you with something?" I asked, wondering what in the world she wanted.

Her upper lip curled with disgust. "Did he meet them here? Any of those women? Did he make a fool of me every single day?"

Ah. Now I understood. She'd already been humiliated by the discovery of her husband's schemes. She didn't want salt in the wound by finding out he'd met his marks in public. "Not that I ever saw," I said, grateful that it was true. I didn't want to lie to this woman, but I also didn't want to make her feel worse than she already did.

"Small favors." She frowned. "People are saying he was poisoned by something he ate here. Ironic, if this was also his *safe* place," she remarked, making air quotes around the word safe. "We were going to reconcile, you know, but there was one woman . . ."

"Yes?" I prompted, trying to come across as nonchalant. She was talking about someone specific, not just one of the many her husband had wronged.

"I'm sure he screwed her over just like the others, but he took it too far with her. She fell in love, poor poor girl. Of course, the feeling wasn't reciprocated."

"How do you know that?" I asked.

"Because she called me. She would sit there on

the other end of the line and not say anything. Or she'd hang up. She harassed me."

"Maybe she found out what he was doing," I suggested.

She scoffed. "I think it was more than that. That woman called and called and called. She *told* me she loved him, and that *he* loved *her*. Now I'm not even sure if he was capable of love."

"But he loved you and his kids."

"Did he, though?"

"At one time, he must have." I hoped he had, especially for the kids' sake.

"If he did, could he have done this to me? To them? They're going to be saddled with his stories. His women and his thieving."

"They have you," I said, hoping she wasn't involved, so that her children wouldn't become parentless.

"I found his burner phone. One of them anyway. He messed up and dropped it when he was playing catch with Brendan a few weeks ago. I heard it buzzing in the grass. Incoming texts that grew more and more frantic. By the time he realized and came back for it, I'd read all the texts between them. I broke that thing into a thousand little pieces. Oh, he was mad." She cracked an almost maniacal smile. "Almost saw steam pouring from his ears."

For a second, I thought of the weighted look that had passed between Josh and Martina when they'd crossed paths the morning of his death. Just as quickly as it had surfaced, it was gone. "Do you know the woman's name?" I asked, holding my breath. Maybe she was Josh's killer.

Another scoff. "Unfortunately, no. I just call her the home wrecker. One of many."

I didn't correct her by saying that, actually, *Josh* was the home wrecker—a bunch of times over. The women he swindled had had no idea he was married. Tracy was mad at the world, and nothing I said was going to change that.

Chapter 18

Tracy Prentiss had been gone for only thirty minutes when another woman from Josh's past waltzed into Yeast of Eden.

Sharon Steward swept into the bread shop with her shoulders back. She stood tall and proud, and could have easily played the part of one of the immortal Amazonian women who lived on Paradise Island in the *Wonder Woman* movies. She wore a black dress—still in mourning, I supposed, despite Josh's lies and deceit.

I spotted her, but she hadn't yet spotted me. What was she doing here? Had she somehow tracked me down, like Tracy Prentiss had? Or maybe she was just here to see the place Josh had spent so much of his time.

I stood at the coffee bar, in plain sight, but turned my back so she wouldn't spot me. If she wasn't here actually looking for me, like Tracy had been, then I had a chance of evading her. I quickly considered my options. I could duck my head and hightail it to the kitchen, but I'd have to pass right by her. The odds of escaping her notice were not in my favor.

I could try to walk backward through the dining area toward the kitchen, but that would be a bit on the conspicuous side. I nixed that plan.

The only other option was to keep my back turned and hope she would be in and out without recognizing me.

I turned my back to the door and crouched down, using the damp towel in my hand to wipe the front of the cabinet. The bell on the door tinkled, and my heartbeat surged. Maybe she'd been following the news articles and had simply come to Yeast of Eden to see the place Josh had spent so much of his time. I took a chance and glanced over my shoulder, my heart constricting when I saw her staring right at me.

She blinked, and her face took on an odd expression. It was as if she was trying to place me, given the out-of-context setting, but at the same time, it was clear she knew exactly where she'd seen me. "Ivy?"

I feigned surprise as I stood. "Sharon? What a . . . wow! What are you doing here?"

"What are *you* doing here?" She registered the apron I wore with the Yeast of Eden logo embroidered on the bib. "You work here?"

I looked around, wide-eyed, as if I was seeing the bread shop for the first time. "Here?"

"Yes. Here," she said, her tone effectively conveying how ridiculous the question had been.

"I . . . yes. Part-time."

She came closer, suspicion and anger commingling on her face. "You said you met Josh on Meet Your Mate dot com," she said, accusation heavy in her voice.

I racked my brain for a way to talk myself out of the lie, but there wasn't one. It would be too unbelievable to say I'd met Josh online and then coincidentally met him here, too. I had linked myself with the five grieving and betrayed women, pretending to be one of them. Now I had to come clean. For the second time that day, I led a heartbroken woman to the table by the window.

Esmé was working the counter this morning, although, at the moment, she was leaning against the back counter reading a book. I caught her eye and held my hand up, opening and closing it twice to indicate I was taking ten minutes. She nodded at me, then went back to her book.

"Would you like anything to drink or eat?" I asked Sharon before I sat down.

"No," she practically snarled. "What I want is for you to tell me who you are. Are you really one of Josh's victims?"

She cut right to the chase. I had to admit, I liked that about her. "Look, I'm going to be honest with you."

"Oh, please do," she said, her sarcasm thicker than a heavy layer of morning coastal fog, but then a lightbulb seemed to go off in her head. She chastised herself. "Oh my God. How stupid. I remember reading your name. You're the one who found him, aren't you?"

Me and my very memorable name. "My dog, Agatha, actually made the . . . uh . . . discovery."

"The news said Josh came here to work. Almost every day. That he was poisoned here."

"He did work here, but our bread did *not* poison him," I said. I pointed to his regular table. "He came around eight in the morning, and worked until about eleven. Sometimes a little earlier, sometimes a little later."

She stared at the empty table as if she'd conjured up his ghost. After a few seconds, she blinked. "Uh huh. And what was he like when he was here?"

I got the sense that she was trying to piece together who the real Josh Prentiss was. How much of the man she knew was authentic versus a part he'd played. Her question was tough to answer, given the new information I had about his online dating ruse and the women he'd duped. "I always thought he was very friendly. Charming. He usually ordered a particular thing on each day of the week." I went through his Tuesday through Friday routine.

"So he had a sourdough roll the morning he died." She looked down, musing. "It would be difficult to lace that with poison."

Exactly. "It sure would."

"He spent the night with me Monday," she said out of the blue. She stared out the window at the cars driving just twenty miles per hour through town. The news vans were gone. No more holdouts for more dirt on Olaya. Not even Marcus Brolin. The narrative had already shifted, and the media had begun telling the story of Josh Prentiss and his deceptions. His favorite-son status was tarnished. Like Tracy had said, carrying Josh's revised story was now the burden of his family.

I considered Sharon Steward more closely. The perfectly put-together black dress. The low-heeled black pumps. The understated makeup and wavy dark hair, a thin line of gray at the roots. No tears. No bags under her eyes. Could she have discovered Josh's game and poisoned him? Was she here playing a game? Was I sitting across from a killer? "So you saw him Tuesday morning?" I asked. "You got to eat breakfast together?" I asked.

She snapped her attention back to me. "No. I live in Santa Barbara. He always had to leave early to get to work. I only saw him on Monday nights. I thought it was all the traveling he did. Or *said* he did. Now I know the truth. He was with someone else on each of the other nights. Probably during the days, too."

"Is that what the other women said? Linda and Peggy and Betsy and Darlene?" And Jeanne and Martina, I added silently.

"Linda said she saw him on Tuesday nights. She's in Morro Bay. That's all I know, but with that many women . . . I don't know how he kept it all straight. I imagine he had women up and down the coast. He must have put miles and miles on his car. And being back with his wife? He was . . ." She trailed off and hung her head, her stoic façade cracking for a moment. She looked up at me, her face resetting. "He took advantage of lonely women. He was a horrible human being."

I couldn't disagree. And she was right. The fact that some of these women were not from Santa

Sofia explained how they didn't run into him at the bread shop or around town. I bet most of his women were from ritzy places like Malibu and Los Feliz. That also explained why he left the bread shop around noon. He probably spent his afternoons getting to those locales. "Sharon, you said you gave him eleven thousand dollars?"

"So stupid, right? You're lucky you didn't actually fall for him. And Peggy, with fifty thousand?"

"If the other women gave him money to invest, too—"

"You *know* they did. Clearly, that's all he was after."

Even with all the evidence against him, it was still difficult to reconcile this new version of Josh with the man who'd been a Yeast of Eden patron for the past few months. Still, I knew she was right. "Why did you come here?" I asked Sharon.

She sighed. "I couldn't sleep last night. I just tossed and turned, fuming about how idiotic I was to trust him. Of course, I wasn't the only one, so it wasn't just me, but that really does not make me feel any better."

"Josh was very good at conning people." I reached for Sharon's hand, covering it with mine. "You might even say he excelled at it. You can't blame yourself."

Once again, her stoic façade cracked. Her lower lip quivered, just slightly, but enough to reveal how hurt she really was underneath her anger and self-flagellation. She pursed her lips and cleared her throat. "He really did," she said. "He really did excel at it."

I hated to ask, but curiosity got the better of me.

"Sharon, how *did* he get you to give him so much money? What was it for?"

"It was an investment. A sure thing, he said." She made air quotes around the words *sure thing*. "It was some company with new technology they were patenting. He said it was going to revolutionize something with cell phone battery life, I think? He said it was a complicated business model, but they had a high rate of return. And returns were guaranteed." She shook her head, that self-reproachment back.

Hearing Sharon explain what little she knew set off alarms in my head. I'd overheard enough of his phone conversations to have heard some of the same investment nomenclature: high rate of return . . . complicated . . . guaranteed returns. "He sold it well," I said. And it sounded to me as if he'd been selling it well for a good long time.

"I trusted him," she said. My mind circled back to my earlier conversation with Tracy. She'd trusted him, too.

Unfortunately for anyone who knew him, Josh Prentiss, it seemed, was wholly untrustworthy.

Chapter 19

The best Mexican seafood in Santa Sofia is at Baptista's Cantina & Grill, hands down. The restaurant was an institution. It had been there for as long as I could remember, at the same location, perched on the pier over a rocky inlet. Miguel had come back to Santa Sofia after his father passed, in much the same way I'd come back after losing my mother. He'd taken over the restaurant and had spent untold time and money renovating it. It was a passion project—one he'd put his entire being into.

Miguel's sister, Laura, helped out in a pinch, and their mother still acted as the head hostess, greeting old friends and new customers alike. But the heart and soul of the place came from Miguel. He created the menu, experimented with new dishes constantly, tweaking old favorites and creating new ones. He worked the line, so he knew what it was like in the trenches with his kitchen staff, and he knew everything that went on in the front of house.

The remodel had started and finished with Billy as the contractor. The Naugahyde booths and worn tables went away. In their place now were rustic tables and chairs. The floor was tiled in an Aztec pattern, and an open fireplace stretched up to the tall ceiling, faced by bold and graphic tile. A long bar stretched along one side of the restaurant, to the left of the entrance and waiting room. Miguel had hired a knowledgeable man as his mezcal concierge. If anyone, ever, anywhere had a question about tequila or mezcal, Jorge would know the answer. The walls were wood-planked, enormous windows gave a priceless view of the pier and ocean, and specially made blown-glass fixtures completed the unique and beautiful interior.

Miguel's father had created a restaurant with a classic menu. Miguel had elevated it. The world-class brisket *queso* remained—thank you, Lord— but the rest of the traditional offerings had Miguel all over them. Seared tuna tostadas; kale and sausage soup; lobster with mole sauce. The menu was a treasure trove for the ultimate gastric experience.

I didn't have my own table in the way Josh Prentiss had had at Yeast of Eden, but if it was a slow night, Miguel would set me up at a table near the kitchen. I arrived on Wednesday night, hoping, for my sake, that that table was available.

Lucky for Miguel, it was not. The murder might have slowed the bread shop's business, but the pall over the town had lifted, and Baptista's Cantina &

Grill was hopping. The people of Santa Sofia had embraced the changes Miguel had implemented, and the tourists loved the place even more, if that was possible. It was packed to bursting. Miguel's mother took names at the hostess station, greeting people in her broken English. Her smile blossomed when she saw me come in, crow's feet sprouting from her eyes. "Ivy, *mija. Hola, hola.*"

I went straight over to her and wrapped her in a big hug. The woman had raised a wonderful son, and I showed her my appreciation for that every time I saw her. I waited for twenty minutes before she led me to a back table near the kitchen. It was a little out of the way, so it gave me a smidgeon of privacy, but more important, it was also convenient for Miguel if he was able to pop out of the kitchen for a quick hello or an even quicker smooch on the cheek or brushed over the lips.

"Thank you," I said to Mrs. Baptista, soon to be my mother-in-law. Holy moly. That was a concept that didn't quite seem real to me, yet, but it would be happening. Soon.

The engagement party! In all the hoopla over Josh Prentiss's murder, the party celebrating Miguel's and my betrothal had taken a back seat in my mind. I hadn't given it a single thought since discovering Josh's body

Miguel's mother left me to my thoughts, and a server familiar with my presence brought over a thick-glassed bottle of water with an attached stopper and a small, clear glass, then returned with a small dish of a decadent, creamy jalapeño sauce, fresh *pico de gallo*, and a rustic woven basket of tortilla chips in three colors. The traditional yellow chips were outnumbered by the blue and red triangles.

I ordered a margarita—perfect for a warm summer evening—and dug into the chips and salsa. I knew Miguel's mother would let him know I was there. He'd come out when he could. In the meantime, I took a small Moleskine notebook from my bag, along with a maroon felt-tip pen, and started jotting down ideas about the party in the park.

Before I could proceed with any planning, I needed to check in with Olaya. With Martina under the microscope, was she even up for the party? Were any of us?

I fished my cell phone from my bag, scrolled to Olaya's name, and placed the call. She answered on the third ring with a clipped, *"Hola."*

"It's Ivy," I said. "Are you okay?"

"Por supuesto, mija. I am just tired. Pilar . . . she cannot sleep. She cannot eat. She is . . . lost. And Martina . . ."

She trailed off, enough said. The image of the bell-shaped flowers of death in Martina's yard pixelated in my mind. It was a coincidence. It had to be.

Suddenly, talking to Olaya about my engagement party was the last thing I wanted to do. "Let me try to help. Come have dinner with me. Both of you. All of you. I'm at Baptista's."

She covered the mouthpiece of her phone, and I heard her speak to someone I presumed to be Pilar. Her muffled Spanish turned slightly cajoling. The talking stopped, and for a second, I thought the call dropped. "Olay—" I started as she said, "We will come. Now?"

"Great!" I exclaimed. "I'm already here, so yes, come now."

We hung up, and I flagged down my server. We'd need a bigger table. It only took a few minutes before another table cleared out and was cleaned up. Once it was, I gathered up my bag, water, and notebook. The server carried the rest. "Your margarita will be ready in a few minutes," he said, before sauntering off to help another customer.

I turned my attention back to my notebook, but instead of brainstorming things for the engagement party, like Olaya's bread wall, the special thing she said she was planning, and the flowers and decorations, I turned to the back and started jotting down the things I knew about Josh Prentiss.

1. He'd been separated but was reconciling with his wife, Tracy.
2. But Tracy was embittered and not keen on reconciling. So why had she agreed?
3. Josh had an online dating profile . . .
4. And he dated several older women in Santa Sofia: Darlene, Betsy, and Linda, all of whose last names I didn't know, as well as Peggy Martin and Sharon Steward.
5. Plus the mysterious Jeanne Pole.
6. According to Sharon and Peggy, they'd both given Josh money to invest. High risk, high reward. Did such a thing really exist?
7. He'd also dated Martina Solis.

*   *   *

I looked up to see that a frosty glass filled with a margarita on the rocks had been delivered. I'd been so lost in my own thoughts that I hadn't even noticed. The culmination of my musings was that I didn't want any of the women involved with Josh to be guilty of his murder. They were the victims in all this. Each and every one of them.

A healthy sip sparked my musings into a different direction. Josh Prentiss had been an athletic booster for the high school. I remembered Nina exclaiming something about how the booster money would get the athletic program a new marquee. Had Josh had something to do with fundraising? Could he have been doing some shady dealings there? If the man was sketchy in one part of his life, it stood to reason he was sketchy in another. Talking to someone on the boosters seemed like a smart next step.

The problem was, I didn't know anyone on the boosters.

But, I thought, I *did* know Josephine Jeffries. Aunt Josie, as Billy and I had grown up calling her, had been my mother's best friend and fellow teacher at the high school. I wrote down her name and drew a little star next to it. Tomorrow I'd stop by to see her. It might be a long shot, given she'd taught in the history department, but maybe she knew something about the athletic boosters.

Someone cleared their throat, jolting me from my thoughts. I looked up to see Miguel sitting across from me, a chip in his hand. I stared. "When did . . . where did . . . how did you get there?" I finally managed.

His mouth curved up in a crooked grin. "Long enough to have a handful of chips," he said.

I'm sure I looked chagrinned. So much for being situationally aware.

"What has you so focused?" he asked.

I turned my notebook around so he could see my thoughts on Josh Prentiss. He scanned the list, then cocked one eyebrow and looked at me. "Are they still looking at Martina?"

I'd filled him in on everything up to this moment. Now a deep frown pulled at my lips. "No stone unturned, basically. I don't think anyone is off the list until they have the right person."

"The guy sure wasn't what he seemed. He was a real charmer," Miguel said.

"A real snake charmer," I amended. I thought about the very grounded Sharon Steward and the very practical Martina. "Able to manipulate even the most reasonable of people."

The way he looked at me made me think he could read my mind. Which maybe he could. "So what are you going to do?" he asked after a few seconds.

I'd been considering this very question. In order to prove Martina was *not* involved in Josh Prentiss's death, the real murderer had to be caught. Olaya needed me to get to the truth, and I wanted to, as well. "So far there are a bunch of duped women with pretty solid motives. I'm going to dig around and see if I can unearth something else." I repeated my thought that if Josh was sketchy in one part of his life—and so absolutely— then he was probably equally sketchy in other parts.

"That's a reasonable assumption," he said. He loaded up another chip with salsa but before he put it in his mouth, he leaned closer. His voice took on a solemn tone. "But be careful, Ivy."

"Of course." I smiled to myself. This was one of the reasons I loved Miguel Baptista. Despite any misgivings about me getting wrapped up in another murder investigation, he was supportive. He'd never try to stop me from pursuing the truth. Not that he could have, but the point was, he didn't try. *I'm all in.* Those were the words he'd said when he'd proposed. He definitely was one hundred percent all in, and so was I—both in my relationship with Miguel *and* in my effort to prove Martina was innocent.

"I have to get back." He stood, then bent and lightly brushed my lips with his. A second later, he disappeared into the magical kitchen of Baptista's Cantina & Grill, and I was alone with my notebook. I absently sketched a drawing of Angel's Trumpet. The ones in the park were white. Bright and fresh. The perfect backdrop to the rest of the flowers along the garden path. Anyone could have plucked a flower from the park. Martina had them in her backyard, but I realized that didn't matter one bit. Angel's Trumpet grew in abundance all over town. Anyone and everyone had access to the poison that had killed Josh. I turned the page back to my list of things I knew about Josh.

"Hola, *mija*." Olaya's voice came from behind me as her hand landed on my shoulder and gently squeezed. "You remember my niece—my god-daughter—Pilar?"

I jumped up, dropping my pen onto the page. "I do! I'm so glad you could join me."

Pilar's smile was thin and tight. She was a beautiful girl, but the tragedy of losing her parents had made her a shadow of what I imagined her former self to be. I gestured to the chair next to me. She pulled it out and sat down.

Olaya's gaze slid to my open notebook. Her nostrils flared. "That man—I have heard the stories. The women—"

"What's going on, *Nina?*" Pilar interrupted. I knew the word *madrina* meant godmother in Spanish, but Pilar used the more familiar term.

Olaya sank into the chair opposite Pilar. "*Mija*, the man who died recently? The one I told you about?"

Pilar nodded. "Yeah, the guy at the park that everyone says was poisoned with bread from the shop."

Olaya pulled a face but continued. "Your *tía* Martina, she knew him."

Pilar, I realized, had discerning eyes. They were deep brown with copper undertones. She looked from her aunt to the drawing in my notebook, then back to Olaya. They went wide. "The police think *Tía* Martina killed that man?"

Olaya and I both shook our heads. "No, no," I said, and Olaya echoed me. "They have a lot of suspects, and they know of a lot of people the man manipulated. Unfortunately, Martina is one of them."

The three of us fell quiet when our server delivered water and menus to Olaya and Pilar, again when he returned to take all of our orders, and a third time when he came bearing a steaming bowl of brisket *queso.* "From Mr. Baptista," he said.

"Tell him thank you from all of us," I said, thinking that this *queso* was yet another reason to love this man. He slow-cooked the brisket, placed a hefty spoonful doused in barbecue sauce at the bottom of a shallow bowl, poured creamy white queso on top, added a dollop of homemade relish, and served it with freshly made tortilla chips. Miguel knew that sometimes cheese was the best solution to any problem—or if not a solution, then at least a pick-me-up. To Pilar, I said, "This stuff is addictive, so be careful."

She dipped the tiniest corner of a chip into the cheese. She flipped the chip around—no double-dipping for this girl—and dunked it again, deeper this time.

"You have to dig down to get the brisket," I said, demonstrating. "And the relish? Pure bliss."

She didn't look convinced, but she promptly loaded up another chip, then another. Oh yeah— I could see the bliss on her face—she was sold. Another brisket *queso* convert.

Olaya watched Pilar eat, shooting me a pleased look, then casually pushing the appetizer closer to her niece. After a few minutes, Pilar slowed down, then gulped down half a glass of water. "That stuff is pretty good," she said.

That was an understatement. "I know. It's my favorite."

She took another bite, chewing slowly. When she finished, she raised her gaze to us. "*Tía* Martina did not kill that man."

I started to close my notebook, but Olaya's hand clamped down on my wrist stopping me. "What is that?"

I looked down. "What?"

"That," she said, and after a long second, she released my wrist and tapped her finger on the flower. "What is this?"

"It's called Angel's Trumpet," I said slowly.

She raised her eyes to mine. "It has something to do with that man's murder?"

I couldn't keep the truth from her. "It does. He was poisoned with this flower."

She dipped her chin and her eyes, flecked with gold, clouded. "This flower. It is in—"

I interrupted her, my words rushing out. "I know, but it's also in the park, and probably a million other places. It grows well in our climate. It's just a coincidence."

"The police may not see it that way," she said.

She was right. Martina already had the motive and opportunity. This coincidence also gave her the means. I felt a rush of panic. "I'll get to the bottom of this, Olaya. I promise."

Chapter 20

As a general rule, I avoided Santa Sofia High School. My mother had taught English there during all of my childhood. The few times I'd been on campus since her death had triggered unbridled memories of her. They ran loose, each packing an emotional wallop stronger than a body punch by Iron Mike in his prime. Thankfully, my alma mater was located off the beaten path, so I didn't have occasion to drive past the building very often.

Today, however, I had to visit. I started by picking up Pilar from Martina's house. Martina lived in a town house on the east side of Santa Sofia. It was more affordable than a single-family home. The size—it was a one-bedroom—fit her perfectly.

"I think she is concerned about Martina because of the flowers," Olaya had said.

Pilar confirmed that theory after I knocked on the door and she let me in. "Follow me," she said. Her long hair flew in a sweeping arc as she spun around and marched toward the small backyard.

I did, stopping next to her. She put one hand on her hip with an attitude only a teenager can muster. "This is *not* Angel's Trumpet," she said, her other hand pointing at the trumpet-shaped flowers.

I leaned closer, looking at the flowers. They were tubular, and the petals flared out just like the flowers in Skyline Park. But . . . "You're right," I said. "They're different."

"These are trumpet vines," Pilar announced triumphantly. "I downloaded a plant app. You take a picture, and it tells you exactly what plant it is. This"—again, triumphant—"is *not* Angel's Trumpet."

The flowers at the park hung down like a weeping willow, whereas these . . . these seemed to sprout upward, like sunflowers reaching for the sky. Trumpet vines. Not Angel's Trumpet. I had one of those plant-identifier apps, but I hadn't thought about verifying the flower growing in Martina's yard. Clever, clever Pilar.

"*Tía* Martina didn't kill that man," Pilar announced.

"Good discovery, Pilar," I said, but my smile felt tight. Olaya and I had both jumped to the conclusion that the flowers in Martina's yard were Angel's Trumpet. The fact that they aren't didn't actually clear Martina of suspicion, though, because the poisonous flower was prolific in the park. Still, it was a relief they weren't growing right in Martina's backyard. It created a degree of separation for her as a suspect in Josh's murder.

I ushered Pilar into my sporty Fiat crossover, which had also been my mother's, and headed for the high school. Pilar sat in the passenger seat. She'd connected her phone to the car's Bluetooth and queued up a playlist.

"It's a great school," I said to her. Our dinner the night before had cheered her up for the briefest moment, but not for the longer term. The grief would be with her like a passenger sharing her body. Baby steps, I'd told Olaya. It would take time, love, support, and more time. "You must enroll for school," Olaya had told Pilar as we'd all left the restaurant.

Pilar's face had crumpled. "I want to go home."

Olaya wrapped her niece into a tight hug and whispered to her. I stood back and waited. Finally, Olaya pulled back and looked Pilar square in the eyes. "It will be all right. I promise you that. I am here with you. Consuelo and Martina, they are here with you."

The idea that Martina was under scrutiny for Josh Prentiss's murder painted a dark cloud over the moment. It wasn't my place to say anything, but I did anyway. "She's right, Pilar. I know it doesn't feel like it now, but your pain and your grief will fade. Eventually. It won't go away, but it will become tolerable." I pressed my palm to my chest. "And your parents, they will always be right here."

She dragged the back of her hands under her eyes, swiping away her tears. Her loss was immeasurable, and nothing anyone said would lessen it. It made me think of Beth and Brendan Prentiss. Their loss was just as real as Pilar's. These kids were all too young to be suffering so.

Generally, I worked hard to consign every memory from the high school, and the emotions attached to them, to a lockbox in my mind, with the idea that I'd revisit them later when I had the time and inclination. So far, that time had not come. Now I felt that familiar tug of melancholy as I pulled into the parking lot. I acknowledged it, and then I firmly chased it away with an audible exhalation. The parking lot held a fraction of the vehicles it did during the normal school year. Summer in Santa Sofia was temperate and blue-skied. The beach called like a siren's song—too tempting to pass up for most. Only those kids who were missing courses for graduation, who had been absent too many times, or who had simply chosen not to do the work during the regular school hours, showed up for summer school.

My mother worked every summer, whether or not she was actually teaching summer school. People thought teachers had it easy. Done by four and holidays and summers off! Not true. I'd seen my mother work from sunup to sundown, planning lessons, critiquing essays, coming up with new resources and methods of reaching her students, and attending professional-development sessions—all for no extra pay. Most of the teachers who worked summer school didn't do it out of passion for teaching. No, they needed to supplement their incomes. It was that or work at Target, Dollar General, or some other retail job, where you'd run into your students and have to smile and explain that working two jobs helped pay the bills.

Growing up, I remembered there being a few times when things were tight. That was when my mother had rolled up her sleeves and taken a second job, leaving Billy and me on our own to roam through Santa Sofia with Emmaline and Miguel and whatever other latchkey kids came along to join us. I'd seem my mom and Aunt Josie collapse at the end of every school year, desperate for the time to recharge their batteries. By the end of the summer, the batteries usually only made it to 75% or 80% charged.

Josephine Jeffries also worked every summer. She did it for the money, pure and simple. That being said, she also loved every last one of her students with every fiber of her being. If there was anything she could do to help them navigate their high school paths, she'd be all in.

I'd sent her a quick text to let her know I was coming to help a friend register for school. It took a solid hour to get Pilar set up for the upcoming school year. We sat with the registrar as she went through Pilar's paperwork and transcripts from her previous high school. So many times I wanted to reach out and squeeze Pilar's hand, to transfer some of my inner strength to her.

But I barely knew the girl, so I resisted the temptation, settling for a gentle squeeze on her shoulder instead. She offered me a reticent smile, but didn't shrug off the touch. It was a start. I was here for Pilar, too.

The registrar remembered me and my mother,

but that wasn't enough to bend the rules. Olaya, as Pilar's legal guardian, would need to come in and sign the paperwork, but we got as much of the enrollment done as we could. By the time we came out of the registrar's office, Josie, as she now insisted I call her, was waiting for us. Her face had always been framed by wavy blond streaks in her short auburn hair. She'd let the blond turn silvery, but it hadn't aged her. She wore a gauzy peachy sundress, her signature karma necklace strung on black leather, and lavender-framed glasses. She was the freshest sixty-something teacher Santa Sofia High School would ever see.

She might just be the freshest sixty-something woman anywhere.

"Darling, darling, darling!" She clutched my arms and stood back to look at me. "You are just the loveliest creature on the planet. And engaged!"

I realized I hadn't seen Josie since Christmas. She released my arms, but grabbed my left hand, happily tsk'ing and shaking her head at the engagement ring my father had given to my mother more than thirty-nine years ago, and that Miguel had given to me. A doleful smile graced her lips, and her eyes glazed. "Your mom would be so proud of you, Ivy. So proud."

She pulled me in for another hug before releasing me altogether and swinging her gaze to Pilar. "And who is this bewitching young lady?"

I waited for a breath to see if Pilar would introduce herself. She didn't, so I did. "This is Olaya Solis's niece."

"Olaya from the bread shop?"

"Yes," I said, remembering that Josie didn't frequent Yeast of Eden the way most Santa Sofians did. "If I succumbed to the magic of that bread, I'd never keep this girlish figure," she'd joked once or twice.

"Any friend of Ivy's is a friend of mine," Josie said, then hooked one arm through mine, the other through Pilar's, and led us from the office to her classroom. I shivered as we stepped in. Josie was hot-blooded and kept her classroom at a chilly sixty-five degrees as a result.

"Pilar is starting tenth grade here in the fall," I said. Aunt Josie *had* always—and *would* always—teach tenth-grade social studies, which meant world history, culture, and geography in the modern world. She threw in mini book studies, working closely with the tenth-grade English teacher. That person used to be my mom, Anna Culpepper. They'd loved connecting Earnest Hemingway and *The Sun Also Rises* to their unit on the effects of World War I. The "Lost Generation"—those who came of age after the Great War—had been deemed irreversibly scarred. In contrast, Hemingway presented them as irrepressibly strong. I'd absorbed everything they'd taught, year after year. To this day, I could talk for hours about the expats in Paris and Gertrude Stein's salon, where Pablo Picasso, Henri Matisse, F. Scott Fitzgerald, Hemingway, and Stein herself had buoyed literature, art, and the intellectual life.

I'd purposely left out any details about Pilar's parents. Aunt Josie was perceptive. I knew she'd picked up on the omission, but she didn't tread into that troubled water. I felt certain she'd work some magic of her own to get Pilar into her history class, and bit by bit, she'd win the girl's trust. I hoped Josephine Jeffries would become a huge influence on Pilar—in the best possible way.

The summer-school day was over, and her classroom was free of students. Pilar perused one of the bookshelves in the back of the classroom. I sat across from Josie, who perched on the edge of her desk. "I saw the news about Yeast of Eden and the supposed poisoning of that man. It's not true, is it?" she asked, her voice low.

"No!" I said with more harshness than I'd intended. "Not an ounce of truth."

One of Josie's perfectly curved brows arched upward. "Do tell."

I'd been replaying the morning of Josh's death since the night before when I'd sat at Baptista's Cantina & Grill, waiting for Olaya and Pilar to show up, and again while I'd lain hopelessly awake in bed. "Usually, Josh sat at his table and did his work. There was some commotion that morning." Mae chasing her mother around the bread shop was front and center in my mind. "But still, I don't see how anyone could have poisoned his food or coffee. He filled his own cup at the coffee bar. I gave him a fresh cup that I'd poured myself." Women who seemed infatuated with him had been there that day, namely Kristin Spelling. That little girl, Tara—her mother had looked smitten, too. Julia had turned Josh down flat. And Taylor had given him a death stare. More important, though, was that none of the women I knew for a fact Josh had dated and stolen from had been there. Tracy had not been there. His children had not been there. Whoever he'd been on the phone with and had planned to meet at eleven o'clock had not been there.

I cupped my hand over my forehead because the person I wanted to be cleared of suspicion *had* been there. Martina.

Pilar's desolate voice sparked an entirely new idea. "What if a bunch of people wanted him dead. Maybe it's like that movie *Murder on the Orient Express.*"

I looked at Pilar and blinked. "*Murder on the Orient Express,*" I repeated.

"It was a book first, based on the Agatha Christie novel of the same name," Josie said. "One of your mother's favorites."

I knew the book. And, of course, Josie was right. I had a distinct memory of going to the public library with my mother so she could check out the last Poirot novel, *Curtain.* Her sadness at seeing Poirot's stories end sparked my own interest in seeing what all the fuss was about. Once I started reading Christie's books, I couldn't stop. They'd spoken to me, too, so much so that I'd named my pug after the Grand Dame of Mystery. Of all Christie's novels, *Murder on the Orient Express* had been one that my mother had read and reread. "It's just so clever," I remembered her saying as she flipped back and forth, examining the clues.

I swung to stare at Pilar. "You mean it was a conspiracy? Maybe the women he screwed over all did it together?"

She drew back, looking a little shellshocked by my stare. "I mean, except *Tía* Martina, but yeah, maybe?"

My mind sputtered. The grieving women who'd

known Josh from MeetYourMate.com hadn't seemed
to know each other at the funeral, but I'd just made
that up in my head. Clearly they *had* known each
other before the funeral, because I'd seen them
together when they'd been a flock of silver-haired
birds cruising down the sidewalk and into Yeast of
Eden.

The notion that any of these women could be a
murderer was alarming enough. The idea that
they were in it together? Horrifying.

I reached into the recesses of my mind, searching for a different answer. I was operating in the
exact opposite way Captain York did. He found an
idea he liked and sought to prove it—in my opinion, to the dismissal of other potential explana-
tions. I, on the other hand, wanted to dismiss the
possibility of multiple scenarios with multiple potential suspects by conjuring up a brand-new solution. I drew a blank, and my mind drifted back to
football and the boosters, the reason I'd come to
see Josie.

"Football?" Josie repeated.

I nodded. "Football."

"What about it?"

"Josh Prentiss was a booster."

"*Okay.*" Josie's tone clearly indicated she had no
idea what I was talking about.

"The guy was a scoundrel and a thief, but that
doesn't mean any of his victims actually killed him
over it. What if we're on the wrong path altogether? What if his murder didn't have to do with
his cougar hunting?"

"Ah, so you need to talk with someone connected to the football program here," Josie said.

"Yes. Exactly."

"Well, sweetheart, I do happen to know the football coach." Josie winked. "If you know what I mean."

From the way she flicked her eyebrows up and her coy smile, I most definitely knew what she meant. Josie had always been single, but I'd never actually thought about her dating. "Aunt Josie!" I put my hand to my chest. "You and the football coach? Be still, my heart."

She winked and flashed that smile again. "Bruno's a great guy."

Bruno. A cliché football coach's name, if I'd ever heard one. "Think he'll talk to me?"

"Sure he will, darling, but he's not on campus right now"

"Is he gone for the day?"

"He is, but luckily this trip is local, so he'll be back this afternoon." Her lips formed a disapproving line. "The scouting these coaches have to do. It's too much." She wagged her finger at me as if I was personally behind the system. "We *should* be focused on the minds of these kids. I tell you, Ivy, our societal values are all screwed up."

She was preaching to the choir. Football had never been my kind of sport, especially after I'd seen Will Smith's movie *Concussion*. "I doubt it'll ever change," I said. "It brings in all the money, right?"

"It does. Those boosters, they're dynamite. That man, Mr. Prentiss, he was a fixture on campus." She continued, saying how Josh Prentiss had been at the high school nearly every day. "He was tight with so many people. The AD. All the other boosters. And, of course, Bruno."

"What's an AD?" I asked.

"The school's athletic director," Pilar said at the same time Josie answered with, "The athletic director. She runs all the sports programs."

That sounded like a path worth pursuing. "Is she here?"

Josie answered by way of picking up the handset of her desk phone. She ran her index finger over what I assumed was the list of room extensions, stopping when she found the one she wanted. She dialed, and five seconds later, she was speaking with someone. "You remember Anna Culpepper?" There was a moment of silence on Josie's end, then she said, "English? Oh, right. I guess she was here before your time."

My mother hadn't been gone *that* long. A thin veil of sadness draped over me at the idea that she hadn't even existed for some of the people here, despite the fact that she'd dedicated nearly her entire adult life to the high school.

I distracted myself from that line of thinking by shooting Pilar a smile. "Are you okay?" I asked.

She nodded and held up several books she'd taken from the shelves. *The Odyssey*. Tolkien. *Dune*. Books with politics and war and quests. Josie's love of history came through in the books she'd selected for her shelves.

I snapped back to attention when Josie said, "Great. I'll bring her down," and hung up the phone. She beckoned to Pilar. To me she said, "She has a few minutes."

"She didn't know my mom?" I asked, unable to keep the question inside.

Josie gave an apologetic smile. "She's pretty new here."

Pilar replaced the books, and we all left Josie's classroom. I shifted the conversation back to Coach Bruno. "Should I come back tomorrow to talk to him? Or can you ask him to give me a call?"

Josie gave me a side-eye glance, followed by a conspiratorial grin. "Tell you what. You and that sweet boy, Miguel, come on over for dinner tonight, how about that? You can talk to Bruno then."

I loved the plan. I'd have the coach's undivided attention, and at the moment, that's what I wanted and needed. "I'll have to check with Miguel to see if he can sneak away from the restaurant, but I'll definitely be there. What can I bring?"

She didn't hesitate. "Bring some of that delicious sourdough from the bread shop." She patted her stomach. "Seeing you, that's worth a splurge. Other than that, just bring your appetite."

"Deal."

We reached the field house, a stand-alone building on the edge of campus, and stepped into another world. The central room had an enormous putting surface and chipping area for golf. Beside me, Pilar muttered under her breath. "Jeez. My school doesn't have this."

I didn't remind her that *this* was now her school. I shared her sentiment, though. I was no golf expert, but this place seemed pretty state-of-the-art. A simulator screen took a large portion of one wall. Barrier netting enclosed the sides, and a life-size, crystal-clear photo of a golf course was on display. I stared at the setup, then at the young man using the simulator. He stood with his side to the screen. His legs were hip distance apart. He choked up on a golf club, cocked his arms, bringing his club back, then let loose. The golf ball that had been on the floor in front of him rocketed to the simulator screen.

"It's amazing, isn't it?" A woman ambled up. She looked like an athlete, with her black Adidas sweatsuit and white sneakers. "We can adjust the wind variable, whether or not we want the course soggy or dry. We can play different holes. It allows the golfers to work on their swings."

Whatever else it did, I imagined it certainly gave the Santa Sofia High School golf team a leg up. "Incredible," I said.

She held out her right elbow. "I don't shake. I elbow-bump," she said. "Mandy Trainer, athletic director."

How punny, I thought. A trainer named Trainer. I bumped elbows with her. "Ivy Culpepper. And this is an incoming sophomore. Pilar Solis."

We chatted for a few minutes, with Mandy Trainer asking Pilar about her interest in athletics and trying to sell her on the women's golf team. Pilar forced a placid smile and just nodded.

"I'll leave you to it," Josie whispered to me. "See you tonight, Ivy."

I gave her a quick hug—because we were closer than elbow-bumping friends. Josie left. Mandy Trainer had coerced Pilar to the putting green, held a putter out to her, and introduced her to another teenager. We left them to putt, and I followed the AD into her office. She gestured toward the round conference table. A whiteboard calendar was mounted to one wall. Next to it was another whiteboard filled with tournament names and dates. Her desk was pushed up against the opposite wall, tucked into a corner. Piles of papers and pamphlets and magazines sat on the desk. A large package of bottled water, another of Gatorade, and a basket of granola bars were pushed up against the wall. She closed a floppy planner as she sat, pushing it aside. It seemed Mandy Trainer conducted her business here at the table.

I sat facing her. She was young for her position. Maybe early thirties. I instantly admired her for having such an important leadership role in the school's sports program, doubly impressive because sports was a male-dominated field. "Thanks for seeing me," I began, not really sure what to say. I felt like I was grasping at straws.

"No problem. What can I do for you?"

I shifted in my seat, wondering how, exactly, to answer that question. Five minutes ago, I hadn't known this woman existed, but here I was trying to glean information from her that would implicate someone in her football program for murder, taking the heat off Josh's female victims. I shoved away any reservations and dove in. "I, uh, knew Josh Prentiss."

She pressed her lips together and gave a sad nod. "Yeah, that was a shock."

To put it mildly. "I know he was a big part of the boosters—"

She waved offhandedly. "Only for football."

"What?"

"Josh was a football booster. Each club has their own. They fundraise and support the coaching staff and team for their particular sport."

"Oh. Right. Of course." I hadn't played high school sports, so I wasn't in the know, but it made sense that each sport had their own parent group supporting it.

Mandy motioned with her head toward the large window separating the office from the main room and the golf simulator. "Our new simulator is thanks to the golf boosters. They are incredibly supportive. Sadly, none of the other boosters come anywhere close."

This flipped my preconceived notion on its head. "I thought football—"

She gave a sardonic chuckle. "Everyone thinks football trumps every other sport. Not true. The football boosters are active, but"—she looked at the simulator again—"it's hard to top that. There's an excellent soccer simulator, but we'll never get one for the team. Not that they need it. Soccer's not big enough here. The boosters managed team-spirit wear last year, but that's about it. The others are about the same. Track. Cross-country. Swimming. Water polo. Baseball. Cheerleading." She paused. "Well, baseball actually does okay. They should be upgrading our batting cages next year."

"What about football, though?" I asked, circling back. I couldn't believe golf brought in more money for the school than football.

Mandy Trainer frowned. "There's been a decline in donations. They do lots of fundraisers. The crab feed in early spring is a big one. An Octoberfest magic show. The boosters *want* to fund an

assistant coach position." The *but* hung there between us. I waited, and she continued. "They're
still saying it'll happen, but so far it hasn't. They
just haven't brought in enough. "

So interesting. "A decline? When did that start?"

"A few years ago, from what I gather. Before my
time."

Right. She was new. "I'm sure they'll have a good
year."

"God, I hope so. The parents and the entire
community *do* show up for Friday night football
games flashing their team hoodies and carrying
their team water bottles. It's just not enough."

I'd come here looking for something that didn't
add up. Maybe I'd already found it. "Is the team
doing okay? About Mr. Prentiss's death, I mean?"

She met my gaze head-on, her brown eyes suddenly more intense. She tilted her head slightly.
"Don't you mean his murder?"

The air in the room turned thick and heavy, but
the word sliced through it like a razor-sharp blade.
I couldn't read her—or her tone. It sounded almost accusatory, but nothing precipitated it. "Right,"
I said. An image of the kid who'd confronted me
outside Yeast of Eden popped into my head. He'd
been volatile. "How is the team handling his murder?"

The dark shift in her countenance evaporated.
"It's off-season. Some of the boys come in to train,
but that's about it, so I'm not entirely sure."

"I'm sure he'll be missed by the boosters," I said.
"I saw how committed he was to the team."

"He *was* committed." We talked for a few minutes about the boosters themselves. "Mr. Prentiss has been on the executive board since Brendan was a freshman," she said.

Josh's son was going into his senior year, so Josh had had three years with the boosters. More than enough time for someone to pick up on any discrepancies in the books. My hope in a new scenario with a new suspect started to pixelate.

Nothing else from Many Trainer was forthcoming, so I pushed my chair away from the table and stood. "It was nice meeting you."

The AD didn't return the sentiment. She just stood and followed me out of her office. I caught Pilar's eye. She handed the putter to the girl next to her and joined me. I opened the door, letting the blinding light from outside shine into the room. I hadn't realized it before, but now I saw that there were no windows to the outside. "It's Ivy, right?" the AD said to me, catching the door and holding it open.

Pilar exited ahead of me. I stood in the threshold. "Right."

She cocked her head again, and this time there was no mistaking the curiosity and suspicion lacing her words. "Maybe I missed something, but why exactly did you want to talk to me about Josh Prentiss?"

I'd been relieved when she hadn't asked me this question. Now I summoned up the answer I'd thought up on our way from the main building to the field house. "There were rumors going around that Mr. Prentiss's death had something to do with the bread shop in town."

Her eyes narrowed. She nodded. "Seems a little unrealistic to me, but I've heard some people say that."

I exhaled the breath I hadn't known I'd been holding. My fear that Mandy Trainer bought into the ludicrous idea that Olaya's bread had been the vehicle for the poison that killed Josh Prentiss evaporated. "It *is* unrealistic, isn't it?"

The sun beat down on my back. Standing there with the door open was letting the paid air out and the warm summer air in, but Mandy didn't seem to mind. I scooted over enough to let a young woman pass by me. "Hey, coach," she said.

Mandy turned her body enough to pat the girl's shoulder. "Work on your putts today, Chelsea."

The girl, Chelsea, smiled and nodded. "I will."

Mandy turned back to me. "What does any of this have to do with you?" she asked.

I debated what to say, but in the end, it seemed pointless to hold anything back. Schools were hotbeds of gossip. Better she hear the truth from me so she could help quash the lies some of the football team might still be spouting. "Olaya Solis is a good friend of mine. She's . . . family," I said, because she, along with Penelope Branford, was part of the family I'd chosen. "She had nothing to do with Mr. Prentiss's death. I . . . want people to know that," I said, leaving out Martina and Josh's other victims.

"Makes sense," Mandy said. "I'd want to set the record straight, too."

"Do you have any ideas about why he was killed?" I asked. I hadn't intended to be so direct, but now that it seemed Mandy was on #TeamJustice, the question popped out.

She stood there for a moment, silent. After a solid ten seconds of her intense gaze, she said, "I don't like to speak ill of the dead, but I never much liked the guy. Wait. Scratch that. It wasn't that I didn't like him. It was more that I didn't trust him."

I felt my brows lift. This was a different perspective—and one that had not been the norm. Until the truth had started to come out, everyone else in Santa Sofia thought Josh Prentiss was the most stand-up man around. Aside from the people he'd wronged and whoever had murdered him, of course. "How do you mean?"

"It's just a feeling, really. I always thought he was putting on a show for people. No one is *that* happy *all* the time, you know? I caught him off guard a few times. No smiles and charm. Even at the booster breakfast, he'd been completely humorless. I'd bet my life that was the *real* Josh Prentiss."

I thought about that. Almost every mental image I had of the man showed him smiling. In fact, there was only one time I could think of when he *hadn't* been his smiling, charming self: when he'd been on the phone that morning planning his eleven o'clock meet-up. I asked myself now: Was Josh always happy?

Maybe, but I'd never really know. I moved on to a bigger question: If he was generally happy, what had made Josh lose that inherent joy . . . or if he was always putting on a show, what had made him drop the façade?

Who had he been on the phone with?

Pilar and I headed back to my car. She slid into the passenger seat and immediately reconnected her Bluetooth to the car while my mind whirled. The unknown phone call. The grieving women Josh Prentiss had wronged. *Murder on the Orient Express.* For all of Josh's charming-man image, there were people lined up who had grudges against him. I caught sight of the old marquee as Pilar and I drove off the high school grounds. The boosters had been trying to replace it for years. That's what Nina had said. So why hadn't it been replaced already? Even if the football boosters weren't as flush as the golf parents, they still had money. This was Santa Sofia, after all. A lot of working-class folks lived here, but an equally high number of wealthy people resided here, too.

I tuned out the music playing as I drove. Instead, I thought about Hercule Poirot the entire way back to the bread shop, while Pilar stared out the window beside me.

Chapter 21

My mom's copy of *Murder on the Orient Express* was on the bookshelf in the study at my dad's house. It was stacked on top of a slew of other murder mysteries, but was, by far, the most worn-out of the bunch. I didn't think it would give me any insight to the murder plaguing my mind, but I pulled it from the shelf anyway. Flipping through the pages revealed my mother's annotations. She'd been fascinated with Poirot's keen ability to lay out the array of clues before him and, from them, deduce the truth.

Poirot was clever.

Agatha Christie was cleverer.

I, on the other hand, felt like a mouse in a maze. I'd die of starvation before I found my way out.

My mother had underlined the clues she'd missed on her first read-through of the novel, jotting exclamation points in the margins, notes about what the clues meant once she knew the truth, and a series of highlighted words. When I read them, one word or phrase after another, they showed just how clever the author had been. Twelve stab wounds to the victim. Twelve people hiding in plain sight, each with a motive leading back to a kidnapped child.

I sighed and replaced the book. Josh Prentiss hadn't been stabbed. He'd been poisoned, and one could only be poisoned once, so while Pilar's suggestion that a bunch of people might have worked together to kill the man, it didn't make sense in reality.

I came back to the fact that Josh had been generally liked.

But he hadn't really been, had he? His wife knew he'd cheated. He'd stolen money from at least a handful of women, and maybe more. Many of them seemed to have figured that out before his death. He'd been a booster, okay, but despite his efforts, there was still no marquee and no new assistant coach. Did any of the executive board have doubts about his honesty? My spine crackled. I needed to talk to more boosters.

It didn't take long to find them. A quick perusal of Santa Sofia High School's website led me to the athletics page, then to the football program, and finally to the boosters. I scanned the names, but none was familiar. Each linked to an email. I clicked the first one, which opened up a new email, and started to type. I didn't get far because I had no idea what to say.

Hi! My name is Ivy, and I work at the bread shop

where Josh Prentiss was just hours before his death. Did he have any enemies? Any people who might have wanted him dead? Did he cheat the football boosters out of money?

If I received an email like that I'd run for the hills.

I deleted the draft and instead wrote down the names of the executive board for the boosters in my notebook. Josh had been the controller. The rest of the names were meaningless to me, but I hoped one might lead to a clue.

As well as an email link, a phone number was listed for each board member. Before I could talk myself out of it, I opened the keypad on my phone and called the president. The call was answered on the third ring. A friendly voice saying, "This is Shannon," took me aback. I forged ahead in my most professional voice, half afraid I'd hang up before I even realized I'd done it. "Hi Shannon. My name is Ivy Culpepper. I'm looking into the death of Josh Prentiss. I believe he was on the executive board for the Santa Sofia High School football boosters?"

There was a weighty pause before the woman released an emotional sigh. "God. He was. I can't . . . I still can't believe he's gone. Dead."

"Murdered," I said shortly, in the same way Mandy Trainer had corrected me.

On the other end of the cellular waves, Shannon Lipsky gasped. "Right. Murdered. I can't believe it," she said again, as if that was the only phrase she could summon up.

"I know. It's shocking. Listen, I have a few quick questions." I held my breath that she wouldn't interrupt me to ask who I worked for and why I was digging into the man's death. "Was Josh generally liked by the board and the boosters?"

"Oh my God, yes. He was so wonderful. He and Cheryl—that's the treasurer—they worked miracles raising money. Josh was just so committed to the student athletes. He will be very missed. Sean, um, Fitzwilliam is going to take over as controller, at least until we can hold an election to fill the position."

I wondered about the *um* between Sean's first and last names, but it was good information. I jotted it down. "Fitzwilliam. He's one of the directors, is that right?" I asked, referring back to the list of names on the website. "Married to . . ."

"Right. To Cheryl, the treasurer. At least that will be an easy transition. He can check over the books in the comfort of his own home."

I asked a few more questions, but Shannon couldn't tell me anything else. I hung up with her and moved on, dialing Cheryl Fitzwilliam. I went through the same introduction, hoping for the same result. I got it, but this time it came with an onslaught of tearful emotions. "It's just . . . I can't . . . I can't believe he's really *gone*," she said, her voice breaking down on that last word in a way that made me wonder if Josh's predilection for older women wasn't hard and fast. Maybe the hesitation in Shannon's voice a few minutes ago was because she knew something had been going on between Cheryl and Josh.

"I know. I'm so sorry," I said, leaping forward with that theory even though I had not a shred of evidence to support it. "Were you and Josh . . . close?" I asked, heavy emphasis on the word *close*.

Instead of answering, she wailed into my ear. "He was . . . oh my God, I miss him so much. Please don't tell anyone. My husband, he'll kill me." She gasped at her own choice of words, and I could hear the sound of her hand slapping over her mouth. When she spoke, her voice came out muffled. "I didn't mean . . . ohhh!"

"Cheryl," I said slowly, "were you and Josh having an affair?"

Her sob said it all. Either Cheryl Fitzwilliam was an award-winning actress, or she was truly in distress over her lover's death. After a few more wailing answers to my probing questions, I hung up and promptly called Sean Fitzwilliam, because if Cheryl felt so strongly about Josh, could she have really kept those feelings from her husband?

This time, there was no answer. His voice mail was pleasant enough. *You've reached Sean Fitzwilliam. Leave a message, and I'll call you back at my earliest convenience.*

I left a message, hoping he really would call me back.

I tried the secretary, the vice president, and the other two directors, talking to two of them and getting nothing new, and leaving a message with the third.

I was confident York was digging into Josh's marks, and dredging up any other women Josh might have gotten his hooks into. Including Jeanne P. And I also knew he'd eventually talk to the boosters. Who knew, maybe he had already.

I had just two lingering questions from talking to them myself: Did Sean Fitzwilliam know his wife Cheryl had been having an affair with Josh Prentiss? And if so, could he have been the one to poison his fellow football booster?

Chapter 22

Dinner at Josie's turned out to be far more enter-taining—and informative—than I'd thought it would be. I'd stopped by the bread shop to pick up the two loaves of sourdough I'd asked Zula to put aside for me, then headed inland to Josie's small, ranch-style home. She wasn't wealthy, didn't come from money, and didn't have a deep desire to move closer to the beach.

What she did have was a mid-century, Spanish-style home with a front courtyard enclosed with a stucco wall. Miguel and I drove separately, because he'd have to return to the restaurant while I headed home for an early bedtime, so I could be up bright and early for the morning bake at Yeast of Eden. He was already there waiting for me when I arrived. He opened the driver's side door, taking the bread loaves from me, then taking my hand as I stepped out. It was a balmy seventy-two degrees.

Still, I had brought a light sweater with me just in case Josie kept her house as cold as her classroom. Miguel set the bags of bread on top of the car and wrapped me up in his arms. "How's the investigation?" he asked after a kiss.

"Inconclusive," I said, "but rife with possibilities."

"And the engagement party?"

My lips pulled to one side. "We'll be ready." I hoped.

I'd talk to Olaya first thing in the morning. Josh Prentiss's death and Pilar were wrenches in the plan, but that didn't mean the show shouldn't go on. Miguel and I were still getting married, and he was right. We'd reserved the park. We'd sent out invitations. It was happening, whether or not we had food and drink and entertainment. Which meant we had to finalize everything.

Josie greeted us at the door. She'd changed from her school outfit to an even trendier pair of torn jeans, a flouncy floral sleeveless top, and slim mahogany flip-flops. Her purple toenails matched her glasses. With her silver-streaked hair piled loosely on top of her head, she looked beautifully wind-blown, like she'd just returned from a walk on the beach.

Behind her stood a man who looked suspiciously like Coach Taylor from *Friday Night Lights*. His dark brown hair was playfully mussed, an appealing five-o'clock shadow darkened his upper lip and chin, and his crinkled eyes and slight smile showed his good humor. It was obvious why he was taken with Josie, but now I could see why Josie was taken with him. He casually draped one arm around her, his hand dangling over one shoulder. "Darling!" Josie exclaimed. "Come in, come in."

She stepped back, causing Coach Bruno to drop his arm and step back as well. Her smile softened. "Ivy Culpepper, meet Bruno Chandler. Bruno, this is Annika's daughter, Ivy."

I smiled at her use of my mother's given name. Only a handful of people had known her well enough to know she'd been named after her great-grandmother. Josie was one of those people.

"It's good to meet you," Coach Bruno said. "I knew your mom. Good woman. She was a very good woman."

Miguel pressed his hand against my lower back, a reassuring gesture that shot out a surge of love from my core like rays from the sun. "Thank you," I said.

Josie swung her arm out to usher us inside. Her home was as colorful as she was. Pinks and oranges and purples were everywhere, pops of white giving a fresh and happy feeling to the space. Even her kitchen chairs were colorful—one green, one yellow, one blue, and one orange. They were placed around a square red table, which Josie had set with equally colorful Fiesta dinnerware.

Josie handed us each a wineglass, each adorned with a charm. Mine was a snippet from what looked like a vintage map of Boston. She led us to her patio. Vibrant periwinkle wisteria blooms hung overhead through the slats of a weather-worn redwood trellis. A built-in brick fireplace grounded the flagstone decking on one side. A wrought-iron patio set, including a coffee table, one chair, a love seat, and a sofa, were situated around it. Miguel and I sat side by side on the sofa facing the fireplace. Bruno and Josie squeezed together on the love seat. As we sipped a dry pinot grigio, Josie asked about the meeting with Mandy Trainer.

"She didn't like him much," I said. "She didn't trust him."

"Him who?" Coach Bruno asked.

"Josh Prentiss," I said.

Josie's arm was extended behind Bruno. She laid one hand on his shoulder. "He was one of your boosters, wasn't he?"

Bruno's eyes grew a little more squinty. The way he clamped his teeth heightened the hollows of his cheeks. "He was." He looked at me. "JoJo said you knew the guy."

I smiled at his cute nickname for Josie. "Only a little bit. He was a regular at the bread shop. Did you know him well?" I asked.

Bruno didn't smile much. His lips pulled to one side in a way that made it look like he was biting the inside of his cheek. "I knew him, but not particularly well," he said. "Smoke and mirrors, you know?"

"What do you mean?" Miguel asked.

"He was a lot of show, but not much substance."

"The opposite of you, my love," Josie said with a peck on his cheek. "You're all substance and no show."

At this, the clamped side of Bruno's mouth lifted slightly, just enough to classify it as a smile. He squeezed her knee affectionately. The guy wasn't a barrel of emotions, that much was clear. But was it strange that he wasn't showing any emotion at the death of someone he worked with regularly?

"Sounds like you didn't like him much, either," I said.

Bruno ran his hand down the front of his gray T-shirt. "I didn't have to like him as long as he did his best for the program."

"And did he?" I asked, because I got the distinct impression that Coach Bruno Chandler didn't think so.

He was noncommittal, though. Instead of a yes or no, he gave a slight shrug and an ambiguous, "Hard to say."

"The golf boosters are sure going gangbusters," I said.

Miguel cocked an amused brow. If Coach Bruno saw through Josh Prentiss's act, he would surely see through my way too heavy-handed probing.

"That's exactly the problem," he said. "Smoke and mirrors. I asked him that morning—the morning he died—where's the marquee? Where's the football simulator? Where's the assistant coach we need? He said he and Cheryl had the new numbers after the spring membership drive, and he'd get the information to me soon. We were supposed to meet up to discuss it. Of course, that never happened."

I thought back to Nina exclaiming at what she'd seen on Josh's computer. *Finally, a new coach? Or a marquee?* What exactly had she seen? And if the money was there, why hadn't the boosters delivered the goods?

A niggling thought tried to break free in my mind, but I couldn't quite pull it out. Or, if it had to do with a disgruntled Coach Bruno Chandler, maybe I didn't want it to surface. I needed another suspect, but Josie's new boyfriend wasn't who I had in mind. "How long have you two been dating?"

Josie threw her head back and released a joyful sigh. "Seven months," she said. "If I've had a rough day, I sometimes walk the track." She grimaced. "The day we met was a particularly bad day."

"We'd already met," he said, "but we hadn't *met*."

"Well, yes, because we're on the same staff. But it's a big school, with a lot of teachers. Not a lot of opportunities for athletics and history teachers to commingle, you know. Anyway, I had a student last year who was really struggling at home. Dad's in prison. Mom's strung out most of the time. This sweet girl is raising her younger siblings and trying to keep her head above water. She is exactly the kind of student your mom would have bent over backward trying to help, Ivy."

I knew Josie was right. Every year one or two students had grabbed hold of my mom's heart. These were the kids she couldn't shake. She talked about all her students at dinner, but a few always surfaced to the top. Over and over, their names came up. Over and over, she gave up her lunch period to devote extra time to their learning. Over and over, she stayed late after school to tutor them.

Bruno picked up the story. "I watched Josie circle the track with her hands fisted. Twice that I saw she punched the air in front of her. And she muttered to herself. She talks to herself a lot. More so when she's angry or frustrated."

I laughed. I knew that to be true about Josie. She was one of those people who not only talked to herself, but also referred to herself in the third person, saying things like, *Come on, Josie. You got this,* or *Josie, Josie, Josie. That was utterly ridiculous.*

"Anyway," Josie said, to move the story along. She leaned closer to Bruno. "This man, he chased after me to ask if I was all right. And the rest, as they say, is history. Pun intended."

Coach Bruno wasn't animated, like Josie was, but his eye crinkles lifted, and that one corner of his mouth tilted up a smidgeon more. The man was smitten.

We took our wine inside and ate a light summer dinner of cold cucumber soup, spinach salad, and the sourdough I'd brought. I watched Josie with Bruno, smiling to myself. Love was in the air. These two. Olaya and my dad. My brother Billy and Emmaline. I reached for Miguel's hand. The two of us. The heartache Josh Prentiss had caused for Sharon and Peggy and Linda and Darlene. For Jeanne. For Martina. I hoped they kept open minds about the possibility of love, because it could happen anywhere and at any time.

An hour later, Miguel and I stood on the front porch. "Nice meeting you, Coach," Miguel said as the two men clasped hands in a hearty handshake.

I laughed at how he slipped into calling Bruno "coach." It was a guy thing. I seconded the sentiment. "Next time we'll have you over for dinner," I said to them.

"It's a deal," Josie said. She squeezed my hand, then pulled me into a tight hug. "We'll see you at the engagement party," she said.

An instantaneous yearning for Miguel and me to move forward with our wedding plans spread from my core. Anxiety was on its tail. Until Martina was off the hook, nothing would feel right. Still, I smiled big, gave her another squeeze, and gave an exuberant, "Yes!"

A short while later, Miguel and I sat on the deck of his bungalow in companionable silence, Agatha on my lap. I replayed the evening, specifically the conversation about Josh Prentiss. Smoke and mirrors. Who was Josh, really?

As I stared at the inky expanse of the Pacific on the horizon, that niggling thought finally surfaced. Bruno had said he'd asked Josh that morning about the marquee and the assistant coach. He said they were supposed to meet, but didn't. Could Josh have been speaking to Coach Bruno on the phone that morning in the bread shop? Could Coach Bruno have suspected that something wasn't on the up and up with Josh and the booster money?

Until I spoke more forthrightly with Cheryl Fitzwilliam, the booster treasurer, I couldn't know for certain that Josh had been skimming from the boosters. My gut, though, told me that that was exactly what he was doing.

Chapter 23

The antiques mini-mall was not a place you went if you knew what you wanted. If you shopped with something specific in mind, you were not likely to find it amid the crowded chaos of old record albums, kitchenware, samurai swords, and the detritus from people's lives, past and present. One person's trash was another person's treasure. That was Nina Blankenship's motto.

I stepped inside, breathing in the peculiar smell of old stuff. A horseshoe counter sat in the front at the center of the store, its shelves displaying antique broaches, silver goblets, and other so-called valuables that were kept safe behind the glass.

Customers milled around, some likely tourists and some locals. Old junk appealed to everyone. I admit, I'd found a treasure or two here, including an old, child-sized red rocking chair, which now sat in a corner in my backyard. Kind of a secret garden find.

I walked around for a few minutes, just in case an antique rolling pin or kitchen scale caught my eye. After ten minutes, nothing had materialized. Neither had Nina. I called her name.

"Ivy? Is that you?"

"Yes! Where are you?"

"Over here, by the dress forms."

I had no idea where the dress forms were, but I headed in the general direction I thought her voice had come from. "Marco," I said.

"Polo," she replied.

I walked deeper into the labyrinth of antiques, stopping short when my gaze landed on a narrow rolling pin. I detoured into the consignment space and picked it up, turning it over in my hands. It was heavy. Solid wood. Even the handles were part of the single piece of walnut. I had to have it. I took it with me as I went back to my search for Nina. "Marco."

"Polo!" she said, and then she popped up in front of me like a jack-in-the-box.

"Oh!" I jumped back, the rolling pin clenched in my hand like a weapon.

"Don't clobber me with that!" she exclaimed.

I felt a blush creep to my cheeks. "Sorry," I said. "I was looking for you, but you still startled me."

"Look what I found!"

Her exuberance was contagious. I peered forward, excited to see. She bent over, then stood again holding a wooden crate filled with sewing patterns. I didn't sew. "Hmm," I said.

"Now, I see you're not enthused by these, but they are pristine. Never used. Never even opened. They aren't worth much to the average person, but to the right customer, they're a gold mine."

One person's trash . . .

"Cool," I said.

She extricated herself from the tight spot she'd been in. Trails of dust marked her dark clothing. Her gaze landed on my rolling pin. "Where'dya find that?"

I pointed behind me, a vague indication that it had come from one of the consignment spots in that general direction.

She grinned, the apples of her cheeks rosy. "Isn't it amazing?" she gushed.

"Isn't what amazing?"

"That the right person finds the right item. I mean, this place is jam-packed. I can honestly say I've never seen that rolling pin before, but here you are, a baker, holding it. It's like it found you rather than the other way around. That's exactly what'll happen with these patterns. Some lucky dressmaker or fashion designer will stop in, and they'll be an unexpectedly lucky find."

She was probably right. "You've really never seen this here?" I asked, holding up the rolling pin.

She shook her head. "Never." She spread her free hand wide. "But look at this place. It's not surprising. A million little treasures lurk here, just waiting to be found."

I followed her up to the front counter. She pulled the tablet she used for transactions from a hiding place under the counter, then rang up a petite floral teapot for a woman, swinging the tablet around so she could sign for her purchase. I was next. The rolling pin cost all of five dollars. I paid for it before broaching the actual reason for my visit. "Nina, remember the morning Josh died?"

The smile fell away from her face, replaced by a heavy frown. "Do I remember! I'll never forget it. The stories people are telling about that man . . . I can't believe all those people grieving for him if what half of what I've been hearing is true."

"What kind of stories?" I asked, wondering if yet more skeletons would be falling from Josh's closet.

Nina pulled the stool she kept behind the counter closer and perched on it, leaning her forearms on the edge of the worktop. "I have heard so many people say that he had"—she lowered her voice and glanced around to make sure no one was within earshot—"*girlfriends*."

"He did," I said. "I've met some of them. He was on a dating site."

She slapped the counter with an open palm. "Meet Your Mate! I heard the same thing!"

"Older women," I said.

"Yes!" Slap. Her voice dropped again. "And I heard that he stole money from some of them."

"Me, too," I said. "From a lot of them."

Nina reached under the counter and pulled out a white bakery box. From the looks of it, she'd visited the bread shop that morning and had left with a collection of goodies. She pulled out a blueberry sourdough roll. She tore it in half, holding out a hunk for me. I wasn't hungry, so I resisted the temptation. "No, thanks," I said, then I redirected the conversation. "I thought I heard you say something about the marquee to Josh. Booster business?"

"That morning?" she asked through a mouthful of bread. She swallowed. "Oh my gosh, yes! He had a spreadsheet up with some incredible numbers. Finally, the football team'll get every single thing they could possibly want. An assistant to help Coach Bruno. The marquee. Maybe even new turf!" Her excitement waned slightly.

"What is it?" I asked.

"It's just . . ." She waved her pudgy hand. "It's probably nothing."

"Nina, what's wrong?"

She tore out a soft tuft of bread from the inside of her roll, pressing it between her fingers. "I'm probably wrong, but when I turned around and saw Josh's computer open and the spreadsheets up—"

"Spreadsheets? More than one?"

She gave a slow nod. "He was flipping back and forth between them, and I could have sworn they both had this year's date at the top. I started talking to someone, and when I turned around again, only one spreadsheet was up. I thought to myself, *Maybe you imagined it, Nina*, but the more I think about it . . ." She tossed the bit of bread in the trash before breaking off a piece of the crusty outside. "I don't think I *did* imagine it, Ivy."

If I'd been faced with this question a week ago, I wouldn't have thought anything of it. Josh was one of the good ones. But with all the new information

I had about him, I couldn't think of a benign reason for him to have two spreadsheets with the same date open.

Nina put what was left of her roll back into the open box and leaned toward me again. "It looked to me like he was changing the numbers on one of them, but he wouldn't—*shouldn't*—have been doing that. Right? I mean, two financial records of the same year? I talked myself out of it then, but there's something definitely fishy about that, right?"

Very fishy, I thought. And just like that, Nina had helped me draw a heavy black line under the question of whether Josh could have been embezzling money from the football boosters. If he was doctoring the books by creating a fake spreadsheet, it seemed likely that I was on the right track.

Could he do that alone? At that moment, something else about Nina's encounter with Josh surfaced. She'd said, *Josh Prentiss, here you are again. We have to stop meeting this way.* They'd often come into the bread shop around the same time, but her comment sounded like it referenced something else. Some other chance encounter they'd had. "Nina, did you see Josh when he wasn't at the bread shop?" I asked her.

The way her lips pulled down carved deep lines on either side of her chin made her face look like a marionette's. "Sure. At booster breakfasts and events."

At booster breakfasts. Coach Bruno had said he'd talked to Josh that morning. It could have been via a phone call, but what if it had been in person? "When was the last booster breakfast?" I asked.

Deep vertical lines formed between Nina's eyes as she pinched her brows together. She pulled her head back as if she was surprised at the question—or that I didn't know the answer already. "That morning. We have a booster meeting on the second Tuesday of the month. We do it early. Too early. Seven AM, but the coaches have to scout after school, and the trainer has other sports she oversees, so mornings are easier for them."

That meant it was likely Coach Bruno had talked to Josh at the meeting, not on the phone.

"That's the thing," Nina continued, and I suddenly realized I'd spoken aloud. "At the meeting, Coach Bruno was asking Josh about the assistant coach position, and the marquee, and a bunch of other stuff the team needs. Josh and Cheryl—"

"Fitzwilliam?"

"Right. She's the treasurer. They said proceeds had been down and expenses were up, but they were working on making things happen. But when I saw the spreadsheets—" She paused.

"Did you get a good look at them?" I asked, not remembering how long Nina had been standing there before her exclamation startled Josh.

Cleared her throat. "Long enough to eat a morning cookie," she said, waggling her brows. "On one of them, it didn't look like proceeds were down to me. It looked like there was plenty of money. On the other, though . . ."

She trailed off, the implication clear. On the other one, Josh was doctoring the numbers. Two sets of books. *Smoke and mirrors*, Coach Bruno had said the night before. which meant my hunch that

Josh was stealing money from the boosters was probably right.

Cheryl Fitzwilliam had been having an affair with Josh. She'd made that perfectly clear. Had they been working together to defraud the boosters? They would have had to, I reasoned. She was the treasurer, he was the controller. I thought about Tracy saying there was one woman who'd fallen hard for Josh. If he'd gotten Cheryl to help him defraud the boosters, she might very well be the one in love with him.

"Who was at the booster meeting?" I asked Nina, the idea surfacing that Sean Fitzwilliam may have become wise to his wife's affair *and* the embezzlement. That certainly gave him motive.

Her frown deepened the marionette lines on either side of her chin. "The usual suspects. The board and the directors. Shannon, the president. The VP. The secretary. Cheryl and Sean Fitzwilliam. She's the treasurer, and he's a director. Josh. He was the controller. And the other directors. Oh. And Coach Bruno. The athletic director— Mandy Trainer. Then a handful of parents. Most of us go for the free food," she said with a shrug.

My brain skittered. Mandy Trainer had mentioned a booster breakfast, but I hadn't connected the dots until now. Sean had been present, and there had been . . . "Free food?"

"It's always a continental breakfast," Nina said. "Fruit, muffins, jam, coffee, juice."

My head felt full of cotton. Did Emmaline or York know about the booster breakfast? Josh very well could have been poisoned there—well before he ever stepped foot in Yeast of Eden that morning. In my opinion, Sean Fitzwilliam was a strong suspect.

This information could prove Martina, as well as the other women Josh had wronged, were all innocent, but on the tail of that thought arose another question. It wormed its way through the thickness of my brain. Why hadn't Coach Bruno mentioned the booster breakfast?

Who else could have become wise to the embezzlement? Had others also become suspicious? Once again, Sean Fitzwilliam's name surfaced in my mind.

Chapter 24

I left a message for Emmaline, telling her about the booster breakfast. From there, I set my sights on Sean Fitzwilliam. It wasn't hard to track down his place of business. He owned a math and reading tutoring center in Santa Sofia. I showed up out of the blue, hoping he'd be there. He was.

Meeting him reminded me to let go of preconceived notions. Because he was a football booster, I pictured him as the athletic type. When I found out he ran a tutoring business, my image refined, and I pictured him as Coach Bruno's twin—a sporty man who was also invested in his students' futures.

Turns out I was wrong on both counts. Sean Fitzwilliam was a middle-aged guy whose shirt was wrinkled and whose pants were slung low under his prominent belly. Football trophies from his high school heyday were displayed around the room. He wore his shiny high school football ring like a beacon to the past. A slick black sports car sat out in the front parking lot. I suspected it was his. He seemed like the type to buy a snazzy car in a midlife crisis.

Students of varying ages sat in little cubbies with headphones on. At scattered tables, adults worked one-on-one with kids. They spoke in low voices, completely focused on the work. He greeted me with a toothy smile that struck me as very practiced. Sean Fitzwilliam spoke to me, but his eyes constantly moved around the room, checking on the kids of varying ages with headphones on working at cubbies, landing on the adults and students working side by side at scattered tables around the room. He was a man who only half paid attention to one thing at any given time.

He brought his focus back to me. He kept his voice at a practiced low level. "How can I help you?"

I'd thought long and hard about what angle to take. I didn't know if he'd been at Josh's funeral, but they'd been on the boosters together, so I leapt with faith. I tilted my head and gave him a puzzled look, like I was trying to place his face. "Have we met?"

He looked at me as if he were trying to remember, then gave his head a little shake. "I don't think so. I would have remembered."

I couldn't decide if the twinkle in his eye was smarmy or just friendly, so I ignored it. I opened my eyes wide and snapped my fingers—a little over-dramatic, perhaps, but it got the message across. "I know. I recognize you from Josh Prentiss's funeral."

His smile turned into a frown. "You knew him, too?"

This I could be completely honest about. "I did. Pretty shocking, all the stuff that's coming out about him."

He remained silent at this. So, not defending Josh. Because he knew the guy had been having an affair with his wife? "I'm looking into his death," I said, quickly moving on with, "Were you friends?"

He tilted his head as if he was seriously considering the question. "That's a little complicated," he said after a moment. Then he gestured toward a door leading to a small office away from the main study room. "Let's go in there. More private."

I followed him, happy he hadn't just shut me out, like I feared he might, or asked me who I worked for or why I was investigating. I had a niggling thought that anyone who was guilty would have asked those questions or kicked me out with no compunction.

The room didn't look like an office, exactly. There was no work desk. No filing cabinets. This was more like a mini conference room. It could have been picked up whole and placed into the high school's field house. Just like the athletic director's office, the main seating was at a small round table. I sat across from Sean. NFL team pennants ran around the room at the top of the wall, each point of one banner touching the edge of the one in front of it. A few more trophies were placed here and there. "From my heyday," he said with a touch of melancholy.

"Looks like you were quite the player.," I said.

Another wistful look slid across his face. "I was. All-state in high school. Full ride to Cal Berkeley." He patted his chest with one hand. "Two years in, and I went into A-fib. And that, as they say, was that. My dreams of the NFL crashed and burned."

I felt for him. Atrial fibrillation was no laughing matter, and football—at least in my opinion—wasn't worth risking your life over. "Looks like you've done really well for yourself, even if you didn't get to go pro."

"Sure. But it's not the same, you know. It's like spending your whole life training to be an astronaut, only to get kicked out on your ass at the last second because Elon Musk is taking your spot on the rocket." He gave a heavy sigh. "I really could have made it. My son's going to."

"Oh yeah? Is your son on the team?"

"He's a freshman. QB. He's going to lead the team to state when he plays varsity. Mark my words."

"I will," I said with a smile. "You were on the boosters with Josh, right? Is that how you knew him?"

"Me and Josh, we go way back. We were at Cal together." He grinned. "Hell, I stole his girl from him."

I stared, wide-eyed. "Really?"

"My wife. She ended up with the better deal . . . you know, given the circumstances."

"Circumstances?" I asked.

"From what I hear, the guy was kind of a prick. All those women? Sheesh. I dunno how he kept it all straight. Plus, you know, he's dead."

The conversation felt a little morbid. He was saying that Cheryl made the right choice in marrying him since Josh Prentiss was a player who'd up and died. Only *why* Josh died was still in question. Extra morbid if Sean Fitzwilliam had had anything to do with it.

"She must be very upset since she worked with him on the booster finances," I said, knowing full well exactly how upset Cheryl Fitzwilliam was.

"She's the emotional type," Sean said. "Cries at the animal commercials on TV. Cries at everything. We have tissues in every room of the house."

From talking to Cheryl, there was more to her emotions than puppies and kittens in need of adoption, but I didn't go there. My goal was to see if Sean suspected anything. So far, it was a big *no*.

"It must be hard to realize he was there one minute—at the booster breakfast, right? And then, bam, gone."

My words felt a little heavy-handed, but if Sean thought anything of it, he didn't let on. "The guy was in tiptop shape."

"So you have no idea who killed him? Who would have wanted him dead?"

He gave an emphatic shake of his head. "None." But then he leaned in a hair. "Then again, I've been reading about all the women he swindled."

I shook my head in solidarity with them. "It's sad. So many of them, their financial security destroyed."

He didn't say anything. His gaze had strayed to the window between his office and the tutoring room. He shifted in his chair. Getting ready to wrap up our little meeting, I thought. "Shannon Lipsky said you'll be taking over as controller. Looking through the books and everything? Hopefully the football program can start to catch up with the golf program."

That brought his attention back to me. His face clouded. "I haven't been able to check out the books yet," he said, his voice quiet and reflective. He ran his hand over his face, and I suddenly realized I had seen him before. That morning—the morning Josh died, Sean Fitzwilliam had been at the bread shop. He was the man who'd ordered a morning cookie, then raced out the door after Josh left, heading in the same direction.

"Were you at the booster breakfast Tuesday?" I asked.

He shook his head. "Summers are busy here. Kids trying to make up credits to pass their grade level. Cheryl went, but I was here. Why?" he asked.

"Oh, it's nothing. Josh was there. I just wondered . . ."

I trailed off, then made my excuses to leave, thanking him for his time. I'd come wondering if he'd known his wife had been having an illicit affair—and potentially committing fraud—with Josh. My blood ran cold. The man came off as clueless about both, but I left feeling pretty sure the answer to both my questions was actually a solid yes.

Chapter 25

Part of me wanted to tell Emmaline everything, but she was very much about distribution of leadership. Captain York was in charge of criminal investigations within the department. If I had something substantial to present to her, she'd listen. But if I came to her with unsubstantiated theories, I was afraid she'd refer me to Captain York. I felt like maybe we'd had a breakthrough at the funeral, but would it last, or would he go back to taking anything I said with a hefty dose of salt? Presenting him with a half-developed theory that he could easily dismantle or disregard felt like the wrong move. Risky since, while he hadn't told Mrs. Branford and me to butt out, he also hadn't given us the green light to proceed. No, I needed more.

I'd added the new information I had to my notebook, filling several pages with information on the booster breakfasts, those who'd been present, the food served, and Nina's story about seeing two spreadsheets for the same booster year open on Josh's computer.

I also added Sean Fitzwilliam's name with a big, bold question mark next to it. He'd probably been at the booster breakfast. He could have poisoned Josh, then followed him to make sure the job was done.

I headed across the street to Yeast of Eden instead. The bread shop wasn't up to normal customer busyness, but the line was six people deep, and the low buzz of normal conversation filled the shop. Mae, done with the morning bake shift, sat at a table. Half-moons darkened the skin under her eyes, more evidence she wasn't adjusting her bedtime to give herself enough sleep. Her lids drooped. Meanwhile, Zula manned the register. "Do you need help?" I mouthed to her.

She flashed me her white-toothed smile and shook her head. "I am fine!" she called.

I heard one of the men in line murmur, "You sure are." I waffled between being offended on her behalf and nodding along with him in appreciation of Zula's extraordinary beauty. In the end, I left it alone and scooted into the kitchen.

"Ivy," Olaya said the moment she spotted me. She had just slid a baking tray into one of the commercial ovens set to LOW BAKE, and now directed her full attention on me. "Come."

She led me to her office, where she immediately picked up several sheets of paper with sketches she'd done. "We have not had time to plan the engagement party for you and Miguel, but I have been thinking about it. This is my plan."

The first sketch was of the bread display she had described to me. Seeing it drawn out allowed me to visualize it so much better. Basically, old crates were stacked vertically and horizontally to create a puzzle effect. Within each crate and in baskets were stacks of different types of artisan breads, all small, manageable choices appropriate for a party. Each type of bread was labeled with a beautiful, hand-drawn sign: CROISSANTS; MULTIGRAIN ROLLS; SOURDOUGH ROLLS; CARDAMON BUNS; CIABATTA SQUARES; and BRIOCHE. The display looked rustic and inviting. The backdrop of the Pacific Ocean in the distance would enhance it all the more.

"It's gorgeous! But, Olaya, you don't have to—"

She waved her hand as if it were a magic wand, stopping my words on my lips. "*Basta.* This is what I do. This is what I *need* to do."

I knew she was being completely honest. She'd gone through her funk, and now the best way she knew how to move forward, rather than being sucked down into some dismal abyss in which Martina slipped away, was to bake. I wouldn't let Olaya lose Martina—or let Martina lose Olaya, for that matter—but I could keep searching for answers, and Olaya could bake. It's what she did best. "Okay," I said.

I caught a glimpse of another set of sketches. "What are those?" I asked, reaching for the page.

She pulled it back. "This is a festive project. Do not worry about it."

My nose prickled, and my eyes turned glassy. I had had no expectations about all the bread at the party, but here she was, even amid all the unrest in her life, planning something special. The gesture helped me understand the depth of the love she felt for me.

If I had to choose a word to describe Olaya, it would be sanguine. She smiled, but not in a toothy way like Zula, and not with an enthusiastic burst of a grin like Nina. Her lips curved upward, and the sides of her eyes crinkled. She looked pleased in a way that was self-assured and wise. I would return that love in the best way I knew how—by proving Martina innocent and absolving the bread shop of any connection to the murder of Josh Prentiss.

I sat at a table in the bread shop, sipping on a glass of unsweetened iced tea. The more I thought about the booster breakfast, the more likely I thought it was that Josh had actually ingested the poison before he arrived at Yeast of Eden the day he died.

I flipped to the page in my notebook where I'd written the effects on a person if Angel's Trumpet was ingested.

- Muscle weakness
- Dry mouth
- Rapid pulse
- Dilated pupils
- Fever
- Hallucinations
- Convulsions
- Confusion
- Excessive thirst
- Difficulty breathing
- Memory loss
- Paralysis
- Coma

A few things struck me. He'd guzzled the water from a disposable bottle that morning ... *and* he'd gotten an extra cup for water. I made a check mark next to *excessive thirst.*

I remembered him squinting, as if the light was bothering him. That was a possible check for *dilated pupils.*

He hadn't seemed confused or feverish or particularly weak, but he *had* jumped out of his chair like he'd been spooked. He'd said he'd felt something hit the back of his head. *Hallucinations?* I added another check mark to the list.

He had seemed a little confused when he decided suddenly to leave. Out of sorts, anyway. Bit by bit, I became convinced I'd solved at least one part of the mystery. I couldn't sit on this any longer. I thought about texting Emmaline, but went for a phone call instead. "Listen," I said quietly. The last thing I wanted was to be overheard as I told her my theory that Josh was poisoned before arriving at Yeast of Eden. "I looked up the effects of Angel's Trumpet. The dilated eyes. Thirst. Hallucinations. It fits."

"Interesting theory," she said. "I'll pass it on to York."

"Are you working the case at all?" I asked, hoping whatever I had to offer wouldn't just be dismissed by the captain.

"Of course. I'm working the financial angle. I have people scouring his accounts. Yes, plural. York's pursuing other leads. I'll make sure he gets this information. Good job, really."

"So Martina—"

"I can't say anything else, Ivy."

"She doesn't have access to those flowers—"

"Anyone has access," Em said, and, of course, she was right. Angel's Trumpet. Trumpet vine. It didn't matter what grew in Martina's yard—or in anyone else's. The deadly nightshade was in the park, poison there for the taking.

"I know, but—"

"Look. I want to cross her off the suspect list as much as you do. I'm close to being able to do that. As soon as I can, I will."

If Em was digging into Josh's finances, she also needed to know my theory about the boosters and Nina's observation about the dual spreadsheets. I filled her in. "Nina Blankenship from the antiques place?" she asked, and I knew she was writing the name down.

"Yes."

"And the treasurer, Cheryl Fitzwilliam, admitted to having an affair with Josh?"

It didn't surprise me that Emmaline knew all the players. She didn't need me to rattle off the names of the people on the booster board. "She did. If they were both dirty, it would have been easy to hide money."

"This guy was too much," Emmaline said. I could picture her shaking her head in amazement at his boldness. Scamming the single older women in the area and screwing over the football team, of which his own son was a part—that was ballsy. And heartless. "We haven't found his laptop," Em said.

Without that, would they be able to prove he was cooking the books? "Sean Fitzwilliam," I said.

"Another booster," Emmaline immediately replied.

"I saw him at the bread shop the morning Josh died." I proceeded to tell her about my meeting with Sean, and recognizing him. "He said he wasn't at the booster breakfast, but he might be lying—"

"He wasn't at the meeting. We've checked his alibi. Aside from a stop at Yeast of Eden, Sean Fitzwilliam was at his tutoring business all day, from six AM until eight PM. He left once, at five o'clock, for a dinner run to In and Out. That's it. Right now. we can't connect him to the murder." We fell into a moment of silence before she said, "A lot of people might have wanted a little revenge against Josh Prentiss. Sean Fitzwilliam might have known about his wife and Josh, but right now he's in the clear."

Chapter 26

Two hearty French lavender plants grew in my backyard. I ran my hand up one of the thin stems, my fingers lightly dancing over the delicate purple flowers. The fragrant scent they released was floral and sweet. Life-giving, I thought, rather than the nightshade Angel's Trumpet, which took lives. Strange to think that something as fragile and beautiful as a flower could be so deadly.

I cut several stems of the lavender and retreated from the lingering heat of the day into my kitchen, with its pale yellow cupboards, honey-colored hardwood floors, a rustic brick arch over the stove, and a window set back in the space and overlooking the front yard. The reclaimed wood of the island's countertop made the space feel warm and cozy.

My goal was to get my mind off the murder for a little while. Maybe with the absence of thinking, answers would come to me. I could hope, anyway. I pulled out containers of flour, sugar, sticks of butter, eggs, and everything else I'd need to make the tea loaf.

Before long, I ran my fingers down the stem of one of the lavender sprigs, releasing the tiny purple buds, letting them fall into the batter. I folded them in gently, distributing them, along with the lemon zest, but careful not to crush them. I wanted the bits of lavender to be recognizable as itty bitty flowers.

Into the prepared loaf pan. Into the preheated oven. Out to cool less than an hour later. And still I had no answers.

I sat at the kitchen table, flipping through my mother's copy of *Murder on the Orient Express.* Agatha slept at my feet, lightly snoring. The doorbell rang, and I jumped. The book flew from my hands and landed with a thump on top of Agatha. She popped up, disoriented from being awakened from her sound sleep. The book skittered under the table, but the doorbell rang again, so I left it.

As I rounded the corner to the entryway, the front door flew open. Mrs. Branford's cane swung out in front of her—never quite finding the ground—as she crossed the threshold. She held a key attached to an old Santa Sofia High School lanyard. I'd given her a house key so she could check on Agatha if I had to be away from the house for too long.

"Ivy!" she exclaimed when she saw me. Her navy velour lounge suit highlighted her pink cheeks. "I've been calling you for hours, but you haven't answered your phone."

"I didn't hear it ring," I said, puzzled. I felt my backside, feeling for my phone in one of my pockets, but it wasn't there. Mrs. Branford closed the door, then followed me back into the kitchen. I searched my purse, the counters, the table, and finally found it under the new salad recipe book I'd recently bought, on silent. I grumbled to myself. Sometimes cell phones had a mind of their own.

When I crouched down to fish out the dropped paperback from under the table, I remembered something else, though. Josh had been in a similar position on his knees, also looking for a dropped book. I suddenly remembered the book I'd found and put in the lost-and-found basket. It had to be Josh's. I had no idea if it meant anything, but what if it did? I thought about my mother's annotations in her Agatha Christie book. A book, I realized, could tell more than one story. Maybe Josh's did. It might be wishful thinking, but it was worth a shot.

Mrs. Branford strolled at a slower pace than I did. She also held onto Agatha's leash. I left them behind as I charged ahead and pushed through Yeast of Eden's door. I paused long enough to register that half the tables were filled. Business was almost back to normal—hallelujah.

I looked around for Zula, but only Mae, wearing one of the front-of-shop aprons, stood at the counter. She waved to me, smiling. "Hey, you're back."

"Yeah, I, uh, forgot something under the counter," I said in what I hoped was an off-handed manner.

She immediately bent down to look, disappearing from sight. Her voice drifted up to me. "What is it?"

"Oh, don't worry about it, Mae. I'll get it. What are you doing out here? Where's Zula?"

She popped back up. "She left early. Something about her daughter. I offered to fill in." She winked. "Keeping an eye out for my mother, you know."

Thankfully there was no sign of Kristin Spelling.

Zula split her time between Yeast of Eden and her job at a hospice center. She also had a fourteen-year-old daughter, Ella. The woman never seemed to need down time. She hopped from one place to the next, her exuberance never waning. When she entered a room, she lifted up everyone's mood with her mere presence.

My plan was to take the book I'd found straight to Emmaline—or Captain York. The problem was, I didn't want Mae to see me taking something from the shop's lost and found. Really, I didn't want to explain that I thought it might have belonged to a dead man.

Mrs. Branford and Agatha took up residence outside at one of the cute bistro tables under one of the equally cute awnings. Agatha's tongue hung from her mouth. The heat had abated some, but it was still hot. "Mae, would you mind taking my dog a bowl of water, please? I'll only be a minute."

She hesitated, as if Felix might barge through the swinging door from the kitchen and fire her on the spot for giving water to a dog in need. The incident with Taylor had spooked her. I thought she might actually refuse and ask why I couldn't do it, which would be an excellent question, but instead she said, "Sure," and disappeared into the kitchen. I'd barely made it behind the counter when she was back, carrying a white bowl half-filled. As she headed outside with it, I looked for the book I'd found the day Josh had died. It wasn't in the lost-and-found basket with the other detritus people left behind.

Had someone come to claim it? Was it not Josh's book after all?

I pulled the basket out to search one more time, but it was instantly clear that there was no paperback novel in it. Then I remembered. That man and his posse had burst through the door as if they'd crossed a picket line, all boisterous and obnoxious. I'd shoved the book, as well as the umbrella and hairbands on the shelf, but they must not have actually made it to the basket. I reached under the counter. The bells on the door dinged.

My hand landed on the paperback's cover. Yes! I pulled it out just as Mae came back behind the counter. "Any luck?" she asked.

I quickly shoved it in my bag and returned the basket to the shelf. "Yeah, got it." I popped up. "Thanks for that," I said, gesturing toward Agatha.

"Sure. No problem."

The people from two of the tables cleared out. "I'm, uh, meeting someone soon," Mae said, "so I'd better get started cleaning up." She held up a folded sheet of paper. I recognized Zula's straight-up-and-down handwriting. "I have a list."

A boy? I thought, but didn't ask. "Need help?"

"Nah. I think I'm good."

"I'll be right outside if you need anything." I filled two glasses with water and went to join Mrs. Branford.

Once I was seated at the bistro table, I pulled the book from my bag. The cover had an old-fashioned look to it, with a colored drawing of a man in a turban and the devil playing poker. *Carter Beats the Devil.* I showed Mrs. Branford. "Ever hear of it?" I asked.

Her face was already a map of wrinkles, but they deepened even more as she took the book from me, turned it over to read the back, then flipped through the pages. "Can't say that I have," she announced. "The man certainly knew how to annotate. Color me impressed. If only my students had done half as good a job."

"I bet they did. I can't imagine any student trying to skate by in your classes with less than one hundred percent effort."

She guffawed—an unusual reaction for the spritely old woman. "Oh Ivy, do you know any teenagers?"

"I know Zula's daughter," I said, although I'd only actually met the girl a few times. "And Pilar!" I practically exclaimed. I'd met her even fewer times, but I'd spent a quality hour and a half with her.

Mrs. Branford tsk'd. "That is hardly what one would call a solid sample set. When you gather up one hundred teenagers who are forced to read and annotate *Romeo and Juliet* or *The Great Gatsby* or *Tess of the d'Urbervilles* because it's part of the high school curriculum, about one-third will do an acceptable job—with a loose definition of acceptable. Another third will give it a mediocre attempt. And the last third will scarcely open the book. And although I would love to say that I reached more than the average number of students, alas, I fear that is simply a fantasy."

"Oh, I think you reached more than the average number of students, and then some," I said, thinking about how many times, when we'd been together, she'd been stopped or recognized by former students, now all grown up. This town had an abundance of love for Penelope Branford. "Remember Sylvia and her love for Gabriel García Márquez? Her connection to literature from Colombia was all because of you."

A pink blush stained Mrs. Branford's cheeks as she handed the book back to me. She couldn't refute what I'd said, so she was choosing to remain silent about it.

I riffled the pages of *Carter Beats the Devil.* Notes in both pen and pencil filled the margins. Single sentences and long passages were underlined. As I skimmed the "Overture," words jumped out at me: President Harding; the Secret Service; a theater and a performance. I kept flipping. The next section began with a quote from Harry Houdini. I read and reread the lines. They seemed to have to do with a circus, but I didn't understand. A few highlighted words stuck out, but the book was so marked up with writing that I closed it again.

"Historical fiction that almost reads like a biography. That is the type of book men favor," Mrs. Branford said.

Instead of calling Emmaline, I got my cell phone from my bag and texted her. *Found a book that I think was Josh Prentiss's. He was looking for it before he left the bread shop. I found it later. Just realized it might be his.*

I waited for her response. *I'll send someone. Are you home?*

My thumbs flew across my phone's screen. *I will be soon.*

She sent me a thumb's up emoji, and that was that.

A short fifteen minutes later, Mrs. Branford and I sat across from one another at my kitchen table. We each had a slice of lemon tea bread and a tall glass of iced tea. We both took it without sugar. My years in Texas had almost made me a sweet tea drinker, but being back in California had brought me back to my unsweetened iced tea roots.

"I may choose this for our next book club selection," she remarked, picking up *Carter Beats the Devil* again. "It looks interesting."

Mrs. Branford's book club was as much a social event as a literary discussion. The Blackbird Ladies were a tight group of women who lunched, gossiped, and read together. I'd been included as sort of an honorary member. I'd been reading the books they choose, but I thought I'd pass on this one. The cover didn't do anything for me, plus I had wedding planning to do.

She moved to the couch and started reading, while I scrolled through the recent photos I'd taken and uploaded to my laptop. We sat in companionable silence until Mrs. Branford said, "Hmm."

I looked up at her. "Hmm, what?"

She wagged one finger at me and kept reading. I went back to my photos of the park, thinking about where Olaya's bread display should go, but stopped when Mrs. Branford pushed herself to a more upright position. "Hmm," she said again.

"Not what you expected?" I asked.

"Ivy, my dear, I believe there is a message in this book."

I stared at her. "What do you mean?"

She flipped back a few pages, turned the open book to face me, and pointed to a highlighted word. *You'll.*

Mrs. Branford turned the page until she found the next highlighted word. *Get.*

There were a lot of underlined words and phrases. Some words were circled. But only three more words were highlighted in the entire book. In order, they were: *What. You. Deserve.*

Chapter 27

It was the end of the lunch hour, but the Yeast of Eden kitchen still had bread and pastries to produce. Janae worked on hearty pretzels—a summer favorite. Felix packaged more freshly ground grain to be sold to customers. Two other men Felix had on his afternoon crew finished the sourdough bakes. And I washed bowls and dishes and anything else we'd dirtied in the last hour.

Mae had gone for her thirty-minute lunch break at twelve fifteen. She was a person of routine. As she always did, she'd gone to pick up a sandwich at a deli one block down and two blocks over. Usually she returned precisely twenty-three minutes later. I glanced at the clock. Ten after one. It wasn't like her to be so late. Add being late as strange behavior, and the idea took root.

I'd wait five more minutes before raising the alarm. Maybe I was off base and she'd just run into her mother and was on another mission to stop her from eating carbs. The thought had scarcely passed through my mind when Mae appeared at the back-door entrance to the kitchen. Her normally pink skin had gone sallow, and she dragged in a ragged breath, as though she'd just run a mile at full speed. The air in the kitchen suddenly felt thick and . . . wrong. Very wrong.

"Mae?" I said just as Janae's sharp voice shot out, "Are you okay, baby?" She'd been sprinkling coarse pretzel salt over the thick dough she'd twisted. For a split second, her arm froze, suspended midair, then she threw down the salt and rushed toward Mae shouting, "Felix, baby, help her."

Mae held onto the doorjamb as she looked around the kitchen, her gaze never landing anywhere specific. There was something about her eyes. They were dark. Unseeing. It was as if she wasn't registering anyone or anything. "I'm s-so s-sorry I'm l-late," she stuttered. She smacked her lips, then pushed her tongue out like she wanted to catch a raindrop. "J-J—" She tried to speak but couldn't push the word out.

It all happened so fast. One second Mae was standing. She reached for one of the stainless-steel work tables, but her hand missed, and she stumbled. I dropped the bowl I'd been washing at the sink and sprinted across the kitchen, reaching Mae just as Felix caught her. He gently lowered her to the floor. "Mae?" Her eyelids fluttered. He gently shook her. Nothing. His eyes darted to Janae. "Call 911," he said, then he looked back at Mae. "Mae? Can you hear me?"

I crouched down and felt her forehead. "She

has a fever," I said. I pressed two fingers against the carotid artery in her neck to feel for her pulse. It raced, like a drummer playing the snare, hands flying in a blur.

Symptoms flashed in my mind. Dry mouth. Dilated pupils. Rapid pulse. Fever. Difficulty breathing. My pulse ratcheted up. It was happening to her just like it had happened to Josh, and she'd been trying to tell us. "She's been poisoned! Oh my God, she's been poisoned!"

Time slowed to a crawl. None of us knew what to do. Janae's voice cut through the thick fog. Her words sounded slow and far away. "*They're onnnn theirrrr waaayyy.*"

"Mae," I said, "stay with us." I shot a glance at Janae. "Get Olaya!"

In a flash, Janae was through the swinging doors to the front of the shop. A second later, she was back, Olaya on her heels. "What is happening?" Olaya asked, her usually calm and sanguine voice strained at seeing Mae on the floor.

"She collapsed," Felix said.

I thought I heard sirens in the distance. "I think it's Angel's Trumpet," I blurted. "Like Josh."

Olaya stared. Blinked. Then turned and grabbed her cell phone from her office. The sirens grew louder. Through my own pounding pulse and the cacophony of other sounds, I heard a thump as Olaya yanked her filing cabinet open. From the corner of my eye, I could see her thumbing through a file. Pulling out a paper. Placing a phone call. Talking. I knew she was calling Mae's mother.

And then Olaya was back, rushing back to the

front of the shop, returning a second later, firemen and paramedics in tow.

Felix and I leapt up and out of the way as the first responders circled around Mae. One of them stayed back, beckoning to us. "What happened?" she asked. Janae told the story with far more detail than I would have managed, but I was drawn back in a minute later. The woman asking the questions turned to me. "Why do you think it's Angel's Trumpet?"

I flung my arms around as if the answer was obvious. She had to be living in a cave to not know about that murder that had happened just days ago. "Because Josh Prentiss was murdered with it."

The reality of what I was saying hit me as the words floated into the air. Someone—presumably the same person who had murdered Josh—had tried to murder Mae. The paramedics had Mae strapped to a stretcher. As they wheeled her out, I prayed they hadn't succeeded.

It all happened so fast. One minute Mae was in the Yeast of Eden kitchen. The next minute she was in the hospital. I sat in the waiting room next to her mother. "Tell me again," Kristin said, her voice quivering. "I don't understand what happened."

I pressed my hand against my thigh to stop my nervously tapping foot. I'd been replaying the moments before and after Mae collapsed to the ground. So much for the theory that she was involved in Josh's murder. "I don't know, Mrs. Spelling," I said. "She was fine when she left for lunch. She came back late—"

"That doesn't sound like Mae. She's very fastidious. Very punctual."

"I know," I agreed. "And when she came in, she . . . she was sick. Pale and feverish. Disoriented."

Kristin clasped her hands together tightly, bringing them to her lips. I could see the amount of effort she was putting into controlling her reaction. She was trying not to cry. Not to completely freak out.

"The doctor, she said Mae was poisoned." Kristin shook her head helplessly. "I don't understand. Who would do such a thing?"

That was the very question I'd been asking myself for the last hour. If I was right and Mae had been given Angel's Trumpet, then it had to be related to Josh Prentiss. It *had* to be the same person behind both. But why?

Other than Yeast of Eden, to my knowledge, Mae and Josh had no connection at all. Maybe I'd missed something. She had gone to the funeral, after all. "Mrs. Spelling, did Mae say anything to you about Josh Prentiss's death?"

The question seemed to send a jolt through the woman. She sat up straighter, adjusting her ample body in the chair to turn toward me. "Like what?"

"Anything at all. Did she know him outside of the bread shop?"

She frowned. Shook her head. "Not Mae. Now the *other* girl, *she* did."

"What other girl?" I asked.

"The blond girl that used to work here. She's

been a thorn in Mae's side, let me tell you," Mrs. Spelling said.

Taylor? I thought. Other than Josh's funeral, I hadn't seen hide nor hair of her. I was surprised Mae would have anything to do with Taylor after their last morning together at Yeast of Eden. "Early twenties?"

"I guess. Around there. Mae's age. Blond. Tall. Thin.—" She chuckled sadly. "Of course, next to Mae, everyone's tall and thin, aren't they?"

I smiled.

A few things clicked into place like cogs in a machine. Tracy McCall Prentiss had come to Yeast of Eden, looking for one of her husband's women. She'd hadn't said why she thought she'd find her at the bread shop. She'd said *poor girl.* Had she known Taylor worked there? I remembered the look Taylor and Josh shared. And then there was the book. When Taylor had been fired, the only things she left with were her purse and a book. It couldn't have been the *same* book I'd found—the one with the message—but it proved that Taylor was a reader.

The message in the book materialized in my mind. *You'll get what you deserve.*

Taylor, Taylor, Taylor.

Taylor had locked eyes with Josh the morning he'd died.

Taylor, who'd collided with Mae, and had no remorse. Taylor, who'd uttered those very words the day she'd been fired. *Karma is a bitch,* she'd said. *You'll get what you deserve.*

Taylor didn't fit Josh's MO, though. Older women

with money. That's who he went after to manipulate. Minus Cheryl.

The image of a woman leaving Josh's funeral surfaced in my mind. She'd been ahead of me as I'd gone out to the vestibule. I'd thought at the time it might have been Taylor. Tall. Thin. A too-short skirt. She'd left the funeral early, just like the other wronged women.

I remembered what else she'd said the day she'd been fired. The young woman was supposed to get money from her parents. A lot of money? Plenty of wealthy people called Santa Sofia home, so a trust fund was certainly within the realm of possibility.

A scenario unfurled in my mind. What if Taylor had painted herself as a young heiress? Or at least a young woman with a decent trust fund? What if Josh broke his own protocol and tried to win her over so he could get to her money?

What if he'd lost interest when he realized she didn't actually have the money in hand?

Or . . . what if Taylor found out about his wife or one of his other women?

I'd seen the girl come unhinged. My head reeled. It had only been an inkling of an idea, but now it took root. Taylor may have been behind Josh's murder. And if Mae suspected the same thing, Taylor may have poisoned Mae to keep her quiet.

Chapter 28

Mrs. Branford and I left Yeast of Eden and walked toward my car, which I'd parked two blocks down. I slowed my pace to match hers, letting Agatha trot ahead of us, her leash locked at five feet. Her coiled tail and the pep in her step showed how happy she was to be out and about on such a beautiful summer afternoon. I wished I could say the same. The message in the book weighed heavily on me, as though my intestines had turned to stone.

Since Taylor didn't work at Yeast of Eden anymore, running into her wasn't going to be an easy thing to accomplish. I had access to her personal information from her employment record, though. "Is it unethical to look up her address or phone number?" I mused.

"Of course," Mrs. Branford said, "but that doesn't

mean you shouldn't do it. This is a life-and-death situation."

I hadn't realized I'd spoken aloud. I'd subconsciously wanted Mrs. Branford's advice, and I'd gotten it. It was all the encouragement I needed. We got to my car, but it was too hot for her and Agatha to wait while I went back for Taylor's phone number and address. We kept going another half a block until we were at the park. "Wait here," I said, and I left them to wait at a bench near the gazebo, while I doubled back to the bread shop.

I speed-walked, trying hard not to talk myself out of what I was planning. If Taylor was guilty, and getting her information helped bring her to justice and exonerate the innocent, wasn't that worth the risk?

As I reentered the bread shop, the big obstacle to my line of thinking hit me. How in the world would Taylor have poisoned Josh? She'd been working in the kitchen, but she hadn't come to the front of the shop. Unlike Mae, Taylor had never even been trained to work the register. She wasn't exactly a people person.

I came back to the *Murder on the Orient Express* idea. Maybe Taylor had had help. Mae. *She'd* been in the dining area that morning chasing after her mother. They'd played a weird cat-and-mouse game, with Kristin Spelling dodging around tables, while Mae tried to catch her . . . all because Kristin had been sneaking carbs? Looking back at it now, it seemed . . . orchestrated.

Could the fallout between Taylor and Mae also have been staged? Could Mae have helped out

Taylor by somehow slipping Josh the poison without him knowing?

Something about that scenario didn't seem quite right, but I shoved the idea away as I entered the shop. Pilar sat at a table, a half-eaten raspberry scone on a plate in front of her. Across from her was Ella, Zula's daughter. For the first time since I'd met her, Pilar was smiling. "Hey, you two," I said, probably a little more enthusiastically than was warranted.

"Hey," Ella said. Even in the face of an attempted murder, she was a bright ray of sunshine in every room she entered, just like her mother.

Pilar's smile was reticent, but I sensed it was genuine. Everything felt better when you had a friend.

"Is that lady going to be okay?" Pilar asked.

I paused and drew in a deep breath. The truth was, I had no idea. Mae was in a coma, which was a typical physiological response to Angel's Trumpet. The doctors didn't know any more than we did, from what I could tell. "I hope so," I said.

I left them and went straight into the kitchen. Something was amiss. The door to Olaya's office was closed, and Felix shook his head when I headed toward it. "She doesn't want to be disturbed."

I looked at him. Back to the door. To him again. "Oh."

"She's okay. She just needs some time."

The mood was still somber. I answered a few more questions about Mae, which mostly consisted of saying, once again, that she was in a coma, most likely induced by the same poison that had killed Josh, and that there was currently no improvement. I had to choke out the words. More than anything, I wanted Mae Spelling to be okay.

I left the way I'd come, disappointed at not getting Taylor's address, but also thinking it was probably good I hadn't committed a felony or something.

Instead of returning to Mrs. Branford straightaway, I took the scenic route by way of the deli Mae had eaten at. I heard Miguel's voice in my ear. "If she's done it twice, she won't hesitate to do it again." He spoke reason, but I was beyond hearing it that at the moment. Mae was hanging on by a thread, and I was hell-bent on taking down Taylor. Josh may have been a creep, but that didn't justify his murder. And Mae *certainly* didn't deserve to die.

God willing, she wouldn't.

I still hadn't figured out how, exactly, Taylor could have given the poison to Josh. Mae's scenario was easier.

I pushed into the deli. They knew Mae there, had heard she'd been taken to the hospital, and immediately bombarded me with questions I couldn't answer. Finally, I was able to ask one of my own. I directed my question to a gangly kid with freckles and carrot-colored hair. "Did she meet someone for lunch? A tall blonde?"

One of the high school boys nodded. "Yeah." He cracked a smile and looked over at one of his high school coworkers. "She was hot, man."

His buddy nodded his agreement. "Too old for us, but yeah, hot as hell."

Taylor was in her mid-twenties. To fifteen-year-olds, that was definitely an older woman. Someone like me, who was on the other side of thirty-five, was over the hill.

"Did they order drinks?" I asked.

The first boy looked up to the ceiling as he thought. "Maybe?" he said after a few seconds. "I don't really remember."

Not surprising. It had been hours ago, and there had probably been fifty customers since then.

I thought again about the *how*. How had Mae ingested the poison? She had come back to Yeast of Eden empty-handed. If she'd had a drink, she'd thrown the cup away between the deli and the bread shop.

Or if Taylor had put poison into Mae's drink, she very well may have taken the cup with her to dispose of the evidence. Either way, that was a dead end. Coming away from the deli with the information that Mae had, in fact, met Taylor felt like a big win. I could go to Emmaline and York with this, and for the first time, maybe Captain Craig York would listen to me.

I dropped Mrs. Branford at home, left Agatha at my house, and forty-five minutes later, I sat across from York in his office. "It's possible," he said, though without the enthusiasm I'd been hoping for. "And before you say anything else, Ms. Culpepper, leave it to us. It's touch-and-go for Mae Spelling. You don't want to end up in the hospital next to her." His lips thinned. "Or worse, in the morgue."

He was right on both counts. "I can get you her home address," I said suddenly, thinking that I could get permission from York to find Taylor's address from her Yeast of Eden employment application.

York flicked back a strand of his flyaway blond hair. He thought for a moment, then finally, he took a card from a holder on his desk, held it between his index and middle fingers, and handed it to me. "Call me directly with it, or text me."

Somehow I managed to keep my brows from shooting up to my forehead. Permission to text Captain York was serious progress. We were turning over a new leaf. "Got it," I said, resisting a salute.

From the Sheriff's Department, I backtracked, once again, to Yeast of Eden. This time I parked in the back lot and went in through the kitchen door. Enough time had passed that I figured Olaya would be out of her office. The office door was open, but there was still no sign of her.

"She's in there," Felix said, pointing toward the back room we used for special employee events, and dinners, and even when the bread shop had been featured on a new reality TV show about the best bakeries in the country.

I headed that way, but Felix stepped in my path. "You can't go in there."

"Why not?" A thread of worry spun through me. The death of her brother and Pilar moving in. Then Josh, and now Mae. "Is she okay?"

"She's okay," Janae said from across the kitchen. "She just needs some distraction and time alone."

The same refrain they'd played before.

I took a hesitant step toward Olaya's office. Stopped. Turned toward the door she was behind. Hesitated again. I wanted to be there for Olaya. I also wanted to respect her need for privacy. I turned decisively back toward her office. Straight to the wooden, two-drawer filing cabinet. To the employee section. Olaya was a neat and orderly person. Each employee had their own folder. Each folder had a white tab, the employee's name written in straight-up-and-down print. I let my fingers run over the tabs until I found the one belonging to Taylor Wilson.

The file was flimsy, with only a few sheets. One was the handwritten application Taylor had filled out. The other two were a written account—one from Felix and the other by Olaya herself—recounting the events that had led to her dismissal.

I scanned them, but neither of them held any new clues. Felix had inserted a few emotional statements in his. *The woman knocked Mae to the ground and didn't even bother helping her up!* and *She looked like she could spit fire. Like she could actually go postal.*

Olaya's was more succinct and, true to form, ended on a positive tone. *Clearly Taylor has a lot of anger. I cannot have that toxic attitude in my kitchen, but I wish her well.*

I sat back in the desk chair, thinking about Taylor. Was there a way to prove she'd been in a relationship with Josh? I skimmed the front of the employment application, snapping a picture of the address with my cell phone. Pulling out Captain York's card, I sent it to him in a message.

I flipped the paper over to give a quick glance at the backside. I was about to put the application back into the folder when I recognized a name in the reference section.

Tracy McCall Prentiss. My blood ran cold. Why was Josh's wife a reference for Taylor Wilson?

Chapter 29

Crossing paths with Captain York for the second time in a day might be pushing my luck. He'd given me an inch. I didn't want to take a mile and make him regret it. Instead of tracking down Taylor to ask her about Mae, Josh, or Tracy McCall Prentiss's name as a reference on her Yeast of Eden application, I decided to go straight to the source. I'd find Tracy and ask her how she knew Taylor.

I replaced the file folder in the drawer and spent a solid fifteen minutes trying to find the Prentiss family address. I came up blank. The only Prentiss was a Carter Prentiss with a bungalow in the general area of Miguel's house. The house was a fixer-upper midway through a renovation. When she'd come to the bread shop, Tracy had said she and Josh had bought a house here. A bungalow with an ocean view had to have cost a pretty penny.

Pennies gleaned from Josh's various cougars, I supposed. What would happen to the house now?

The house had to be worth a million plus, but it was an unassuming place. Once the reno was done, however, the value would skyrocket. I made my way through the scaffolding and stacks of lumber, climbing up the steps to the unobtrusive front door. It opened before I could knock, but it wasn't Tracy McCall Prentiss who answered.

A man with a round face, ruddy cheeks, and a thinning hairline stood there. He wore board shorts, a tattered gray T-shirt, and rubber flip-flops. The smell of stale smoke seeped from the old house. He didn't speak, just raised his brows at me, waiting for me to state my business.

I cut to the chase. "I'm looking for Tracy Prentiss. Is she . . . does she live here?"

"Prentiss?" He shook his head. "Nope. Wrong house."

"How about a Josh Prentiss?" I asked.

Now the man expression turned to bafflement. "That guy who died? You want to know if he lives here?"

"I want to know if he used to live here. If his wife still lives here," I said.

His expression cleared and brightened, as if a lightbulb had lit up above his head. "Oh! Geez. I know who you're talking about. You're about twenty-five years too late," he said. "My folks bought the house after the man—James? Jules? Jack? Something like that. He took off, and the woman croaked. Heart attack. All the neighbors said she died of a broken heart, if you can believe that. I don't. From what I heard, the guy left them penniless. Like, he took everything. Sold the house. My folks felt bad, but they didn't know about any of it till the mom died. By then, it was too late to make things right. Plus, you know, the guy was gone."

What a bastard. To leave your family for another woman was bad enough. To sell their house out from under them and leave them destitute, that was the lowest level of low.

"I never heard the name again till the dude just died."

I left and drove aimlessly, thinking. The Bungalow Oasis place had been Josh's family home. That made sense. Even if Josh was trying to chase down his demons by coming back to Santa Sofia, chances are he wouldn't have come back to the same area where he'd grown up.

He'd go to the complete opposite area.

He'd go to the hills.

In the end, it was Aunt Josie who helped me find the Prentiss house. I called her up to see if Coach Bruno might happen to know where his boosters lived. He did.

And I'd been right. Josh and Tracy Prentiss lived in the Santa Sofia Hills. With the address committed to memory, I pulled into a beach parking lot. Before I could turn the car around, Mrs. Branford called. She had a sixth sense, somehow psychically aware anytime I ventured into covert activities. "I'm just leaving the south beach lot," I said.

"Wait there," she said, and hung up before I could ask her why, and what she was up to. Five minutes later, a zippy, bright blue hatchback pulled up. The passenger door opened, and a pair of pink-velour-covered legs swung out. Spiffy, white orthotic shoes hit the ground. A cane followed, a strong and veiny hand clutching the handle and using it as leverage. The rest of the pink-clad body appeared. Mrs. Branford.

I thought she'd need an afternoon of rest after our morning adventure. I should have known better.

She'd switched out her navy outfit, and now, with her snowy white hair perfectly coiffed, as always, she looked like a bubblegum ice-cream cone topped with a dollop of whipped cream. "I was on my way downtown to find you. Looks like I came at just the right time," she said. She looked back into the car she'd arrived in and waved. "Thank you, Lee."

He didn't meet Mrs. Branford's eyes, but gave her a quick wave.

"Try that book, Lee. As a numbers person, I believe you will relate to Christopher John Francis Boone. He's an excellent character. I believe it will hit all the right notes for you."

"One of your former students?" I asked as Lee drove off.

"No. Too young for that. But a bright, if awkward, young man who seems to have lost his way. I think *The Curious Incident of the Dog in the Night-Time* might be just the thing for him."

Mrs. Branford was a special woman. I'd seen her be completely at ease in the basement of a local bar with a crew of seedy poker players, making merry with the Blackbird Ladies, her group of contemporaries, in Olaya's kitchen, and chatting with old students. She found common ground with people, often through books, and equally often simply through conversation. She was an active listener, and that made people feel comfortable.

"I imagine you're right," I said.

Although I hadn't planned on company for my visit to Tracy Prentiss's house, I knew how this worked. I circled the car and held open the passenger door for Mrs. Branford. She scooted her backside in first, swinging her legs around and strapping in as I shut the door and came back around. A minute later, I had Tracy's address loaded into the navigation system, and we were on our way.

"Tracy McCall Prentiss. This murder gets curiouser and curiouser," Mrs. Branford commented. "Tell me what you're thinking since I last saw you"—she flipped her wrist to look at her watch—"seventy-three minutes ago."

This was not an easy question to answer. It was at times like this that I wished I had the mind and deductive skills of Sherlock Holmes. I was much closer to Betty Crocker. I had a feeling, and if I added eggs and flour and mixed the ingredients all together, maybe I'd end up with a cake. I might end up with something no better than a mud pie, though.

My notebook helped me organize my thoughts. I'd learned this from Mrs. Branford, who had a dedicated notebook for each mystery we'd been involved in solving. I hadn't had time to organize my thoughts in writing, though, but having her here in person was better anyway. She became my sounding board. Without any preamble, I launched into the backstory of why we were visiting Josh

Prentiss's widow, including my false start at the Prentiss family home and Josh's mother dying from a broken heart. "I would have gone to see Taylor, but York might be on his way there."

"And an encounter with the captain is not desirable. Enough said."

"Right. But since Taylor put Tracy down as a reference, clearly Taylor has *some* connection to the family, not just to Josh," I said. "First of all, isn't that strange and unexpected? And second of all, why wouldn't she have mentioned that after Josh died?"

"And going with the hypothesis that Taylor committed the murder, this connection might lead you to a motive."

I had theories, but no hard proof of anything. "Exactly."

Turns out the Prentiss house was in a swanky area of the Santa Sofia Hills reserved for the wealthy. The sprawling, Italian-style house looked like it would be owned by a Hollywood star rather than an accountant turned wealth manager. Josh had made a boatload of money. He had his hands in all kinds of buckets of sand. Pooled together, they made an entire sandbox of misdeeds.

I'd half-expected a live-in maid to answer the door, but Tracy appeared, just as worn out as she had been the previous two times I'd seen her. From the dark smudges under her eyes and her blotchy skin, it didn't look like she was getting much sleep. She took us both in, but let her gaze linger on Mrs. Branford. The Pepto Bismol pink was a little hard on the eyes. Tracy arched her brows and dipped her chin, an expression of utter disbelief on her face. "Don't tell me you're another one of—"

Mrs. Branford stomped the base of her cane on the stone porch, interrupting her. "Good heavens, no," she said. She'd jumped into just that role when confronted with Sharon and Josh's other victims in the church, but in the immortal words of Kenny Rogers, Mrs. Branford knew when to hold 'em and when to fold 'em. The woman could read a room. "I am Ivy's friend and neighbor."

Tracy accepted the explanation and turned to me. "I didn't expect to see you again," she said, sounding none too pleased that she was, in fact, seeing me again, and on her very own doorstep.

I contemplated doing jazz hands and giving an exuberant, "Surprise!" but I thought better of it and went with the much more respectable, "Same."

She waited, not inviting us in, and also not prompting me as to why I had come to her home. I often used the tactic of providing silence that people then filled. That conversational strategy had garnered helpful, mystery-solving information on several occasions. Today, however, was not one of those days. I remained silent for ten seconds. Twenty seconds. An awkward thirty. Forty. Tracy's eyes narrowed, but still, she said nothing. Torturous fifty. Whatever Tracy had needed to say, she'd gotten it off her chest the day before. That had been a visit on her terms, with her agenda. Right now, we were playing a game of chicken, and finally, I blinked. I didn't think a casual chat would get Tracy to drop her defenses, so I went for the straight truth. "Taylor Wilson put you down as a reference on her job application for Yeast of Eden."

Again, silence. I imagined her saying, "So?" which prompted me to continue. "I didn't know you knew her. That she knew your husband."

Tracy's face screwed up as though she was trying to figure out if I was actually asking her a question. I was about to rephrase when she threw up her hands. "Her mother and I are sorority sisters. The Wilsons are family friends. They always have been. So, yes, we know Taylor."

Taylor's presence at the funeral suddenly made more sense. Her motive for murdering Josh? Not so much.

Mrs. Branford suddenly wobbled on her feet. I'd seen her swoon before, and each time I worried that it was real and not the act I thought it might be. She held tight to her cane, as if it was the only thing keeping her upright. I wrapped my arms around her waist. "Mrs. Branford, are you okay?"

Her dramatically fluttering eyelids beneath her silvery brows clued me in. This was subterfuge, pure and simple. She managed a focused look at Tracy. "I'm feeling so faint. Could I trouble you for some water?"

"Maybe you should sit down?" I suggested, joining in on the ruse.

Tracy didn't look overly concerned, but she did swing the door open and step back so I could guide Mrs. Branford inside. She pointed to a sitting room off to the right. Four upholstered club chairs sat at each corner of a square coffee table. The decor was tasteful and pleasant, but didn't have the character of Miguel's rattan accents or the antiques I had scattered about my house, courtesy of Nina and the mini-mall.

"Are you really okay?" I whispered to Mrs. Branford after Tracy disappeared, just to be sure.

She waved her hand dismissively. "Of course, Ivy," she said, but slipped right back into her feigned exhaustion the second Tracy's heels thunked against the hardwood floor. She returned holding two glasses of water. I debated taking the first glass and pressing it to Mrs. Branford's lips, but it felt like a step too far. Tracy might end up calling 911 if we played this game too well.

I took the first proffered glass and handed it to Mrs. Branford, then took the second and sipped it. We sat awkwardly until Tracy finally broke the silence. "What is this really about? Why are you asking *me* about Taylor?"

I debated how honest to be. Suspecting Taylor and knowing for certain that she'd killed Josh were two very different things. Information that would give Taylor motive was the goal. I had no idea if Tracy could provide it. And even if she *could, would* she?

I went with a partial truth. "I'm sure you heard that Taylor was fired?"

Tracy frowned. "I *hadn't* heard that."

"She was. A few days ago."

"I can't say I'm surprised," Tracy said. "Working the early-morning shift at a bakery didn't seem like her kind of job. Beneath her, if you know what I mean. She's grown into a bit of an entitled princess."

Taylor herself had made that very point. "Yeah, it wasn't really for her."

I could see the curiosity on Tracy's face, despite her view of Taylor. "Why'd she get fired?"

"I don't think it was just one thing. More a final straw, you know?"

"Okay, so what was the tipping point?"

"Do you know Mae Spelling?" I asked. "They worked together at the bread shop."

Her eyes sort of pulled together, but her forehead remained smooth, nary a line in sight. Botox, I guessed. When she didn't respond, I continued. "Taylor and Mae had a little . . . tiff, I guess you could say. Taylor kind of went off. That's when she was fired. And now Mae is in the hospital."

Tracy didn't looked surprised, but she answered carefully. "I still don't understand why you're here. We don't actually *see* Taylor much anymore."

"I saw that Taylor listed you as a reference on her job application."

She visibly relaxed. "Oh, that. Of course. A while back, Taylor asked if she could use me as a reference. I've known her since she was a baby. Her mother and I are friends. Of course I said yes."

"Wow. Since she was a baby." My friendship with Emmaline came to mind. My mother would have gladly been a reference for her, and I knew her parents would do that same for me if I ever needed it. "That's a long time," I said.

This brought a small smile. "Her mom and I

were sorority sisters. Jeanne's one of my best friends."

My thoughts came to a grinding halt. Surely it was a coincidence. Taylor's last name was Wilson. I felt my jaw tense, but I worked to keep my expression neutral. "Jeanne Wilson?" I asked in a way that suggested I might know her.

"Not anymore. Taylor's last name is Wilson. Jeanne remarried—widowed now—but she has her late husband's name. Poole."

"Finally. The elusive Jeanne . . . Poole," I said softly.

Tracy cocked her head. "Elusive?"

Out of the blue, Mrs. Branford perked up. "I'm feeling much better," she said. She knew everything I did, including about the woman named Jeanne my father had overheard in the market. "Thank you for the water."

Tracy was too smart to be so easily distracted, though. She glared at me, wheels turning behind her eyes. "I'm going to ask you again, what is this about? How do you know Jeanne? Is Taylor in trouble?"

I'd come here thinking that she was very much in trouble. Now I wasn't so sure. "That depends," I said.

Mrs. Branford stood and shuffled toward the door as my mind sorted through this new information. The fine hairs on the back of my neck pricked. Jeanne Poole was Taylor's mother. Jeanne Poole was Taylor's mother!

Tracy jumped up and blocked Mrs. Branford's progress. "What do you mean, that depends?"

My hypotheses had led me to believe Josh might

have seduced Taylor to get her trust-fund money. Now a different scenario reared up as truth. My father had overheard Jeanne Poole talking about her relationship with Josh. That relationship suddenly became clearer. He was married to Tracy. Tracy and Jeanne were longtime friends. He had to have known she'd inherited money. She was a widow. He probably saw her as an easy mark. He'd clearly been a high-risk, high-reward kind of man. The fact that she was his wife's sorority sister and a longtime family friend had no bearing.

I remembered Taylor's hateful stare at Josh, the way she'd marched out and said something to him, followed by another angry glare. What if she'd found out about Josh swindling her mother? Maybe she'd been protective of her mother, or maybe it was that it was supposed to be her money one day. Either way, it was gone now, thanks to Josh.

That might be enough to send Taylor over the edge.

"What is happening?" Tracy demanded.

Instead of answering her question, I asked one of my own. "Where does Jeanne Poole live?"

Chapter 30

Tracy McCall Prentiss was a tough nut to crack. She refused to give up her sorority sister's address unless Mrs. Branford and I agreed to let her come along. I looked at my sleuthing partner. She looked back. The silent communique between us had me agreeing to Tracy. A few minutes later, I followed her Land Rover to an equally fancy house in an equally hilly neighborhood about a mile and a half away. After another minute, we were knocking on an equally beautiful front door.

A woman with flyaway, nut-brown hair piled in a messy mop on top of her head answered the door. She looked at the three of us—Mrs. Branford in her pink velour, me in my floral sundress, and Tracy McCall Prentiss in expensive jeans and a blue chambray shirt with the color turned up. We were an odd trio. "Trace?" Jeanne said, her shock evident. "It's good to . . . uh, what a surprise. What's"—she gestured to us—"this?"

Her voice held the slightest tremble. I'd never met her, so I didn't know if it was simply the way it normally sounded or if some intense emotion had brought on the quiver. If I had to guess, I'd go with the latter. The three of us on her doorstep was certainly enough to shake her.

"Something about Josh and Taylor," Tracy replied.

Jeanne gaped. "Josh and . . . *Taylor*? What about them?"

Tracy pushed her way past Jeanne. Jeanne spun around and followed her. I shot Mrs. Branford a look, and we stepped inside, quietly closing the door behind us.

It turned out Tracy McCall Prentiss had easily put two and two together. She just blurted it out. "Jeanne, were Josh and Taylor having an affair?"

Jeanne stumbled backward. She reached one arm out to the back of a chair to steady herself. Her voice came out as a hoarse whisper. "What?"

Tracy gestured to me and Mrs. Branford. "These two showed up, asking questions about Taylor. And this one"—she pointed to me—"nearly had a heart attack when I mentioned your name."

And here I'd thought I'd kept my cool under pressure.

"If you know something, Jeanne, you have to tell me. We're Alpha Chi Omega. We're sisters."

"If I know something about what? About Taylor and Josh? There's no way. He wouldn't do that to me. That's just sick."

Tracy's head jerked back. She looked like she'd been slapped. "He wouldn't do that to *you*? What do you mean by that?" she asked, but the question on her face cleared suddenly. She'd figured out the truth. "Oh my God."

"Tracy—"

"Oh. My. God. You were one of them, weren't you?"

Jeanne's whole body shook. "Tracy, I never meant—"

Tracy's face suddenly burned with fire. She reared back like an injured animal. "Weren't you?!" she roared.

Jeanne backed away. Tracy advanced. "You slept with my husband," she screamed.

"I—"

Tracy pressed her hands to her head, her fingers clawing her own scalp like she was physically fighting a migraine, willing it not to come. When she looked up at Jeanne again, the flames in her eyes had died down. "You. My best friend. You slept with my husband."

Tears streamed down Jeanne's face. She cried, her mouth agape as raspy sobs escaped.

"I hated him for all the cheating and the lying and the stealing," Tracy said, shaking her head. "But he betrayed me with *you*, my best friend. And you let it happen."

I suspected that a lonely widow didn't have much of a chance when faced with the attentive charm of Josh Prentiss. That didn't excuse Jeanne's betrayal, but it went a long way toward explaining it.

As Jeanne collapsed into a crumpled mound, Tracy whirled around to face me. "What does any of this have to do with Taylor?" she asked, but realization hit her like a slap to the face. "No. Oh no. You don't think—"

Jeanne dragged the back of her hand under her faucet of a nose as she pushed herself up from the sofa. "What? You don't think what?" she croaked.

Finally, I spoke. "Mrs. Poole. Jeanne. Did Taylor find out about your affair with Josh? Did she know about how he defrauded you?"

Her eyes sparked. Grew wide. And then she started shaking her head, slowly at first, then more forcefully. Over and over and over. "No, no, no. Taylor did *not* do this. Could *not* have done this."

Chapter 31

It didn't take long for Emmaline and York to find Taylor Wilson because she wasn't in hiding. York had a team stake out her mother's house. By nightfall, she was in custody, and several hours later, she was released. "Not enough evidence, Ivy," Emmaline said over the phone. "Plus she seems to have an alibi for the time period Mae was poisoned."

"Yeah, but—"

"Whoever Mae met at the deli, it wasn't Taylor."

I'd gone to bed feeling frustrated and back to zero. The only good thing was that business at Yeast of Eden was back to normal. The line was ten people deep. It inched forward as Zula and I took care of the customers. Nina eased up to the counter and ordered an array of breads and pastries. "I can't resist!" she said.

Zula filled up the box. "As it should be. The bread, it is irresistible."

I rang her up. She paid with her credit card, took her pastry box, and stepped aside, waiting for Julia, who was next, cash in hand. "Ready for the party?" she asked.

The words had scarcely left her mouth when Nina whirled around. "Oh my lord, that's right! The engagement party! Of course I would have remembered, but it had momentarily slipped my mind. Will Mae be able to come?"

My smile faltered. "She's still unresponsive."

"I hope the city yanks out every one of those plants at the park," Nina said. "It's absolutely absurd that we've been living with such a poisonous plant in our midst."

I had to agree. "So far, Mae's lucky. The doctor thinks she'll come out of the coma. He said it's just a matter of time."

We all fell silent, each of us, I imagined, saying a little prayer for Mae's recovery.

"Olaya is making spectacular breads for the party," Zula said after a moment. "It will be wonderful. We will save some for sweet Mae."

I smiled, anxious to see the special bread she had planned. "I am making something I have never done before," she'd said more than once, piquing my interest.

At the very least, the trauma of finding Josh's body in the park would be replaced with the joy of the engagement party. While I didn't want him forgotten, I also didn't want the memory of seeing him there to be the thing I thought about whenever I passed by the park. A much happier memory would take its place.

Several more people bought their bread to get their morning carb fix. A child's squeal brought my attention to further down the line. "Magic! Again, again!"

It was the little girl, Tara, and her blond-haired mother. Julia had backtracked in the line. She held a box of eight crayons. She did a theatrical wave of her other hand and *presto!*, the crayons disappeared. She waved her hand again, turned the box around in a willy-nilly sort of way, and *presto!*, the crayons were back.

I helped the next person in line, keeping one eye on Julia's magic tricks. "I should have hired her to perform tomorrow," I whispered to Zula. Little Tara clapped as Julia made a scrap of paper disappear, replaced by a folded one-dollar bill.

A teenage boy stepped up to the counter. His head was turned toward Ella and Pilar, who sat at a table acting grown-up with scones and cups of coffee, and he smiled shyly at them. They giggled, glancing over at him, then quickly away. I immediately recognized the kid with his red hair and freckles.

He turned to look at me, but he was a product of the cell phone generation—easily distractible. Some sound or other caught his attention, and he looked the other way. In the back of the line, Julia ruffled Tara's hair. The bells on the door tinkled as she left. "That was cool," the boy at the counter said.

The person next in line cleared his throat and muttered, "Come on, man."

The boy seemed to suddenly realize he was holding things up. He refocused on me, ready to place his order, but recognition hit. "Hey! I know you. From the deli."

"Right," I said. "What can I—"

"How's that lady?" he asked, interrupting me, the line behind him forgotten again. "Mae something?"

"Spelling. Mae Spelling. She's still in a coma, but she's doing a bit better. She may come out of it."

He made a sad face as only a teenager who isn't really invested in a situation but wants to do the right thing can do. "Ah, that's good."

Indeed it was. "What can I get you?" I prodded.

With the snap of a finger, his expression changed. "I'll take a chocolate croissant," he said.

Zula and I exchanged glances. If the situation for Mae weren't dire, we might have laughed at this boy's effort. She bagged the pastry for him, and I collected his money. "Enjoy," I said.

"I plan to." He started to walk away, directing another shy smile at Pilar and Ella. The man next in line stepped forward, but the red-headed kid stopped and looked back at me. "Did you talk to her?"

I felt my brows pinch. "Who?"

"You asked me the other day who Mae Spelling met at the deli. Who she sat with."

I nodded, suddenly on high alert.

"She was just here." The freckly, carrot-top kid

glanced at Tara and her mother. "The lady with the magic tricks. Sleight of hand." He chuckled. "It's so easy to fool kids."

The world around me seemed to spin out of control. *She was just here. The woman with the magic tricks. Sleight of hand.*

Julia.

Chapter 32

"Oh my God, oh my God, oh my God!" I ripped off the nitrile gloves I'd been wearing. "Can you handle things?"

"Of course," Zula said. She didn't ask me any questions, clearly seeing how desperately I needed to go.

"I'll help, Mama!" Ella jumped up.

"Me, too!" Pilar followed Ella to the counter. Her smile was genuine, her excitement real. There would continue to be a lot of ups and downs, but for the moment, Olaya would be so happy to know Pilar was having an up moment.

I ran past the line of customers to the front door. Out onto the sidewalk. I searched the street in both directions, looking for the tall, thin blonde. Looking for Julia.

I didn't know what I would have done if I'd seen

her. Tackle her like one of Coach Bruno's football players?

She wasn't anywhere. Where had she gone?

I couldn't answer that question, so I let another thought take over.

I exhaled. Coach Bruno was innocent! Martina was innocent! Sharon and Linda and the rest of the women Josh had manipulated and stole from were all innocent.

Even Taylor, who by all accounts was a rather horrible young woman, was innocent.

The second those thoughts passed through my mind, another one slid in. Panic careened in right behind it. Mae was still in danger. If she awoke from the coma she'd been in, she'd be able to identify Julia as the person she'd met with at the deli, and as the person she'd seen putting something in Josh's coffee.

I raced back into the bread shop and through the kitchen, grabbing my purse and car keys on my way out the back door. I sat in my car, heart thumping, nerves ratcheting as I thought and re-processed the events of the last week.

I'd been so intent on proving Martina's innocence that I'd done exactly what Captain York had done to Miguel—I'd glommed on to the idea that Taylor was guilty, and I'd viewed everything through that lens. Taylor—the one who'd been wronged by Josh and who'd gotten her revenge. Taylor—the one who'd been fearful of whatever Mae knew or saw and who'd tried to shut her up. Taylor—the one who'd shot daggers at Josh.

But now I was seeing things in a completely different way. I replayed the moment of Mae stumbling into Yeast of Eden's kitchen. In my mind's eye, I saw her peaky skin, her unnaturally dark eyes, and her parched lips. She'd started to say something before she'd crumpled to the floor. "J-J-J." I'd thought she'd been trying to say Josh's name. That she'd been poisoned, just like he was? J-J-J. My mind stuttered. What if she'd been trying to say Julia?

I thought about how Josh's death came about. Everyone had been blaming Olaya's bread. The kid from the deli said Mae had met Julia at lunch. She could have easily dripped poison into Mae's cup when she wasn't looking. It could have been the same with Josh.

One thing kept coming to mind. Sleight of hand.

Julia making a quarter materialize out of thin air from behind little Tara's ear. Making the crayons in a box vanish. Turning a scrap of paper into a dollar bill.

Julia, who'd bumped into Josh's table. It had been a distraction! The broken plate. Everyone's attention on Josh and the broken plate, and not on her putting something into Josh's coffee cup.

Everyone except Mae. She had been there, chasing her mom around the dining tables. She could have seen the incident at Josh's table but not even realized what it meant. Yet.

I'd never been able to place Julia's age. Somewhere between thirty and mid-forties. Kristin had also said the woman Mae had been meeting with was blond, tall, and thin. Taylor hit the mark on the first two. She was curvy, though, with a booty that would never be described as small. Julia, on the other hand, was almost stick straight.

The image of a woman leaving Josh's funeral surfaced in my mind. She'd been ahead of me as I'd gone out to the vestibule. Something about her had been familiar at the time. My mind had gone to Taylor, but it had taken me in the wrong direction.

The cogs that had previously fallen into place rearranged themselves. The book. *Carter Beats the Devil.* "My dad was an amateur magician," Julia had said when I'd asked her about the quarter trick. I plunged my hand into my purse and pulled it out. For the first time, I flipped it over and read the back. It was about a magician. A true story about Charles Carter, an American stage magician.

Julia had had a book when she'd arrived. She'd surreptitiously left it with Josh. A proclamation that *she* was a magician, he was the devil, and the message inside telling him that *he'd get what he deserves.*

Yet again, I replayed the scene from the bread shop the morning Josh had died. Mae had chased her mother around, but it was the moment after that which now drew my attention. Josh said he felt something hit him in the back of the head. It made him jump. Bump into Julia. The vignette played like a movie in my head. Julia crouching to pick up the broken plate. Josh helping her stand. Julia yanking her hands free of his. At the time, I thought she'd looked abashed, but her emotions must have run much deeper than that. Somehow, he'd screwed her over, too. But how? He'd flirted with her, like she was someone he'd like to get to know, not someone he already knew. She couldn't be one of his victims.

I broke every speed limit in Santa Sofia as I rammed my foot against the gas pedal and sped toward the sheriff's station house. I jerked the wheel, making a hard turn into a parking spot, then raced into the squat beige building.

The same deputy who had been on duty the last time I'd been there looked up from her computer. She had the most edgy haircut I'd ever seen on someone in law enforcement. It was shaved close to the skin on either side of her head, a mop of curls growing in a stripe down the center. It was almost a mohawk, except she let the curls fall over the closely shorn skin. We were on a first-name basis now, or at least *she* was with *me*. She was still Deputy Hall to me. She took one look at me and stood. "What's going on, Ivy?"

"I need to see the sheriff! Or Captain York!" I said, trying to catch my breath and tame my racing pulse. "I—I—I—" I caught my breath. "I think I know who killed Josh Prentiss!"

Deputy Hall's thin eyebrows rose up. "What's that?"

"I think I know who killed Josh Prentiss," I repeated, more in control of my breathing this time.

"Ivy, they're both in the field. I'll call them—"

But I was already running toward the door.

Chapter 33

I still didn't understand Julia's motive as I raced to the door. At the moment, it didn't matter. A single question careened through my head. Where was she now?

As I grabbed hold of the handle, the answer hit me like a bag of Felix's flour to the head. Julia had been right there at the bread shop counter when Nina asked me if Mae would be able to come to the engagement party. Julia had heard me say that she was still unresponsive, but that the doctor thought she'd wake up. And that it was only a matter of time.

I'd wasted precious time by going to the Sheriff's Department. I turned back to Deputy Hall. "Tell them to meet me at the hospital!" I yelled, and without another word, I sprinted back to my car, threw myself in, and tore off.

The hospital was on the same side of town as the

Sheriff's Department. I was a mere 6.8 miles away, but those miles stretched on and on. Finally, after what felt like an eternity—I could have made bread dough and let it rise—I finally made it to the visitor parking lot of Mercy General. My long walks on the beach with Agatha didn't make me a runner. I was good and winded by the time I got to the automatic doors. Inside. To the elevator. Pushing the UP button. Again. And again.

Finally, the elevator arrived at the first floor. I leapt inside and impatiently pressed the button for the fourth floor, where Mae was peacefully sleeping off the poison in her body.

The lift made a stop on the second floor, but it had been a phantom rider. No one was there to get on. Someone had probably pressed UP when they'd meant to press DOWN. I held in the aggravated scream climbing my throat.

I nervously tapped my hands against my outer thighs as I waited for the door to close. As the elevator kicked into motion. As it stopped at floor four. As the doors slid open.

Finally.

I careened into the hallway. Kristin stood at the nurse's desk. "Ivy—" she started, but I couldn't take the time to stop and talk with her. If my instincts were right, there was no time to waste. I made a hard right, nearly crashing into the wall, making the turn as though I were a race car taking a curve on two wheels. A nurse glared at me. I slowed to a speed walk, breaking into a run again once she was out of sight. Left at the end of the hall. I kept going, passing patient rooms until I got to Mae's. The door was closed.

"Ivy!" Kristin called, lumbering from somewhere behind me.

I ignored her. Turned the handle, pushed it open—

There she was.

Julia stood with her back to the bed. My body wanted to freeze. To stutter in disbelief, because I'd been right.

Somehow, my legs took me forward in a rush.

Julia had turned her head when the door to the room opened. She *had* frozen. Caught in the act. The moment's hesitation was enough. I leapt, plowing right into her back. The small glass vial she'd been holding flew from her hand. It landed on the linoleum floor, shattering, a small amount of liquid spilling out.

"Get off me!" Julia screamed. Her limbs flailed, one hand flopping against her face, but I held tight, dragging her to the ground, far away from Mae.

"Oh my—!" I heard Kristin's shrill voice in the doorway.

"Get help!" I yelled.

I heard her voice in the deep recesses of my mind. "Help! Someone help!"

I had a few seconds to grill Julia. I seized them. "Why, Julia? Why did you kill Josh? Did you date him?" I asked, thinking that explanation didn't make sense because she'd clearly shut him down.

She barked out a vicious laugh. A cackle, really. The adorable woman I'd known from the bread shop was all but gone. In her place was this vengeful creature. "He didn't even recognize me. My own br—" She shook away the word that had been on her lips. "I thought if he only . . . then maybe . . . maybe . . . But he didn't. He took everything from me, and he didn't even recognize me."

"Recognize you from where?" I asked, but even as the question formed, an answer configured itself right alongside it. Josh had looked at Julia strangely. I'd thought his ego had been bruised because of her rebuffing him, but what if it was more than that? What if he *knew* her but couldn't *place* her. He'd left his family twenty-five years prior. That was a long time. When she'd talked to him at the bread shop that morning, his demeanor had changed briefly. Had he experienced some flare of recognition?

The guy at the Prentiss's old house had tried to summon up the name of Josh's father. James? Jules? Jack? James? Jules? Jack? James? Jules—

"Jules," I muttered aloud. "Jules. Jules . . . Jul . . . ia." I dragged in a shocked breath. "Julia!"

Something about the beach bum from the Prentiss's Bungalow Oasis home circled in my head. He'd said, *The guy left them penniless.* We'd been talking about Josh Prentiss's father—or at least *I* had. But what if the guy who'd sold the house out from under his mother and siblings . . . the man who'd left them penniless . . . what if that had actually been *Josh*? His father ran off with his assistant, sure, but what if Josh ran off, too, taking with him whatever money his mother had left? What if his propensity for financial crimes had started way back then, with his own family?

And what if he'd left a sister behind to deal with it all on her own?

Seconds later, people spilled into the room, like ants swarming around a discarded piece of birthday cake at a park.

A nurse was at the bed checking on Mae. Kristin rounded the bed. "Is she all right? Please tell me she's all right."

"She is," the nurse said. "Her vitals are strong."

"Step aside," a male voice said. Instant relief coursed through me. Deputy Hall was as good as her word. She'd called York and relayed my message to meet me here. And he'd come. He'd actually come.

I heard the thud of heavy footfalls. I saw a pair of black boots first. I craned my neck to follow the legs all the way up to Captain York's wonderful face. I'd never been so glad to see him. And I might never again. "Ms. Culpepper, you can get off of her now."

"I need a little help," I said. I was lying on top of Julia, who was immobile. Her body was twisted, contorted so her hands pressed up against her face. Her gloved hands. Her damp, gloved hands.

I swung my gaze to the broken vial and the liquid on the floor. "Oh my God." I scrambled back. Felt a sturdy arm lift me the rest of the way off.

With my weight off of her, Julia was able to flop onto her back. She scooted back, horror clear on her face. "Help me!"

Everyone stared at her, but no one moved. "Help you with what?" York asked, a grim look on his face.

"It's in my mouth!" she shrieked, her voice a hundred times louder and more panicked than

Kristin's had been. Her gloved hand had been pressed against her face, I realized. Her nostrils flared as panic set in. "I need a doctor!"

I glanced over my shoulder at York, thinking he might take over, but he rocked back on his heels, his arms folded, his lips pushed out.

"What's happening here?" Another man's voice. The man himself, wearing a white doctor's coat, stethoscope around his neck, worked his way through the gathering crowd.

"What's happening here, Julia?" I asked in drippy saccharine voice. "You better tell the doctor what was in that vial. What you got in your mouth." I could have said: You brewed poison juice from Angel's Trumpet and had it in that vial. You were going to finish the job.

But there was no way I was uttering those words. This would be her confession.

Julia's eyes grew dark. Her pupils dilating. One of the symptoms of the poison. She remained stubbornly silent.

"Think the extreme thirst will come next? Or the disorientation?"

I caught York smirk from the corner of my eye. The doctor, though, was not amused. "What the devil is going on?" he repeated.

Carter Beats the Devil.

Not this time, I thought. "Maybe it'll be the hallucinations or—" I pressed my palm against my chest dramatically. "I hope you don't slip straight into a coma like Mae—"

"You bit—"

"Tsk, tsk," I interrupted.

She started to lift her arm, but it dropped back down to her side. Her eyes flared with panic.

"That'll be the paralysis," I said.

"Enough!" the doctor bellowed. He spun around to one of the nurses. "Clear these people out of here."

Julia sat slumped against the wall, her legs outstretched in front of her. She looked like a rag doll ready to fall on its side. The doctor started toward her, crouching and reaching for her wrist.

"Be careful there, doc," York said.

The doctor shot a questioning look. Julia and I had been in a game of chicken. I blinked first. "It's pois—" I started, but she drew in another strained breath and spoke in a hoarse voice. "Angel's Trumpet. It . . . is . . . A-A-Angel's . . . Trumpet."

The doctor started. He drew gloves from his pocket as he began barking orders. York stood back to let the man work, but he cleared his throat and said with no ifs, ands, or buts, "Doc, I'm going to need to talk to her once she's stable."

Chapter 34

Josie swept into the bread shop, Coach Bruno holding the door for her.

"Josie!" I'd been sitting at one of the tables, laptop open, flipping through photos of the park. I jumped up. Her arms came around me like a life-giving cocoon. "What are you doing here?"

"We heard everything. The second poisoning. The apprehension of the killer. Quite a week for Santa Sofia."

It had been, and I sincerely hoped things would now settle down. I wanted to bake bread. Take photographs. Get married. Maybe have a child with Miguel. I'd be happy if murder was never again in the mix.

"We just came from the sheriff's station house," Josie said. She tapped Coach Bruno on the arm. "Tell her what you discovered."

He pressed his lips together and gave his head a little shake, as though he still couldn't quite believe what he was about to say. "I scoured the books with the school's bookkeeper. The numbers didn't match. Josh . . . he swindled the boosters. With the treasurer, Cheryl Fitzwilliam. They stole thousands. Tens of thousands."

I slapped my hands together triumphantly. "I *knew* it! I mean I couldn't *prove* it, but, yeah, I suspected." I told them what Nina had said about the spreadsheets and the doctored set of books."

Coach Bruno's lips thinned. "That bastard."

"And you went to the authorities," Josie said to me as she patted her beau on the arm. A statement, not a question.

I nodded. After leaving the hospital, I'd rounded up Nina and taken her to the sheriff's station house. I suspected Sean Fitzwilliam would give his ten cents, too, when called upon. "Emmaline's bringing in a forensic accountant to audit the books."

Josie and Coach Bruno shared a look. "That explains it."

"Explains what?" I asked.

"It explains why we felt like we were preaching to the choir. It wasn't a surprise to them."

"Just icing on the cake of Josh Prentiss's character. He had us all fooled."

Sharon had come by the bread shop after she'd read the Marcus Brolin piece in *The Scout*. It had exonerated Yeast of Eden of all wrongdoing, and he'd even gone so far as to issue an apology for throwing the bread shop under the proverbial bus. "They've been able to trace all the money to some offshore account," Sharon said with a disbelieving snort. "That man should rot in hell."

I didn't know about that, but all his crimes would be publicly revealed, one by one, and his victims would get their recompense. I hoped that would be enough for Sharon and the others.

For Julia, it was too late.

Coach Bruno's head rotated on his thick neck. "This is going to make national news. 'Treasurer and controller take boosters to the cleaners,'" he said, making air quotes around the headline.

Well, then. I thought back to my conversation with Sean Fitzwilliam. It looked like Cheryl had bet on the wrong man after all. My heart went out to the jilted husband.

Josie and the coach got in line for bread. "A rare treat," Josie said.

I put my things away under the counter and stood at the register. I threw in an extra croissant for the coach and a morning cookie for Josie, then said goodbye with air kisses and a wave.

Coach Bruno held the door open for a woman coming in at the same time. She had chestnut ringlets, streaks of blond woven throughout. Her hair was pulled into two low ponytails, and square-framed glasses perched on the top of her head. I immediately recognized the crate under her arm. The pristine patterns Nina had discovered. "Did you get those at the mini-mall?" I asked the woman when she made it to the front of the line.

She glanced at them, her face breaking into a wide smile. "That place across the street? Yes! Do you sew?"

I spread my arms wide. "No, no. I bake. Not like

Olaya, but I try. But I saw them the other day. Nina said they're quite a find."

"Oh my goodness." She gazed at them with open adoration. "*Such* an amazing find."

"I take it *you* sew."

"Oh yes. All my life. I have a little shop in a small little town in Texas. You've probably never heard of it."

"I went to UT," I said with a wink. "Try me."

"No! Small world, right?"

"Right," I agreed.

"I live in Bliss. It's a little place. Quaint and colorful."

"I've heard of it! Kind of like Granbury."

She beamed. "Exactly. I have a dressmaking shop there. Buttons and Bows."

"You're a long way from home," I said.

She turned to glance at the man coming up behind her. Tall. Olive-skinned like Miguel. Baseball cap backward. And a wedding band. He took the box from her to hold. "We're on vacation. My great-grandmother, Loretta Mae, once told me about this bread shop. And"—she spread her arms wide—"here it is! She said the bread is"—she leaned in and lowered her voice—"magical."

I laughed. "A lot of people say that." And it was a lot better than people thinking our bread was poisonous. Thankfully, those rumors hadn't spread far and wide. This couple from Texas proved that point.

She pulled something from her wallet. A business card in the shape of a dress form. BUTTONS & BOWS / HARLOW CASSIDY, DRESSMAKER.

"If you're ever in Bliss, look me up," she said.

"I definitely will," I said, and I meant it. I felt an instant kinship with Harlow. They picked their bread and left the shop. All the while, I kept thinking about what Nina had said. "The right person will find it." She'd been talking about the box of patterns.

Maybe she was talking about people, too.

Chapter 35

My phone rang early Saturday morning. Too early for regular humans to be awake, but I was up with the birds. The engagement party was that afternoon. My dad, Billy, Emmaline, Zula, Esmé, Ella and Pilar, Mrs. Branford, and, of course, Miguel would be meeting me at the park to set up the bistro tables and the bread-wall display. With Nina's help, I'd been collecting antique milk bottles for the table decorations. Each would hold a spray of summer flowers.

"It's too early," I said to Emmaline.

"Thought you'd like to know. Mae woke up."

I bolted upright in my bed as if a puppet master had yanked the string attached to my head. My leg bumped against Agatha, who gave a squeaky complaint and rearranged herself. After a week, I'd almost given up hope. "Have you talked to her? What'd she say?"

"Whoa, Ivy. Settle down. I called to let you know I'm heading over there right now with York. If you—"

I was already out of bed. "I'm on my way!"

Fifteen minutes later, I was retracing my steps to Mae's room, only this time my urgency stemmed from relief that she was okay. The door was closed. A feeling of déjà vu washed over me as I grabbed the handle and pushed. This time, though, Mae was sitting up in her bed, sipping water from a straw inserted into a pink plastic cup. Her mother sat in a chair, holding her free hand. Emmaline and Captain York were already mid-interview. York had a notepad out. They both glanced at me as I walked in. Emmaline smiled. York, surprisingly, gave me a nod. No scowl. No chastisement for having gotten involved. In fact, I thought I saw a trace of a smile on his lips.

I grinned back at them both before focusing on Mae. The second she saw me, she jerked into movement. "Here, Mom," she said, thrusting her cup of water at Kristin and freeing her other hand. She reached both arms out to me. "Ivy, Ivy, Ivy. You saved my life!"

Kristin was out of her chair now, rounding the bed and pulling me into a bear hug. I felt the warmth of her tears against my cheek. "You really did. You saved her life."

I hadn't expected this. I'd come to check on Mae and hear her story. Tears pooled in my own eyes. "I'm—Mae, I'm just so glad you're okay." I pulled away from Kristin, looking at her. "She *is* okay, right?" Back to Mae. "You *are* all right?"

Mae's voice was hoarse, but she managed a laugh. "I'm going to be okay."

Emmaline cleared her throat. "Mae, if we can keep going, please. You were telling us about the morning Josh Prentiss died."

Kristin squeezed my hand, then let me go. She pulled the other chair in the room closer to hers and guided me into it as Mae leaned back again. "Well, my mom—" She broke off and sent a chastising look at Kristin. "She was sneaking carbs when she shouldn't. She's got type two diabetes. Bread is *not* on the diet."

Kristin's cheeks stained a blotchy pink. "It's just hard, sweetheart. You know it is," she said, but not with any defensiveness. "The bread shop is just too enticing."

Mae screwed up her lips and nodded. "I know it is."

"You saw your mom and ran after her?" Emmaline prodded.

Mae looked back at Em and York. "Yes. It was extreme. I know that, but she just—well, never mind. I went after her to get the bread from her. I was going to drag her outside. That's when Julia bumped into Josh's table."

"And what happened next?" Emmaline again.

Mae's face clouded. "It just seemed so odd. Her hand sort of hovered over the table. It wasn't till later, after Josh died, that I came back to that moment. I just wasn't sure, though. I thought I saw her put something in the coffee, but then I second-guessed myself and thought there's no way. Julia seemed so nice whenever I'd seen her. It didn't make sense, so I thought I must have imagined it."

"What happened at the deli?" York asked.

I leaned forward to listen. Mae picked up her water from the bed table and took a sip. "I had, uh, just sat down with my food. Suddenly Julia was there sitting across from me. I saw the look on her face, and I knew I hadn't imagined it."

York's pencil stopped moving, and he looked up. "She had never joined you before?"

Mae shook her head with more gusto than I imagined she'd have at that moment. "Never. She was a customer, and she was friendly, but we weren't . . . friends. And there she was acting like we were."

"You didn't see her put anything into your drink?" Kristin asked in a tremulous voice.

Mae tilted her head down, giving her mom a placating look. "No, Mom. If I had, I obviously wouldn't have drunk it."

Kristin fluttered her hand. "No, of course you wouldn't have. Stupid question."

"What did Julia say to you?" Emmaline asked.

Mae closed her eyes. I could see how tired she was, the poison that had wracked her body still taking its toll. A shiver visibly shook her, sneaking into her voice as she spoke. "She just asked what kind of sandwich I got, then she said how funny I'd been with my mom. Then she brought up Josh Prentiss."

I scooted to the edge of my seat.

"What did she say?" Emmaline asked.

"She said that people got what they deserved."

A shiver wound through me, too. The words highlighted in the paperback book Julia had left with Josh.

"I remember saying that Josh hadn't been such a good guy, but that he didn't deserve to die." Mae swallowed hard. Her eyelids fluttered. "He didn't deserve to die," she repeated, "but Julia just laughed at that. She said of course he deserved to die. He'd tricked so many women, cheating them out of their money. She'd really loved him once, she said, but he'd cheated her, too. She said she'd done womankind a favor by getting rid of a man like Josh."

Another involuntary shudder washed over Mae. "I never saw her do it. Put poison in my drink. I never suspected. Then she asked what my mom would do without me. *What would your mom ever do without you?* Those were her exact words. I think I knew at that point, but I already wasn't feeling very well. She gathered up my sandwich and my drink, and she walked with me partway back to Yeast of Eden. I was stumbling. Everything went a little fuzzy. And then she wasn't there anymore, and I didn't think I'd make it, but I did. Barely." She opened her eyes and found me. "And when she came to finish the job, you saved me, Ivy."

And then we were crying. Kristin. Mae. Me. Even Emmaline's eyes had gone glassy. York turned his back on us, and I had the fleeting thought that he might be choked up, too.

Miguel and I stood in front of the gazebo in the park. The bread display was every bit as beautiful as Olaya had said it would be. Baguettes and batards. Rolls and pastries. They were all artfully stacked in the crates and baskets. Plenty to eat during the party, and more than enough for our friends and family to take a loaf or two home at the end. The whole display was like a giant new-fangled charcuterie. Olives and hummus, nuts and chocolate, cheeses and meats. It all worked together to create a casual and festive celebration of our upcoming wedding.

A light ocean breeze had blown in. It carried the low and happy chatter of our guests. They gathered around the tall bistro tables we'd rented, eating, drinking, and generally making merry. The lingering sadness of Josh Prentiss's murder and Julia Prudell's subsequent arrest had brought the festive mood down a notch, but Mae coming out of her coma had raised it back up.

I spotted Martina, Consuelo, and Freddy. Martina waved, then pressed her crossed hands over her heart. A thank-you. I pressed my fingers to my lips, kissed them lightly, then sent the kiss across the park to her. She smiled. A sad smile, the bitterness at what had happened with Josh still there, but a smile, nonetheless. She had her sisters. She had her niece. She had me. Martina would be okay.

"Vicente is back," Olaya whispered.

I nearly choked on the sip of punch I'd just taken. Vicente Villanueva was the man Martina had been in love with. "He is?"

She pointed to the opposite side of the park. A man in his early sixties, with dark hair, tall and thin, walked across the grass. I saw the moment he spotted Martina. He broke into a smile, and he took his steps faster. He bent to kiss Martina on her cheek, then rocked back on his heels, his hands deep in the pockets of his cream-colored linen pants. She turned, wary at first, and then she registered who stood before her. She smiled. She laughed. She clasped her hands over her mouth. And then they fell into a desperate hug.

I nodded my silent approval. Martina and Vicente had been close. Maybe moving toward marriage, but he'd left. Then she'd been burned by Josh. It would take them a fat minute to fall into a comfortable rhythm with each other, but I could see that they were already on their way.

In the middle of the park, I spotted two more people, and I beamed. Mrs. Branford shone like the North Star in her bright white velour lounge suit. Her silvery hair glistened in the waning light. By her side was Mason Caldwell. Room 315. Chemistry. The elderly man had a distinct twinkle in his eye when he looked at Penelope Branford. They'd reconnected on MeetYourMate.com, of all places. Mrs. Branford didn't want to give up her poker nights or her Blackbird Ladies so she could hang out with a man. No, if she dated, it would be on her terms. From the looks of things, they had come up with some mutually beneficial terms that suited them both.

Olaya disappeared for a few minutes. I spotted her again as she walked toward the front, where Miguel and I stood. She wore a muted periwinkle caftan with colorful handwork embroidered down the front. She was festive and stunning, her olive skin clear and shimmering, her iron-gray hair silvery. She carried a wooden tray covered with a tea towel. She set it in the one open spot on the table. "Ivy. This is for you," she said.

I held my breath as she lifted the linen towel. I gasped. And stared. And nearly cried. There sat the most magical bread I had ever seen. Even in the midst of her distress over Martina being involved with Josh, not to mention Pilar and her trauma, Olaya had spent time secretly working on a special bread for the engagement party. Now I gazed upon it—a work of art. It was heart-shaped and two-tiered. The bread itself was baked to a golden brown, but the delicate three-dimensional roses adorning the entire thing made it magical. Each was created from bits of dough pressed and shaped as the petals and leaves of the flowers. Delicate swirling lines and miniature daisies made the whole thing look like a celebration.

"It's a masterpiece," I said.

"And too beautiful to cut," Miguel added, wrapping his arm around Olaya in a touching hug.

"Nonsense," Olaya said. "That is precisely what you are meant to do with it. We must eat it and take in the blessing." She took my hand. "This is called a Ukrainian Korohvie. It is part of the Ukrainian wedding ritual. The kneading, it represents the blessing for the new family being formed. The flowers on top, they will bring you good fortune. A happy marriage. Traditionally, relatives from both the bride's and the groom's family work together. That is what we did."

I spotted my father from the corner of my eye. He walked up, smiling, his eyes glassy. "You helped with this?" I asked him.

"We all did," he said. He pointed to Billy and Emmaline. My sister-in-law had changed from her sheriff's uniform to a summery sheath. They came up to us at the same time Mrs. Branford and Miguel's mother did, with Miguel's sister, Laura, her husband, Sergio, and their two kids in tow.

"I don't understand," Pilar piped up, coming to stand next to Olaya. "They're not Ukrainian."

Tears had welled in my eyes. I wiped them away. Miguel moved closer to me, a rock by my side. "Actually, my mother was Ukrainian on her father's side, so I have a little bit. Her name was Annika, but she went by Anna," I said with a smile. But it wasn't about how much I had in me. It was about my mother *being* here.

I had never told Olaya that bit about my mother's background, so for a short second, I wondered how she had known that little fact about me, but then I saw my father's sentimental smile. Of course. He was sharing his history with Olaya, and that history included my mother.

Through the fabric of her caftan, he lightly touched the small of Olaya's back. She was his future, as Miguel was mine, but *this* bread, this Korohvie that Olaya had honored my mother with, it brought her into this moment of my life in a tangible way. She was here with me on this incredible day, proof that she wasn't gone. Anna Culpepper lived on through this celebratory bread tradition. This was a moment I would always remember.

Recipes

Olaya's Morning Cookies
(naturally gluten free!)

Ingredients
- 6 tablespoons unsalted butter
- ¼ cup granulated sugar
- ¼ cup light brown sugar, lightly packed
- 1 large egg
- ½ teaspoon salt
- ½ teaspoon vanilla extract
- ¾ cup oat flour
- ½ teaspoon baking soda
- ¼ teaspoon ground cinnamon
- 1½ cups extra-thick rolled oats (or substitute old-fashioned oats)
- ¼ cup golden flaxseed meal
- ½ cup dried cranberries
- ½ cup chopped walnuts
- Other add-ins of your choice

Add-Ins
- Raisins
- Pecans
- Slivered almonds
- Golden raisins
- Dried cherries
- Dried blueberries or other dried fruit
- Chocolate chips
- Sweetened dried coconut

Directions

1. Preheat oven to 350°F.
2. Prepare 2 baking sheets by lining with parchment.
3. Cream butter and both sugars together in a large bowl.
4. Mix in the egg, salt, and vanilla.
5. Stir in the flour, baking soda, and cinnamon until combined.
6. Add the oats, flaxseed meal, cranberries, and walnuts (or other add-ins). Stir until just combined.
7. Using a spoon, form cookie dough into small to medium-sized balls. Place on the baking sheets. Press down slightly to flatten.
8. Bake for 12–15 minutes.
9. These cookies keep for 2 or 3 days in an airtight container.'

Blueberry Cornmeal Cake

Ingredients

- 1½ cups all-purpose flour or gluten-free flour
- ½ cup medium-grind yellow cornmeal
- 2 teaspoons baking powder
- ½ teaspoon baking soda
- ½ teaspoon salt
- 1 cup granulated sugar
- ½ cup unsalted butter, softened
- 2 large eggs
- Zest from 2 lemons
- ⅔ cup buttermilk
- 1½ cups fresh blueberries

Directions

1. Preheat oven to 350°F. Butter or grease an 8-inch springform pan. You can also cut a parchment round to fit the bottom of the pan.
2. Stir together flour, cornmeal, baking powder, baking soda, and salt. Set aside.
3. Cream sugar and butter using stand mixer or hand held mixer until light and fluffy. Add eggs, one at a time, beating well after each addition. Add lemon zest.
4. Add dry ingredients to butter mixture, alternating with buttermilk. End with flour mixture.
5. Pour batter into prepared cake pan. Sprinkle fresh blueberries on top.
6. Bake at 350° degrees for 40–50 minutes. The cake should start to pull away from

the sides of the pan and spring back when lightly pressed in the center with a fingertip.

7. Cool in pan for 10 minutes. Remove cake from springform pan; serve warm or at room temperature.

Lavender Tea Bread

Ingredients

- ¾ cup milk
- 3 tablespoons finely chopped fresh lavender
- 6 tablespoons butter, softened
- 1 cup white sugar
- 2 eggs
- 2 cups all-purpose flour
- 1½ teaspoons baking powder
- ¼ teaspoon salt

Directions

1. Preheat the oven to 325°F. Grease and flour a 9-inch x 5-inch loaf pan.
2. Combine the milk and lavender in a small saucepan over medium heat. Heat to a simmer, then remove from heat, and allow to cool slightly.
3. In a medium bowl, cream together butter and sugar. Beat in the eggs until the mixture is light and fluffy.
4. Combine the flour, baking powder, and salt.
5. Stir the flour mixture into the creamed mixture, alternately with the milk and lavender, until just blended. Pour into the prepared pan.
6. Bake for 50 minutes at 350° or until a wooden pick inserted into the loaf comes out clean.
7. Cool before serving.

Visit our website at
KensingtonBooks.com
to sign up for our newsletters, read
more from your favorite authors, see
books by series, view reading group
guides, and more!

Become a Part of Our
Between the Chapters Book Club
Community and Join the Conversation

Betweenthechapters.net